Karen A. Miles is a 47 year old English teacher and mother of three currently living in Italy. She has lived abroad all her adult life and has constantly found herself in difficult, challenging and life changing situations. Her writing is a careful balance of experience and fantasy, but which is which, is a closely guarded secret.

This book is dedicated to my amazing family whose love and support continues to give me the strength to keep going, to the rest of my family and my dear friends who keep me smiling and to my incredible Mum whose personal courage was, and will always be, an inspiration.

Karen A. Miles

TORN BETWEEN

AUSTIN MACAULEY
PUBLISHERS LTD.

A CIP catalogue record for this title is available from the British Library.

ISBN 9781786126993 (Paperback)
ISBN 9781786127006 (Hardback)
ISBN 9781786127013 (E-Book)

www.austinmacauley.com

First Published (2016)
Austin Macauley Publishers Ltd.
25 Canada Square
Canary Wharf
London
E14 5LQ

Chapter 1

"Champagne? Miss? Would you like some champagne?"

Mel looked up at the air hostess.

"How much is it?" Mel reached for her bag that was wedged in under her seat.

The air hostess smiled, "It's complimentary Miss, would you prefer orange juice?"

Mel, glowing pink from embarrassment, held up her hand to take the glass from her, "No, champagne is fine, thank you."

The hostess handed her the champagne and placed a small white napkin on the tray in front of her, then she gave her a tiny bowl of mixed nuts and moved on to the row behind.

Melissa sipped her champagne and rested her head back on the cushion. She looked around her, the majority of the other passengers were men. The man in the seat to the left of her was reading intently and scribbling notes in the margin of the book; Mel glanced over and saw the title. 'How to Get Ahead.'

On the other side of her was a Chinese looking gentlemen also reading, he was immersed in a copy of 'Strategic Finance'.

'So this is business class, thank you Rob's boss!' she thought taking another sip from the flute, 'Not bad, not bad at all.'

"Ladies and gentlemen, welcome on board this BA flight to Singapore. Our flight time to Dubai is seven hours, where we will have an hour stopover before continuing on our way to Singapore with a further flying time of eight hours and fifteen minutes. My name is Rupert and I am the cabin manager, today on board we have an expert crew here to help you and make sure you're comfortable. At the front here with me is Jane and at the rear of the cabin are Simon and Scott. Today in business class we have Judith and Elaine and first class today is being looked after by Ryan."

Melissa listened intently to the speech, she was feeling excited but a little apprehension was starting to creep in.

"I would like to remind all passengers to check you are in a smoking section of the aircraft before lighting your cigarette and remember smoking is not permitted in the toilets.

Now I ask for your full attention as we take you through the safety instructions."

The aeroplane began to move off towards the runway at low speed. Mel's heart began to beat faster, she finished the champagne in the glass and placed it on the tray table. The hostess passed almost immediately to take away the glass and place the tray back in its upright position. Mel began to breathe deeply, she held onto the arm rests with a tight grip and closed her eyes.

This was the first time she had been on a plane and she felt a sudden surge of panic. The safety demonstration that was taking place in front of her was only adding to her anxiety and she realised in that instant that she was afraid of flying.

'In case of a landing on water' it went on. She began to shake, her hands gripping the arm rests even harder.

'Why the hell would anyone tell you there was a chance this plane would have to land on water? How are you supposed to enjoy the flight thinking about that!'

The plane came to an abrupt stop and she leaned forward to look out of the window to see what was going on. She saw the crew take their seats and the plane began to move again.

It picked up speed and the engine noise was almost unbearable, faster and faster, the plane was now at full speed, everything was rattling.

Mel felt sick, her heart was exploding in her chest, suddenly the plane tilted upwards and they were in the air.

"Oh God, oh shit" she exclaimed out loud. The men on either side glanced up to look at her, they both smiled and went back to their books.

Mel heard a loud banging noise coming from underneath the plane and jumped in her seat.

"It's just the wheels," one of the men explained, smiling, "they're just putting the wheels away, nothing to worry about."

Mel smiled back at him desperately trying to pull herself together.

After what seemed like an age, the plane straightened out and there was a clicking sound as the passengers undid their seat belts and began to get up from their seats. Mel opened her eyes and her breathing slowly returned to a normal rate, she released her tight grip on the arm rests and wiped her sweating palms on her trousers.

A few minutes later the air hostess appeared once again.

"Would you care for another drink Miss?"

"Yes, champagne please."

Mel practically snatched the glass from her outstretched hand and knocked back the contents, emptying it in one go. She was reminded that that is not actually the way you're supposed to drink champagne, by the look of disapproval on the air hostesses heavily made up face.

Maybe it was the effects of the champagne but she finally found herself starting to relax a little. She looked around her again, she still couldn't believe it, here she was on a business class flight to Singapore! She was on her way to Paradise to be with Rob.

"Mel, let's go out tonight, I want to talk to you about something important."

Rob had called her early, at around eight thirty, from the office.

She remembered clearly that it was the sixth of March and more importantly that it was a Friday, her favourite day of the week, the day Rob came home from London and they could spend the whole weekend together.

"All right, where do you want to go?" she had asked curiously.

"Let's go to Anton's, be ready for 7 and I'll pick you up," he said excitedly.

'Wow, Anton's, posh and expensive, it must be about something really important' she decided, her mind doing overtime.

At twenty past seven they were seated at a romantic table in the corner. Rob scanned the wine list and ordered a bottle of Asti Spumante.

Mel that evening was dressed to kill, she was wearing a black and white dress which buttoned up the back and accentuated all her curves.

Not bad for a dress that had cost £5.99 at the market.

Her mind was still racing, they never came here unless it was a birthday or some other special occasion. They had been together almost three years and now he had something important to talk to her about.

Obviously he had gotten the hint after the great Valentine's sulk, when, convinced that the box Rob handed her contained an engagement ring, she was unable to hide her disappointment and had cried as she opened it and saw it contained only a pair of earrings.

She sat in silence while the waiter poured the Spumante and then handed them a red leather bound menu.

They clinked glasses and she took large sips from the half-filled glass.

"So," he took hold of her hand, "I have to talk to you about something big."

Rob was grinning from ear to ear and Mel's palms began to sweat.

"What is it? What's so important?"

She braced herself for the proposal and began to ponder how she should reply. Should she say yes straight away or should she wait a few minutes or maybe even say that she would tell him tomorrow? It was a difficult one. The way she gave the answer was important as she didn't want to come across as being too keen or unsure.

Rob reached into his pocket, Mel leaned forward slightly to be ready.

"Okay, here goes." He still had his hand in his pocket. "Well, I've been thinking for a while of making some changes in my life, I want to have something more Mel, I need to have something more." He continued smiling.

Mel nodded in agreement and smiled back.

'Here it comes'.

"I've been offered a job in Singapore, a good position in the company and in Singa-bloody-pore, for two years, isn't that great?"

Mel sat for a minute not able to speak until finally she found the strength to form the words.

"Yes, that's great," she lied, the corner of her mouth trembling slightly as it formed a half smile.

"You could come out at Christmas if you like and visit me. The lads said they might be coming, it'll be fun. What do you reckon?"

The room began to spin a little. Mel stood up, holding onto the table to steady herself.

"Excuse me a minute please Rob, I need to go to the ladies' room, that Spumante's gone to my head a bit."

She walked unsteadily towards the bathrooms and found the toilet occupied. She stood there in front of the mirror staring at the pathetic creature staring back at her.

'How could she have been so stupid? This was worse than Valentine's. She was so convinced he was going to propose this time.

'She could go and visit him at Christmas!'

That was over nine bloody months away. Did the last three years mean nothing to him? And the lads were going! That meant he had talked to them before he had talked to her. She let out a large growling sound just as the toilet door opened and a rather surprised looking woman stepped cautiously out.

Mel dashed past her into the stall and locked the door, then once inside she let out another even larger growl and gave the door a kick.

When she returned to the table Rob was looking at the menu.

"So what are we having?" she smiled.

"Oh Mel", he said reaching back into his pocket, "I almost forgot, this is for you."

She leaned forward again in rekindled anticipation as Rob pulled a key out and placed it on the table in front of her.

"It's my spare car key. I'd like you to look after it for me until Dad manages to sell it."

"Of course Rob, no problem." She replied, devastated.

And that was that, without further discussion, the centre of her small and chaotic universe left ten days later. He had a huge send off at the pub, with his mates going as far as to get him a nurse stripagram who had finished up completely naked, except for her little white hat.

Mel looked on, smiling awkwardly, while Rob was being straddled.

She cried as they said their goodbyes at the airport, a few tears rolled down her cheeks but were quickly wiped away.

"I'll write," he promised "and send you some photos, look after the car."

He kissed her on her forehead, like a father saying goodbye to a child, then turned and walked away towards security.

True to his word he did write; letters and postcards arrived which had pictures of exotic beaches, palm trees and sunsets. There were also photos of beautiful hotels and bars, lots of bars.

He always wrote more or less the same thing;
Dear Mel.

Hot as hell, work good, place great think of me in your 'alone' time!' etc. Occasionally there was a *'miss ya'* thrown in at the end and several obscene doodles.

Alone time! He was so sure she was alone, but was he?

After just six weeks Mel was resigning herself to the fact that she would probably never see him again, his letters and phone calls had already become much less frequent.

After a lot of nagging by her Mother she even accepted an invitation to go out for a drink with John.

John was her Mum's friend's next door neighbour's son, or something like that, an up and coming estate agent. He was sweet, quite cute and generous, but the whole evening was a disaster because she couldn't get past the feeling that she was cheating on Rob.

"Oh for God's sake!" her mother tutted when she recounted the awful, awkward evening she had had.

"Robert's gone, he's in Singapore, probably chatting up hundreds of beautiful Singaporean women. You really need to get over him!"

Mel had always despaired of her Mother's bluntness, but she was beginning to admit that maybe, once again, her mother was right.

That's why it came as such a shock when she got the call.

It was one Wednesday evening in the middle of May, Rob had been gone over two months and she only had some kind of contact with him about once a week.

She was sitting watching a repeat of Fawlty Towers when she heard the phone ringing.

"I'll get it!" Her sister Gill yelled from the kitchen.

"Oh hi Rob, yes she's here, of course she's here, where else would she be? I'll pass you to her. Mel, phone!"

Mel walked into the kitchen and glared at her sister, snatching the phone and covering the mouth piece she mouthed 'idiot' to her, to which her sister Gill replied by poking out her tongue.

"Hi Mel, how's life in the good old UK?" Rob's voice was loud and Mel detected a drunken slur.

She checked the clock, it was almost seven thirty, that meant that it was two thirty or three thirty in the morning there, she couldn't quite get the hang of the time difference.

"Hi, yes fine thanks, are you okay? It's late there."

"Actually it's early if you wanna be picky. Listen a minute, I've had an idea, are you listening? Why don't you come here to Singapore, come and live here with me, it'll be great."

Mel stood in silence for a few moments.

"Mel, Mel, are you still there, Mel? Bloody hell the line's gone dead."

She could feel her heart pounding in her chest and there was a strange ringing sound in her ears.

"No, yes Rob, I'm here. Are you being serious? Am I about to make a complete fool of myself by saying yes just so you can tell me it's a wind up?"

"No straight up, I want you to come here, I miss you. What do you say?"

Mel was blushing from the chest upwards.

She had the urge to do a little dance right there in the kitchen and scream yes, yes, yes down the phone but she decided it was best to play it a bit cool.

"I need to speak to Mum, I can't give you an answer now, it's a lot to think about."

"Have you got a passport? I need you here by the fifth of June, if you want to come my office will pay for the flight."

"Yes I've got a passport, but why the rush? I said I'll need to think about it Rob, and talk it over with Mum."

"Okay, you have until Friday, I'll call back then. I gotta go, I have a meeting in the morning at eight and I need to get some sleep. Think about it, bye babe."

And he put the phone down.

She stood holding the phone, listening to the continuous buzzing sound of the disconnected line on the other end.

Just then her Mum came into the kitchen.

"Mel, is everything all right? You look like you've seen a ghost!"

Mel put the phone back on the hook and sat on one of the bar stools.

"He's finished with you hasn't he? I told you he would. Can't say I'm sorry, I don't know what you see in him to be honest. I've always thought he wasn't to be trusted."

"Actually Mum he wants me to go there, to Singapore and live with him."

"What? Really! When?"

"In a few weeks."

"Well there's a turn up for the books. Why?"

"He says he misses me, I was really surprised myself. Mind you he did sound a bit drunk."

"Ahh, well that explains it then, he'll wake up tomorrow with a huge headache, realise what he's done and take it all back. Expect a grovelling phone call by lunch time."

Mel went to bed that night but couldn't sleep, she lay there thinking about what she should do. This is what she'd always wanted, to be with Rob, to see him every day and to move away. But maybe her mother was right and she shouldn't get her hopes up, but what if?

The next day she had pounced on the phone every time it rang but it hadn't been him.

Rob true to his word, called early on Friday morning.

"So, have you made a decision? Are you going to come here Mel?

"Rob It's a big decision and it's a long way."

It was a long way, but she'd already decided, the second he'd asked her.

"Mel you'd love it here, I've got a new apartment with a pool, a tennis court, an expense account, shit, what more do you want?"

"Do you love me Rob?"

"What? What kind of a question is that! You know I do."

"But you've never said it, you've never actually said 'I love you.'"

"God, what is it with you bloody females? Are you coming or not?"

Mel looked around her, outside the rain was lashing down, whipping the windows and there was a cluttering sound coming from the back garden as the wind played with the blown over rubbish bins.

"Okay Rob, I'll come, I'll come to Singapore."

Chapter 2

"Cabin crew, take your seats for landing."

Mel sighed with relief as the long and difficult journey finally came to an end and not a minute too soon. She had slept really badly, waking every time there was the slightest turbulence, and to make matters worse the man next to her was a snorer.

The plane landed heavily on the runway and Mel gripped the arm rests again, digging her painstakingly manicured nails into the imitation leather.

It slowed to a speed that enabled her to see the airport outside more clearly. There were many big shiny planes with various coloured tails lined up along one side, as her plane turned she lost sight of the other planes but she could see a row of palm trees in the distance. The plane lurched forward as the captain applied the brakes.

Waiting for the seatbelt light above her head to go out she flicked open the buckle and stood up, her back was aching. She caught sight of herself in the refection in the window, her hair was a disaster, all flat on one side and sticking up on the other. She would have to find a bathroom immediately and sort herself out before Rob saw her. Rob! She felt a surge of excitement and her stomach filled with enormous butterflies.

Mel trailed out of the airplane with everyone else, the still-immaculate hostesses were lined up smiling and telling her to have a nice evening, she smiled back and thanked them politely.

'I'm sure I will', she smiled to herself.

As she stepped outside the plane the heat hit her, it was seven o'clock in the evening but it was hot, really hot. She walked down the steps and onto the waiting bus which was cold in comparison. She untied the cardigan from her waist and slipped it around her shoulders.

As she arrived at the terminal she was struck by how new and shiny everything looked.

She lined up with the other hundreds of people at passport control until finally it was her turn. Mel handed over her passport and the man behind the glass glanced at the photo, then at Mel then back to the photo.

"Purpose for the visit?" He enquired.

Mel smiling replied, "I'm here to live with my boyfriend, he works here, he works for Rawlings and Fitch."

The man nodded and stamped an empty page of her passport.

"Welcome to Singapore."

She walked through and followed the signs for baggage claim, spying a toilet she dashed inside and saw her real reflection in the mirror.

Mel quickly took out a brush and a lipstick from her handbag, she was a mess. She dabbed some cover up onto the dark circles under her eyes, brushed her hair and after a few minutes had returned to a reasonable condition. She would have liked to have been perfect but she had just spent the best part of a day traveling from one side of the world to the other. It would have to do!

She found her luggage, already on the belt, and hauled it off with both hands, God it was heavy. She had packed everything except the kitchen sink, photos, books, clothes, shoes and a quite a few cassette tapes of homemade compilations.

Her Mum had used her charm on the man at the check in desk who had tried to insist that she would have to pay excess baggage to the tune of sixty pounds. After a few minutes and choice words her Mum had worked her magic and managed to convince the man to let her off. She was great at that sort of thing and had been able, many a time, to get out of speeding tickets and parking fines with the aid of only a smile.

Mel put the suitcase on a trolley, perched her handbag on top and pushed it, with some difficulty, through the doors into the arrivals hall. She looked desperately round for Rob's face but didn't see it among the sea of anxious relatives. He had had all the flight details and had promised to be there to meet her. As she scanned the crowd one more time she saw a sign being held by a small Indian-looking man. 'Melissa Harrison, Rawlings and Fitch.'

She struggled to get the trolley over in the direction of the sign.

"I'm Melissa Harrison", she told the smiling man.

He took the trolley from her and beckoned towards the exit.

"Come please Miss, follow me, Mr Robert asked me to take you home, he is very busy with work, come, come."

Mel felt a lump form in her throat. She had come all this way and he couldn't even be bothered to meet her at the sodding airport.

She followed the man outside to the waiting car where he struggled to put the suitcase in the boot. Mel stepped forward to try to help him but he waved her back.

Once inside the car she sat back and felt the tiredness take over from the previous adrenaline-driven excitement.

She glanced out of the window, it was getting dark and she noticed the amazing sunset in the distance, the deep oranges and pinks were reflecting on the sea, so beautiful!

The car drove past lines of tall apartment buildings and there were perfect rows of perfect trees along the road on both sides.

After twenty minutes the car stopped in front of a large gate with a blue number 10 painted on white tiles next to it.

"We're here Miss Harrison, I will ring for the caretaker to open the gate."

He got out, walked over to some buttons on a panel nearby, and after a few seconds the gate slowly opened inwards. The car entered, drove along a path and stopped at the bottom of the first of the three high rise buildings. Looking up, Mel estimated there were about 12 floors. She hoped they weren't on one of the higher ones, she wasn't good with heights.

The man dragged the suitcase out of the boot making a small grunting noise as he did so. He then took out a small bunch of keys from his pocket and handed them to Mel.

"I'll leave you here Miss, you need the seventh floor, the lift is just inside. Mr Robert said to say he will be home around ten o'clock. Good night."

He drove off back down the path, she watched the gate slowly opening then turned and entered the building. With the weight of the suitcase and the intense heat she was sweating heavily, walking up to the lift she pressed the button and the door immediately opened.

Mel stepped inside pulling the suitcase in with her, just in time to avoid it jamming in the door as it closed, to Mel's relief there was air conditioning inside.

The lift moved up and she was soon standing in the hallway on the seventh floor where there was a door to the right and another to the left. 'Great, which one was hers?'

Her question was soon answered by the noise of children shouting loudly behind the one on the right.

She walked over to the door on the left and took out the keys, she tried the first one but to no avail, the same with the second, Mel started to cry, it was just a bloody key and it had reduced her to tears.

'He should be here with flowers and champagne, he should be here.'

The third and last key opened the door and she stepped into the apartment, dragging the suitcase behind her.

The first thing she noticed was the faint smell of fried food mixed with a stronger musty smell. She walked over to the French doors and pushed on the latch, the door slid open and she stepped out onto the balcony, what she saw below her took her breath away.

Down on the ground there was a huge rectangular, turquoise swimming pool lit up with lights under the water and large round lamps around the outside. A couple of men were straightening the sun loungers on the grassy area surrounding the pool.

To the left, two illuminated tennis courts were standing unoccupied and to the right were a few buildings mainly in darkness, it was difficult to make out what they were. There were another two towers to her right, all the same height with half circle balconies on the front, then there behind the buildings, was the sea. It was a velvety blue black colour and the moonlight was shining down on it, creating a magical scene.

Suddenly Mel didn't feel angry or upset anymore, she felt peaceful, she felt at home.

Returning inside she began to explore. The lounge was quite big, it had a large glass dining table in the middle with a high backed chair placed on each of the four sides, and there was a ceiling fan hovering directly above. Against one wall was a green leather sofa and a large ceramic white elephant at one end with a beer can balanced ungracefully on top.

Mel walked through into the corridor, there was a door to the left, one to the right and another straight ahead. She pushed open the door to the left. Immediately she saw a large double bed against the wall, on the bed there was a sheet crumpled up on one side and a couple of pillows. She stepped further inside the room and saw a tall chest of drawers standing next to the door which Mel noticed had a covering of dust on the top.

'He could have cleaned and tidied up a bit.'

Opposite the bed was a large double wardrobe with mirrored doors and there was another large rattan ceiling fan over the bed.

Over by the wardrobe were French windows which, Mel was thrilled to discover, led out onto another smaller balcony.

She peeked outside, same fabulous view. Looking around the room she found a lamp on the bedside table and pulled the string, the room glowed pink. She noticed another slightly smaller chest of drawers on the other side and next to them yet another door.

Opening the door she quickly discovered the source of the musty smell. There were three damp and dirty towels on the floor of the bathroom so she quickly picked them up and threw them into the wash basket in the corner of the room.

Apart from being damp and rather dirty the bathroom was new and modern. A large bath with a shower head over it was covered on two sides by a black and white shower curtain and there was a double sink and a large mirror on one wall. The toilet seat was up and she could see it hadn't been flushed, she pulled on the handle and fresh water filled the bowl. Rob had always been really untidy, that's what had given him his nickname at home: 'Rob the slob.'

She could see she was going to have her work cut out for her, but she couldn't wait to get started on sorting out her very own home.

She moved back out into the corridor and peeked inside the other rooms. There was a smaller bedroom with a large single bed that was buried under a mountain of washed but not ironed clothes, an ironing board set up but no iron, and a bedside table. There was no ceiling fan in there but a small portable fan was placed precariously on top of the bedside table.

The door at the end led to a small bathroom containing a shower without a curtain a toilet and a sink. This one was untouched, no towels, no soap and no toilet roll.

She went back to the lounge, picked up the phone and dialled her Mum's number but was met by only the answer machine.

"Mum, hi it's me, I'm here and it's amazing, I'll take some photos and send you them. Miss you already, Rob says hi. Love you Mum, speak soon."

Putting down the receiver the feeling of sadness crept back up on her.

She walked through into the small but well laid out kitchen. There was an oven with a hob where a frying pan had been left sitting there filled with used cooking oil and floating, burnt bits of egg white still inside.

In the corner was the biggest fridge she had ever seen, she walked over to it and pulled open the door. Inside she found two cans of Tiger beer, a bottle of gin, not yet opened, and half a bottle of tonic. There was also a packet of butter, three eggs, a strawberry yogurt almost a week out of date, and a carton of milk.

She reached for the gin and the tonic and then began opening all the cupboards looking for a clean glass. Eventually she found one and poured out a large measure of gin. The tonic made a pathetic hissing sound as she unscrewed the cap and Mel realised it had gone flat, oh well it would have to do.

She found the ice cube tray but it was empty, shit! She filled the tray from the tap and put it back in the freezer and closed the door. Then she immediately reopened the freezer door, 'could she drink tap water here?' She wondered. 'Better safe than sorry.'

She took the tray back out and threw the contents into the sink.

Mel carried her drink out onto the balcony and sat there for a while breathing in the heat and the strange, new smells.

Draining the bottom of the glass she went back inside, turned on the ceiling fan, which gave a little relief from the heat, and curled up on the sofa. She glanced at her watch and saw it was nine p.m. so she decided to have a quick nap before Rob arrived home.

Mel awoke to the sound of a key in the door.
She sat bolt upright,
'How long had she been asleep?'
She looked again at her watch, twenty past twelve.
She had played out this scene hundreds of times in her mind, the big romantic reunion, him sweeping her off her feet and swinging her round like they do in the hairspray adverts.
Mel jumped up and ruffled out her hair with her fingers.
Rob staggered in through the door carrying the most pathetic wilted bunch of flowers she'd ever seen and a parcel wrapped in beautiful red and gold paper.
"Meeel, you're here! These are for you."
He lunged forward and grabbed hold of her waist, pulling her in close to him and shoving the flowers under her nose.
"Hello Babe, how was your flight? Sorry I couldn't pick you up, had a really important meeting with some Japanese clients over from Japan. Really, really bloody important, couldn't get out of it."
He kissed her hard on the mouth and Mel could smell the scent of whisky.
"I've been here for hours Rob waiting for you to get home, alone and starving hungry, there's nothing to eat here."
"Mel, Melissa, love, don't start, there's a good girl. I told you I was sorry, I had a big meeting, closed a big deal today. Big meeting, big, big deal but I'll make it up to you. We'll go out tomorrow night I promise and I'll show you around a bit, what do you say? Come on smile, you're in

Singa-bloody-pore Mel. Have you seen the view from the balcony? Oh it's amazing, come here."

He grabbed her hand and dragged her outside where they stood on the balcony looking down at the lit swimming pool and the moon reflecting on the sea.

"Isn't that just the best Mel? Eh? Eh?"

He elbowed her hard in the ribs and Mel nodded.

"Here, open it."

He handed her the parcel and she carefully opened it, not wanting to tear the paper. Inside was a dark green embroidered silk dress with a mandarin collar and splits up each side.

"It's lovely Rob, thank you, I'll try it on tomorrow."

Mel managed a smile, the view was breathtaking. The warm scented air wafted around her and she closed her eyes to concentrate harder on the perfume. He was still holding onto the condemned bunch of flowers in his hand.

"Rob it's beautiful here, really beautiful." She leaned over and kissed him on the cheek. "I'm going to go and find a vase for these," she said, taking the flowers off him and walking into the apartment.

"Yeah, okay, good luck with that!" Rob laughed. "And I'm going for a piss, back in a sec."

He walked forward a few steps and stopped just a few centimetres from the closed part of the glass door.

"Shit, that was close, nearly walked into that bloody door."

He staggered off down the hallway and into the darkened room on the left.

So much for the big romantic reunion, but still, he was home now and they were together again.

In the kitchen, as predicted, Mel was unable to find a vase so she rinsed out a beer bottle she found in the bin under the sink and half filled it with water. With a bit of effort she squeezed the stems into the small neck of the bottle and carried the pathetic display through to the lounge and placed them on the centre of the dining table.

She pulled the glass door across and pushed down on the lock again, as she did so she caught her reflection in the glass. She looked nice, a little tired but nice and he hadn't said a word about her appearance.

'He's obviously had a long, difficult day' she said to herself, justifying his current state and lack of attention.

She walked into the still darkened bedroom and before she turned on the light heard the familiar and very disappointing sound of snoring.

Mel turned around and walked back into the lounge, and crossing to where the telephone was, she picked up the receiver.

Carefully she dialled the number and after a few seconds heard the ringing on the other end.

"Hello, hello, who is it?"

"Mum it's me, it's Mel."

"Oh thank God, where have you been? I've been waiting for a call from you for hours. I said to your sister that it's strange we hadn't heard from you, your plane was due in hours ago. How was your trip? How's Singapore?"

"Oh Mum, I'm sorry, I left you a message, didn't you get it on your answer machine?"

"I never listen to that thing, your sister usually does it for me."

"The flight was great, they really looked after me, and here it's amazing. The place is fantastic, really gorgeous, you'll have to come over here and see it for yourself. I'm really sorry I didn't call back before but Rob took me straight out for this amazing dinner and we've only just got home. He's having a shower at the moment but he said to say hi."

"Oh sounds lovely, I can't wait to see the photos, make sure you send lots over. Anyway Mel I've got to go, the news is just about to start and you should be getting to bed it late, isn't it?

"Yes it's late Mum and I'm really tired."

"Call me again in a few days, and take care. Love you."

"I love you too, bye Mum."

Mel put down the phone and walked back over to the bedroom.

'I miss you.'

Chapter 3

The next morning when Mel woke up she was disorientated and took a few moments to realise where she was.

She looked over and saw that Rob was not in the bed.

'God, don't say he's left without saying goodbye!'

Just then he walked out of the bathroom, he was already dressed in his suit.

He leant over and kissed her tenderly.

'Sorry babe about last night, I'm a shit I know. But to say sorry, I'm taking you out for dinner tonight, I'll take you into town. There's a great Chinese restaurant on the top of the Pan Pacific hotel near the centre. It's really good, loads better than the 'Jade Dragon' in the high street, you'll love it. Get a taxi at seven to the Pan Pacific hotel in Marina Square and I'll meet you there at the entrance. I have to get to work now, why don't you go down and have a swim, relax and introduce yourself to some of the neighbours. I'll call you later."

He leant over to kiss her again but Mel recoiled.

"I thought you were taking a few days off when I arrived Rob, you promised!"

He smiled. "Mel I can't control when interest rates will move, bloody busy right now, gotta go but I'll see you later. Have fun."

And he grabbed his wallet and keys and left.

She couldn't wait to get down to the pool. She rummaged around in her suitcase and eventually found her bikini and sun tan lotion. She grabbed the best looking towel she could find from the pile in the spare room along with her sunglasses and headed downstairs.

Passing the flower gardens, Mel noticed how immaculately kept they all were. Very different to the three or four sad looking pot plants she had at home. At the pool there were neat rows of virtually empty sun-loungers, she picked one in the far corner but as she went to lay her towel down a short man appeared from a little shed carrying a blue and white mattress and laid in onto the plastic sun bed. He smiled warmly at Mel.

"Welcome to Mandarin Towers Miss," he said. "Let me know if you need anything, all right?"

Mel thanked him and he disappeared back into his little hut.

The water was lovely and cool on her overheated skin. She held her nose and, leaning backwards, hair trailing out behind her, immersed her face in the water.

She loved it here, the big comfortable sun loungers, the big fluffy towels and this huge turquoise and blue mosaicked pool that wasn't too busy.

Her previous pool experiences had been in the local cold, over-chlorined public swimming bath, with its freezing changing rooms, cracked and chipped tiles and overzealous life guards with a whistle blowing fixation.

Mel swam a few lengths, she was quite impressed with her speed, she had never been overly sporty. At school she had come almost last in nearly all the running races and managed to improve her average in the cross-country only by finding a short cut through the boy's school playing fields.

She was, however, quite good at hockey and finally made it onto the team in the 4th year. Who knows, if she had stayed on and finished the sixth form, where she could have ended up?

Mel climbed out of the pool and lay down on her sun bed, where the sun dried her skin almost immediately. She closed her eyes and reflected on her last few months of school...

"Mel, Mel, do you want another Malibu and coke?"

Stella was shouting over to her from the bar.

Stella always went to the bar as she was the oldest looking of all of them.

Mel and Stella went every Saturday to the local disco. It was full of fifteen and sixteen year olds, even though the official age limit was supposed to be eighteen.

That evening they were going to the St. Valentine's disco, accompanied by Stella's boyfriend Mark and his friend Tom, who was desperately trying to 'get off' with Mel.

She wasn't in the slightest bit interested in this weedy little thing who stank of Brut. He had done more than 'splash it on all over' - he'd showered in it!

"Oh I love this song, come and dance."

He grabbed her hand and dragged her onto the dance floor.

"*Karmkarmakarma chameleon, you come and go, you come and gooooo, Love would be easy if your lalalalalalala dream.*" He sang out at the top of his newly broken voice and twirled her around violently.

She looked over desperately in Stella's direction, begging her with her eyes to help out but Stella beamed and gave her a thumbs up sign.

"I need to go to the bathroom a minute Tom, I'll be right back."

Mel broke free of his grasp and escaped into the toilet. There was the usual queue of four girls, all spraying their wildly backcombed hair into even higher styles and applying the fifth layer of mascara and yet more eyeshadow with their fingerless gloved hands. Mel glanced in the mirror and noticed one of her huge electric pink earrings was missing. Damn! It must have flown off while that idiot was spinning her around just now.

She finally emerged from the ladies' and was greeted in the corridor by Mark, Stella's boyfriend.

"So what do you think of Tom? He's all right, right?"

Mark was very cute, not that bright but Mel was happy for Stella.

"He's ok. Not kissable though!" Mel began to laugh just as Mark leapt forward pinning her to the wall and kissed her firmly on the lips.

"What the hell are you doing?" she protested, pushing him off.

"Oh come on Mel, you know I like you. You're hot and a good dancer and I know you like me."

Mel was shocked, "Stella is my best friend, she's your girlfriend! Stop being an arsehole!"

She went through into the main room where "The Reflex" was blasting out. She adored Duran Duran and would have usually raced over to the dance floor, but right then she didn't feel much like dancing.

Tom came bounding up to her like a puppy with a stick to throw.

"I found this on the floor," he beamed holding up her earring,

"Come on let's dance, I love this song", he began singing badly at the top of his voice.

"Oh the Reflex is a lonely child, who's walking in the park..."

'Noooooo! Aaaahhh! Those aren't the words!' she screamed in her head, 'this evening's just getting better and better.'

On Sunday morning she woke up and went immediately to call Stella, poor Stella! She hoped she was okay and that Mark hadn't said anything. She would try and convince her to dump him but it wouldn't be easy and she sure as hell wasn't going to tell her what happened. She had seen Stella angry on more than one occasion and knew better than to get on the wrong side of her.

The phone rang a few times before being answered.

"Oh hello Mrs. Shaw, it's Mel, is Stella there?"

"Hello Mel, no I'm afraid she's not, I'll tell her you called."

And the phone went dead.

Mrs Shaw was a right snob, she always made a point of talking about her new this and her new that, and asking how they were getting on the council estate, but Stella was good fun and gave Mel loads of clothes and records that she no longer wanted and certainly wouldn't miss.

Monday morning and Mel arrived at school at her usual time of quarter to nine. A group of her classmates were standing together outside on the netball court so she walked over to join them. As she got near one of the girls saw her approaching, spun round and spoke to the group, at which point they all turned, glared at Mel and quickly marched off.

Oh charming! she thought, not thinking that much of it. When she got in the classroom she sat down at her desk. Her heavy desk lid was full of etchings. 'John Taylor for ever', 'Duran Duran number 1 fan!' And then she saw a new fresh carving in the corner, 'BITCH'. She turned around to notice that all eyes were on her. She lifted the lid of the desk and saw on top of her books a pink piece of paper with the words, "Such a f****ng slag. We hate you. Signed 'the whole school!' P.S. We'll get you for what you did!

Mel looked back around the classroom, five or six girls were staring in her direction and the others were all pretending to be busy in their desks.

Just then Stella walked in and she had obviously been crying. Some girls jumped up and went over to hug her whilst looking daggers at Mel. She stood up and tried to talk to Stella but her 'minders' kept her at a distance.

"Stella, talk to me, what's going on? Stella?"

Stella began to cry again.

Tracey Hogging moved away from the group and placed her face in Mel's.

"As if you don't know! Leave her alone! I mean it, or you'll have me to deal with."

Everyone knew that you didn't mess with Tracey Hogging. Someone once made the mistake of laughing at her surname and Tracey 'accidentally' broke two of her fingers the next time they played hockey by bullying off much too high.

And that was it, Mel had been sent to Coventry. Over the next two months she was stabbed with a compass, received twenty or so threatening notes and spent every lunch and break time on her own.

She had to be accompanied by her Mum to school and picked up every afternoon.

Her Mum went to speak to the headmistress who assured her that she was on top of the situation, that was the day before the compass incident.

Stella's Mother had called asking Melissa's Mother to keep her "slutty council house kid" away from her precious daughter.

Mel grew tired of the bullying and so, consequently Mel dropped out of school and didn't complete the sixth form. That meant that she didn't get to finish her A' levels and kissed goodbye to her dream of studying law at University and becoming the next female Quincy.

The following summer Mel met Rob while she was out with some new friends. She had been invited out for a drink by a girl from work and her Mum had encouraged her to get out of the house.

She was insecure and vulnerable, and he was charming and funny and had a job in 'the city', not to mention he had a car, albeit a beaten up old Vauxhall! And that was it, she was totally swept away.

Her trip down memory lane was interrupted by a cold shower caused by 'the smoker', as Mel had decided to call him because he had had a cigarette constantly in his mouth from the moment he arrived, diving clumsily into the pool.

After the initial shock she took pleasure in the cooling down it had given her. She closed her eyes once more and returned to her memories.

It was the night in a pub a couple of years later when Clare Turner, a former school friend and 'gang' member came in. Mel was out on the town with Rob and a group of his crazy work friends who had come down from London for the weekend.

They were loud and crude making Rob seem almost timid in comparison.

She froze the moment she saw Clare, the intimidated 16year old once again, but then, pulling herself together, got up the courage to be the bigger person and say hello. Much to Mel's amazement Clare smiled and came over to her table.

"Hi, Mel, how fab to see you, you look great!"

Clare also looked good, too good!

"Who's this?" Rob asked, practically drooling into his beer but Mel didn't get a chance to reply.

"Hi, I'm Clare, one of Mel's best mates from school, God we had some laughs didn't we Mel? Do you remember that thing with Stella?"

Mel winced at the still painful memory of the event that changed the course of her life. How could Clare be so blasé about it all?

"Did Mel tell you?

Rob shook his head.

"Oh...my...God...it's so funny,"

Clare slid indelicately onto the bench seat next to Rob, nudging him and forcing the whole row to shift along.

"So, what happened was," she continued, hardly taking a breath.

"Stella, Mel's other best friend, had this boyfriend, a bit of a pig really. Anyway, he dumped her one night after some disco thingy and told her that he wanted to go out with Mel! Well imagine poor old Stella, heartbroken and humiliated. She called Tracey and me to tell us and the next day we went over to her house and spent ages forging a letter from "Mel," she did the inverted commas thing with her fingers, "saying that Mel was madly in love with Mark and had kissed him at the disco. So we made out Stella had finished with *him*. Genius!"

Mel's heart began to pound, her hands formed into a fist shape and under the table her foot was tapping at a hundred beats a minute.

"Anyway," she continued proudly, "she took the letter to school and they all fell for it, believed every word, what a laugh! Poor old Mel got quite a lot of stick over it, hey Mel? Still girls will be girls!" She raised her glass in a 'cheers' motion at Mel.

Mel's eyes were welling up at the thought of all 'the stick' she had been given. Quick as a flash she stood up, grabbed Rob's almost full pint glass and threw the entire contents into Clare's grinning face.

Mel turned over on the sun bed and unfastened her bikini top, she smiled to herself at the image of Clare stood there dripping wet, over streaked, over-hairsprayed hair now flattened with lager running down her heavily made up and no longer grinning face.

Her smile then turned to audible laughter as she remembered Clare tottering out of the pub in tears.

'Oh, girls,' she said to herself, adjusting the makeshift towel pillow under her head,

'If you could see me now.'

Chapter 4

Mel stood under the cool shower enjoying the temporary relief from the heat. She squeezed out some shampoo from a virtually empty bottle onto her hair and rubbed her head for a few seconds. Then she reached for the shower gel and squirted a bit onto her hand and began to wash herself. She grimaced as she passed her hand over her shoulders and felt the sting of burnt skin, the same happened with her shins and her arms and she could feel the cool water creating steam down her back as well.

After a few minutes she reluctantly pulled back the curtain and climbed out of the shower, gasping as she saw her reflection in the mirror.

Her whole body was red except for very clear white, bikini shaped areas. She stepped closer to the mirror, her nose was glowing.

'I could get a job pulling Santa's sleigh' she smiled.

She grabbed the towel from the side and wrapped it gently around her. Walking back into the bedroom she sat on the bed for a while and waited for the warm air in the bedroom to dry her naturally. She couldn't bear the thought of rubbing the hard towel over her sore skin.

After just a few minutes when she was dry, she stood up and went over to the wardrobe.

'What to wear?' The present from Rob was out, far too scratchy today.

She flicked through a couple of the things she had had time to hang up but they all seemed too heavy or too clingy for a hot evening and sunburn! Then she remembered her little black dress that was still waiting patiently somewhere in the suitcase.

Remembering it was somewhere at the bottom she thrust her hand in, felt around and pulled it out and shook it, luckily it wasn't too creased because she couldn't face the steam iron right now.

Then she hunted through back through her suitcase trying to find her new underwear.

The week before leaving her Mum had taken her shopping to buy some new bits and pieces to take with her.

"You need some new undies." Her Mother had pointed out while she was helping Mel pack.

"All yours are falling to bits. Let's go into town this afternoon and get you some."

Mel loved shopping with her Mum, she always told her the truth about what suited her and what didn't, she knew that if her Mum said something looked good or awful, as was usually the case, then it really did!

In the shop Mel began to picking out underwear that she thought looked comfortable. There was a set of three, high leg, cotton knickers in pretty plain pastel colours and another set the same but in darker shades. She was about to put them into the basket when they were snatched from out of her hand.

"Absolutely not!"

Her Mum replaced the offending items back on a random rail and proudly held up her find. She had an assortment of black and white, lace and satin, very skimpy knickers. Mel glanced down at the price tags.

"Mum, why is it that the less material you use the more expensive things become?"

"If you're going to go and live in Singapore with Robert and be all grown up then the least you can do is act all grown up. These are much more suitable Melissa, trust me, you want to keep your man happy in the bedroom otherwise it's never going to work."

"Mum!" Mel almost shouted, glowing with embarrassment. "I don't really want to discuss this with you, it's weird!"

"No it's not, stop being such a prude about it, now let's get you some decent bras, something to maybe push you up and out a bit."

Her mother stood staring at her chest looking almost sorry for her.

"Unfortunately Melissa you didn't inherit my boobs, brains yes, boobs definitely not!"

And she marched off on a mission towards the bra section. Mel trailed reluctantly behind, glancing sadly down at her 34Bs as she went.

After a few minutes of more digging around in the case she eventually found a black lacy pair of knickers and slipped them on, followed by a matching bra. Her back smarted as she did up the bra and twizzled it around, and the pulling up of the straps was accompanied by 'ouches' and 'aaaahhhs.'

She walked over to the full length mirror and stood admiring her shape.

Mum had been right about the underwear, she did look hot, in every sense! Her reddened skin was now bordering on crimson.

She gently pulled her dress over her head and smoothed it down, her hair was virtually dry already. Mel grabbed the brush from the top of the chest of drawers and picked up the hairdryer that was lying on the floor, finding the cold setting she finished drying her hair. When she passed the brush through her hair she grimaced again, even her head felt burnt, she didn't know that was even possible.

She reached for her make up bag and pulled out a few items, on finding the cover up she dabbed some gently onto her nose and forehead area and very, very slowly she rubbed it into her skin. Looking again in the mirror she was satisfied that it had taken away a little of the redness. She was now sweating visibly so she grabbed the can of deodorant and, digging around under her dress, sprayed a lot on her armpits and a bit on her bra-enhanced cleavage, jumping slightly as the cold spray hit the skin.

Going back to her makeup she brushed some gold eyeshadow onto her eyelids and added a bit of bright pink in the outer corners. Then she took a black pencil and drew a line under her eye, and with the back of her hand she wiped away a little trickle of sweat running down her cheek.

Finally she applied some waterproof mascara and finished the look with a light pink shiny lipstick. Done!

Mel checked herself closely in the mirror, not bad!

She sat back down on the bed feeling extremely hot and uncomfortable, she was also starting to feel a bit sick. Taking a deep breath and pulling herself together she stood up and walked out of the room.

She looked at the clock, it was ten to seven.

Mel took the lift down, the air conditioning giving some temporary relief to her glowing skin.

Arriving at the ground floor she stepped outside and immediately had the urge to run back inside and spend the evening in the nice, cool lift.

She hunted around in her bag and found the compact mirror which she flicked open and used to check her make up once again. She was convinced of finding it all sliding down her face but to her relief it was fine except for her nose was visibly red again so she dabbed on a bit more cover up.

Mel didn't have long to wait for a taxi, one arrived almost immediately.

As she climbed in she began to feel very excited about spending a romantic evening with Rob in this exotic location.

"Pan Pacific hotel please."

She was so impressed by everything she saw out of the taxi window, she still couldn't really believe she was actually there, she wanted to pinch herself but resisted as she was in enough discomfort right then.

By the time the taxi arrived at its destination her burnt bottom cheeks had melted through her dress and were now fused with the plastic seat in the back.

Peeling herself off the cab she stepped out into the bright lights of the hotel entrance and, looking up, she saw that the doorway was flanked on either side by two huge marble pillars and she saw Rob was standing next to one of them.

She was wishing the lights weren't quite so bright as she started to walk over towards him, Rob saw her approaching and came over to meet her.

His smile turned to a puzzled expression as he got closer.

"Hi Mel, blimey what happened to you?" He hugged her and kissed her tenderly.

She was in pain but smiled and kissed him back.

"Oh nothing serious, just overdid the sunbathing today a bit, I'm not used to it."

"Shit! It's like hugging a hot water bottle, are you sure you're okay?"

Mel nodded and took hold of his hand.

"Our table's waiting upstairs, you'll love the view, you can see almost the whole city."

"Sounds romantic," she said squeezing his hand.

A man dressed in a uniform complete with white gloves and a hat opened the lift doors for them and Mel noticed that amazingly there wasn't a bead of sweat anywhere on him, she wiped another trickle from her cheek.

The lift eventually opened and they stepped out into the circular restaurant.

There was a lot of hustle and bustle, waiters were dashing around carrying plates and trays and many tables of people were chatting and laughing loudly.

Mel happily noticed that the lights were quite dim so her radiation burns would be less visible.

There were large tanks of various live fish and crabs of all sizes along one wall. She had never understood this passion of fish eaters to choose their food, she would never dream of walking into a field and picking out a cow!

Rob noticed her looking worriedly at the fish tanks.

"Don't worry, they do meat as well here, wouldn't want you getting a seafood allergy tonight on top of the sunburn would we?"

Mel shook her head and smiled.

"I managed to get us a table over by the window so we'll have the best view."

Mel smiled again but bit on her lower lip. The lift had taken them to the thirty-seventh floor and she really wasn't good with heights, still she wasn't going to let the sunburn or the vertigo spoil her romantic, long awaited evening with Rob.

A waiter approached them, "Rawlings and Fitch" smiled Rob.

'Using the company name, probably to get the best table.' thought Mel proudly.

"Good move!" she said as the waitress asked them to follow her to their table.

Rob took hold of Mel's hand and she felt her heart jump in her chest. The waitress crossed the large room and stopped at a large round table where four Asian gentlemen were sat. The waitress pulled out one of the empty chairs and indicated to Mel to take a seat and as she did so the four men politely stood up. Mel turned to look at Rob not knowing what to say.

'So much for our romantic dinner!'

"Mel I'd like you to meet some people, this is my boss Vincent, his Boss Sal and those two over there are my unfortunate co-workers, Eric and Matthew."

Mel nodded and smiled timidly.

"And this is my woman, Melissa."

"Hello, hello" smiled the men in unison.

They all sat back down.

"So," Rob clapped his hands together.

"Let's get some drinks in. I'll have a Tiger beer and Mel'll have a G and T, right?" He turned to face her.

"No, really water is fine thank you."

"Water! Water is for fish, let's get you a gin and tonic Melissa" Insisted Sal.

"Yes okay, perfect, thank you." She lied.

Her sun burn was now at maximum strength and her stomach didn't feel good at all.

The waitress gave a quick nod of her head and left the table.

"So Robert this is your girlfriend, is it?" Sal asked in a strange accent while pouring wine into his glass.

"She seems too good for you, you know! Are you sure she is your girlfriend or you just paid her to be here to impress us?"

All present laughed very loudly and Mel joined in awkwardly not really sure if that was a compliment or if he had just called her a prostitute.

Rob grabbed her thigh under the table and gave it a squeeze, then he moved his hand slowly up to the top of her thigh where it rested. Mel shuddered, a little from the sensation of his hand and a little from the chill that she had from the air conditioning.

After a while and a large gin and tonic later, she began to relax a little and her initial disappointment at his surprise dinner began to subside.

"You had too much sun today I think" exclaimed Vincent, or was it Matthew? She was terrible with names.

"Yes." agreed Mel. "I need to remember this isn't UK sun. I'll go out tomorrow and get some much higher protection sun cream or a wet suit maybe."

The gathered guests laughed politely.

"That looks painful, are you burnt everywhere?" Asked Sal smirking visibly. The five men at the table giggled like school girls. Mel decided to play along and leaned in close,

"Well almost everywhere" she whispered seductively.

Mel was feeling quite jovial and she was actually enjoying all the attention.

"Yeh, there will be some interesting white bits I'm sure." Rob burst out. "I'll let you know tomorrow when I've had a chance to explore the situation further!"

"Oh Rob, you're so lucky you know!" exclaimed Vincent.

Mel was lapping up the compliments.

"Although," Rob's voice was getting louder, "some white bits are not as big as they could be!"

He put his hand back on her thigh but this time Mel brushed it off.

More raucous laughter from everyone at the table which caused the other diners to turn and stare, everyone that is, except Mel.

Rob had an annoying habit of talking about their personal life in public and she didn't like it. Some things, she thought, should be kept private! But as this wasn't the moment to tell him she decided to let it slide.

Mel, mortified and suffering terribly from the sun burn, began to sweat visibly, she glanced around at the neighbouring tables trying to ascertain who had heard his comment. The woman at the next table gave her a look of sympathy and shook her head.

'Well she had *definitely* heard!' Mel sighed to herself.

Her stomach still wasn't feeling good so she just sipped at her second drink lightly.

At that moment the waitress appeared and put a large pitcher of what looked like water in the centre of the table, then another waiter came over carrying a large plate of large, grey prawns. Mel looked on in disgust as she saw the prawns were still moving around.

"Oh good, the drunken prawns!" cried Vincent excitedly.

Then he picked up a twitching prawn and dropped it into the pitcher.

"It's vodka you see, the prawns stay inside a couple of minutes and they get drunk, like Rob does every Friday."

He then took out the prawn, now hardly twitching, and popped it into his mouth.

Mel retched and felt vomit rising in her throat.

She excused herself from the table and walked quickly to the bathroom. Once safely inside she was no longer able to hold it back and she vomited violently into the toilet. Sweat was now pouring out of every pore and she sat there trembling on the floor trying to get her breath.

She heard someone come into the room and struggled to her feet just as she heard Rob's voice.

"Melissa are you okay?"

She opened the door and brushed her damp hair from her dripping forehead.

"You look terrible, come out and sort yourself out."

He seemed angry.

Looking in the mirror she caught her pathetic reflection, bright red and soaked with sweat.

"Rob, I'll be fine, go back to the table and I'll be there in a minute."

"All right but don't be long, this is yours" he gave her her handbag.

She ran the cold water and splashed it on her face and chest, then she dried herself off with the hand dryer. Grabbing a crocodile clip from inside her bag she twisted up her damp hair, blotted her face with a hand towel and applied more cover up and lipstick and checked her reflection once again, almost as good as new.

Opening the door she took a slow, deep breath, walked slowly back to the table and apologised for her long absence. The men didn't seem too worried and Rob, now smiling, gave her a wink. To her relief the prawns were almost finished.

The other food arrived and Mel slowly began to feel better. The feeling of sunburn began to subside, and the small amount of food she managed to eat was really delicious.

Rob had been right, it was much better than the 'Jade Dragon.'

Mel, despite everything, had miraculously continued being charming and witty throughout the evening.

In the cab on the way home Rob leaned over.

"You were great tonight, vomiting aside, I was proud of you. My colleagues all really liked you, I liked you, come here."

He grabbed her and kissed her roughly on the mouth and the neck.

"You're still boiling, we need to get out of these clothes."

Mel returned his kisses passionately, she wanted him, it had been a long time.

Once inside the apartment Rob undressed quickly and slipped under the sheet.

"Strip for me" he asked, his hand already occupied under the sheet.

Mel obligingly pulled her dress slowly up over her head, then she undid her bra behind, sighing with relief as she did so and threw it onto the floor. She put her fingers in the sides if her knickers, like she'd seen them do in the cheap porn films that Rob liked them to watch, and slowly pulled them down to her ankles. She stepped out of them and flicked them off in the direction of the door.

Rob smiled as he saw her white areas.

"Nice bikini" he laughed.

She climbed under the sheet as he began running his hand over her breasts and squeezing them playfully. Then he took hold of her hand and pulled it down under the sheet to his awaiting erection. Melissa began caressing him slowly. After just a couple of minutes of foreplay their excitement was at fever pitch. Rob climbed on top of her and passionately kissed her neck. Mel moaned with pleasure at the feeling of his lips on her.

"You're boiling, don't worry, I'll be gentle" he whispered, then unable to contain himself any longer, he was inside her, his hands gently pinning hers to the sheet, finally after months of waiting they were making love.

Mel tried not to think about the pain, her overindulgence at the pool was causing her in that moment and she shut out everything except him.

Rob was good in bed, at least she thought so, and he always took time to make sure she enjoyed herself.

Their breathing was deep and rhythmic, in sync with their movements and the couple held onto each other and kissed urgently.

This, this is what she had missed. This is what she needed, it was him and his love making. She liked feeling wanted, being needed and desired and she liked being able to satisfy her man.

Before meeting Rob her experience had been with horny teenage boys with plenty of urge but no technique. Rob had patiently taught her so much in the time they had been together, and she had had been an A grade student.

After just a few more minutes they lay panting and soaked in sweat, staring up at the static ceiling fan, both too tired to get up and turn it on. Mel turned painfully over onto her side and, smiling to herself, fell into a deep, peaceful sleep.

The next day when she woke her skin was still glowing red but was much less painful to touch. Rob was already in the shower. She got up and pulled on one of his discarded shirts that was draped over the chair in the corner of the room. The shirt smelt of him and she breathed in deeply to capture the scent.

She went into the kitchen and after hunting around in the cupboards found what she needed to make a cup of tea. When the kettle whistled she poured the steaming water into two mugs and dropped in two tea bags. She found a tea spoon in the sink and rinsed it clean. Today she was going to dedicate herself to cleaning the apartment; it didn't look like it had been touched in weeks.

Rob walked into the kitchen dressed for work.

"I've made a cup of tea, where do you keep the sugar, I couldn't find it?"

"I'm out. Anyway it doesn't matter, there's no milk."

"There is, I saw it in the fridge yesterday."

She opened the fridge door and took out the carton, Rob took it off her and poured some out into the sink. The milk fell out in large, stinking lumps.

"Like I said, no milk! It doesn't matter Mel, I'm late and I haven't got time to drink it now anyway. If you go downstairs there's a mini market near the pool, I have an account there so get what we need and then just give them my name."

"Okay Rob, what time are you home this evening? I'll cook us something and we can have a romantic dinner on the balcony."

"Actually no need, good news, we've been invited out again to dinner this evening, I have to dash now but I'll call later with the details. Have a good day and keep out of the sun."

'Good news for you maybe,' thought Mel disappointedly, she was really hoping to spend some time alone with him.

"Oh and can you have a bit of a clean-up in here today?" he added, "I haven't had a minute to do it and It'll keep you busy."

Great! Now it would look like it was his idea, and instead she had wanted to surprise him.

He kissed her.

"I'm glad you're here" he smiled, opening the door.

"So am I" she beamed back, blowing him a goodbye kiss as he closed the door.

Chapter 5

The cab drew up outside a huge iron gate, between the bars the lights which lit up a long tree lined driveway were glowing an iridescent orangey yellow. She opened the cab door and the hot air blew in like the opening of the oven door, she was sure she would never get used to this temperature, the stark contrast between the cool cab and the steamy night air was incredible.

Cab paid, they walked up to a panel on the gate where a dozen neatly typed names were displayed next to their own little illuminated button.

Rob pressed the bottom button on the right hand row with the name, Phillips. T, and a light above their heads came on.

A woman's distant voice could be heard coming out from the panel.

"Hi guys come up, you remember the apartment Robert, don't you lovely? Second stairwell, second floor, follow the noise."

The evening hadn't started out very well, firstly Rob had been late home from work.

"Make sure you're ready for half seven" he had insisted when he had called later that morning, "and look gorgeous, wear that green dress that I got you, okay?"

The Thai silk dress was beautiful, but she wasn't very comfortable in it. Rob had explained that like hand-made shoes and fresh water pearls, Thai silk was an expat's girlfriend's uniform and must be worn proudly.

So, as instructed, at six forty five she showered, dried her hair and put it straight up in a clip and did her makeup, by which time she needed another shower.

'Why the hell couldn't they have proper air con instead of this creaking, noisy ceiling fan that in the dead of night sounded like a small light aircraft circling just above the bed!'

Dressed to order she prepared a 'small' gin and tonic and sat on the balcony taking great pleasure in the light breeze. She looked out over the sea, the sun was going down leading to a small but much appreciated drop in temperature. Mel took a deep breath,

"Another shitty day in paradise" she laughed.

Seven forty five and still no Rob, so she poured another G and T, slightly larger than the first, then finally at eight the door buzzer went,

"Come down quickly, I've got a cab waiting."

'And hello to you too' she thought.

She finished the last drop and placed the empty glass in the sink, turned off the portable fan she had perched on the kitchen worktop and walked out into the hallway.

The lift was up on the tenth floor, she pressed the button and waited a few seconds for it to arrive. Stepping into the lift she sighed with relief as the cool air caressed her bare neck and arms, she loved this lift.

The walk from the lift to the cab was short but just long enough for her to feel the sweat accumulating on her chest and trickling down her cleavage, what little, as her Mother delicately pointed out, there was of it.

She didn't wait for the electric gates to open entirely, just until they were wide enough for her to squeeze through.

"Hurry up Mel, get in the cab, we're late!"

'God he can be such an arsehole, he's almost half an hour late and he's acting like it's all my fault.'

"It wouldn't kill you to be civil, 'Hi! How are you my love? Did you have a good day? Blah, blah, blah. Since when have you been so worried about being late? And why are you so late anyway?"

"I just want to make a good impression, this guy is one of my biggest customers and his wife owns a huge catering company, she might be able to get you a job if you are still insisting on working here."

'Perfect,' she thought, 'I can't boil an egg, but whatever!'

She decided it was better to let the snide job comment go as there seemed to be enough tension in the cab right then.

"You still haven't told me why you're so late."

"I had a late meeting, Mel what's going on with your hair?"

Mel used her reflection in the taxi window as a mirror and took out the clip, combed her hair through with her fingernails before twisting it back up neatly while admiring her new freshwater pearl earrings and necklace.

"It's the humidity" she apologised timidly.

She gazed out the cab window at the perfectly lined up trees which marked the way along the pristine streets which to Mel looked almost fake.

The high rises in the distance signalled the position of the Central Business District which was the centre of commerce and the domain of almost all expats working there. The majority of the brief journey was spent in an awkward silence except for Rob's brief instructions to the cab driver. Mel noticed that he looked very tense and agitated and began to be concerned.

"Is everything all right?" she said quietly, breaking the deafening silence.

Rob nodded and held her hand.

The cab turned into a small street called Arab Street. Hanging outside every shop were all manner of things made exclusively from rattan and silk. Mel decided then and there that this would become her favourite place to spend an afternoon.

The taxi then turned into a larger, more modern street.

"Stop at Victoria Heights, that apartment building just after the restaurant please" Rob instructed.

The cab stopped in front of a low building and in an unexpected gesture Rob spun Mel around to face him, and had a strange expression.

"Come on, let's have some fun, be charming and don't let me down."

He squeezed her hand, he was still smiling but she noticed that he looked very tense.

She imagined that these people were important to have such an effect on him, she didn't remember seeing him that nervous before.

That probably meant that they were in for a boring night.

Come on Mel, she scolded herself, at least you're out meeting people, mingling, who knows you may even enjoy yourself and meet someone interesting.

Melissa had been hoping to meet some other English people and chat about the weather and what was going on in EastEnders. She'd never done it when she was in England but suddenly she had an impelling urge to do just that. She hadn't been out of the apartment alone since her arrival, and she had spent most of the day watching seventies TV programs with Chinese subtitles and trying, with little success, to understand the cooking programs that were demonstrating dishes with ingredients she wouldn't be able find in Sainsbury's.

Her new, more amusing and frustrating hobby was practicing with chopsticks. After the dinner with Rob's bosses when she realised her total inability to work the smooth ivory sticks she had been given, she was determined to master the art of the slippery buggers. She grimaced remembering the scene at dinner, struggling with the chicken and water chestnuts in the bowl, managing to balance the meat precariously between the sticks and bringing it up slowly only to see it tumble onto the table just two millimetres from her mouth.

The training involved two bowls, about a hundred peanuts and the longest, slipperiest, smoothest and most challenging looking chopsticks she could find. She practised transferring all the peanuts from one bowl to another without dropping them. So far, after two hours of exhausting practice she had managed to successfully transfer about half the bowlful.

Walking up the path to the second stairwell, they passed a beautifully manicured lawn. She noticed a huge oval shaped pool surrounded by dwarf palm trees and wooden deck chairs. Behind the pool was a floodlit tennis court on which two grunting figures were knocking seven bells out of a tennis ball.

There was a lift but they decided to climb the two floors, this usually would not have been a problem but it was currently about 30 degrees and extremely humid.

As they reached the second floor the music of Phil Collins could be heard blaring out.

'I can feel it comin' in the air tonight', he crooned.

Mel had always loved this song.

She remembered that she had been woken many a night by the drum bit in the middle pounding on the walls as her Mum whacked it up to full volume.

A door to the right flung open before they had a chance to ring the bell.

"Darling, ciao, you made it, and this lovely young lady with you must be Melanie, so great you brought her this time!"

She leaned forward and kissed them both on each cheek,

'Don't you have to be Italian to do things like that, like in The Godfather?' Mel wondered.

"Hi Alison, yes this is Mel, Mel this is Alison, and may I say how lovely you are looking tonight as always."

A stupid smile broke out on his face, well not so much a smile, he looked more like a puppy dog waiting for someone to throw him a ball.

'Fetch!'

Mel was trying to remember the last time he'd said something like that to her.

"Oh Rob, you charmer." she beamed, then turning to Mel and extending a hand, "Alison Phillips, that's Phillips with two Ls."

"Come on in both of you, Mel we've heard *so* much about you", she slipped her arm through Rob's and led him into the hallway, Mel trailed behind.

"You're from Cambridge Melanie aren't you?"

"Well no actually I'm from Canterbury, and it's Melissa."

"That's right, I knew it was a place with a university or cathedral or something."

Alison led the way along the Buddha lined Hallway into a modern, state of the art kitchen where a group of people, mainly male, were swigging gin and tonics or sipping wine from enormous glasses.

As they entered the kitchen everyone stopped chatting and turned to stare, awkward!

At that moment, in a bizarre, surreal moment all the men, dicky bows an' all, turned towards Rob, let out a shout and in perfect synch started doing the New Zealand rugby team's Hakka.

Mel looked on amused as Rob took the lead, she had no idea he knew how to do that! He had never played a game of Rugby in his life, he'd always been a Cricket man.

Word of her arrival soon spread through the house and one at a time a long line of people queued up to greet the latest addition to the community.

The music was loud, there were a ton of canapés, 3 or 4 Philippine looking waitresses serving the 20 or so guests and the trays of glasses filled with wine and cocktails were never ending.

She wandered around the huge apartment making small talk with bank employees, C.E.s or C.O.s, brokers, but of what she wasn't quite sure, and insurance agents.

She found out that Alison's catering company was called 'Fine Dine' but that she didn't actually do any of the catering, just the organising side. She was then bombarded with a long list of names of wives and girlfriends.

Everyone was commenting on how funny Rob was and how he was such a breath of fresh air. She listened intently to all their comments,

'One of the lads,' 'a real riot" and she realised that in the two months they had been apart her man had been busy, no wonder he had had little time left for her.

She listened, captivated, while Tony, one of the brokers, told a story of his and Rob's exploits to a small captivated audience.

'It had been an especially lively night, when after two bottles of champagne they had gone to the Palm Bar and danced on the tables, dropping their trousers while singing the national anthem'. Hysterical apparently!

It was only after a few minutes that she realised he was talking about Wednesday, the night she had arrived.

He said he had been out with Japanese customers Wednesday, so she checked.

"You did all that in front of Japanese customers?"

"What? God no, it was just us."

Seeing her surprised expression he twigged he'd said something wrong and immediately backtracked.

"Just us and the customers, yes, the Japanese, they loved it, they're real party animals when you get them drunk. Will you excuse me a minute I'm just going to check on Laurel, lovely meeting you, I'll catch you later."

Mel watched him slink out onto the balcony and make a bee line straight for Rob. She couldn't see Rob's expression but she could imagine.

She observed them for a few minutes getting their stories straight and then went back into the kitchen to grab another toothpick with something exotic skewered on it and another glass of gin. She wondered how often he would actually have real appointments with customers.

She couldn't really be angry, she convinced herself, he was a wild spirit after all. That's one of the reasons why she'd fallen in love with him, and at the end of the day he had asked her to come here, and she did have an apartment with a pool...

Pushing past a small group of men, she felt a hand slide deliberately over her right buttock, she decided to ignore it and resisted the urge to turn around and see who was responsible. She then wandered out onto the balcony where she found Rob propped against a pillar deep in conversation with a really big gentlemen with obvious signs of excessive living. As she approached she heard the words, 'interest rates' and 'Bundesbank' mentioned and turned to go back inside, happy to leave them to their riveting conversation but just as she did so the man grabbed hold of her wrist.

"Well, well, who do we have here? Fresh meat, how delightful," and then grabbing a handful of backside, "and tender too!"

She froze on the spot, stunned by this forward behaviour; she looked pleadingly at Rob, her man and protector, to help her out but he just laughed.

"Malcolm Andrews, this is my girlfriend Melissa."

"Ah yes the famous Mel, so lovely to finally meet you, heard a lot about you but Rob never mentioned you were this charming. How come you've never introduced me to this lovely piece of arse before?"

She tried a polite smile, 'I think you've just answered your own question, pig,' she thought.

Malcolm and Rob burst into raucous, over the top laughter.

She escaped back into the lounge where a group of women were chatting together, she decided to join them, thinking it would probably be safer.

"Hi, my name's Melissa, Melissa Harrison, I'm here with Rob."

The women stopped chatting and all turned to face her. Mel estimated they were all in their late twenties and early thirties, although they were all quite heavily made up so it was difficult to tell.

"Hello, lovely to finally meet you Melissa," a tall, attractive woman with long dark hair stepped forward.

"I'm Debbie, Mark Reese's wife, this is Sue, Dan's wife, that is Laurel, Tony's wife and that lucky lady is Tess, Harry's wife, oh, and that poor unfortunate over there near the kitchen is Mary, Malcolm's long suffering spouse. And Lizzie is around here somewhere and she's married to Stuart, and Alison, our hostess with the mostest is Tim's wife."

She didn't have a clue who most of those men were, although she had remembered Rob mentioning a Tim and a Harry that he worked with or for, some important directors or something.

Mel cringed, she was really terrible at remembering names. She scanned the group again mentally repeating their names.

"How are you doing here? How are you settling in?" asked Tess politely.

Mel was wondering what qualified her as 'lucky', except for her fabulous figure, that is.

"Hell, if she's anything like me," interrupted Laurel, "she'll be shell shocked for months, thank God for G and T's."

Mel noted she had an Australian accent, or it could have been New Zealand.

She smiled, "Yes, it has been strange, I *am* still a bit shell shocked to be honest and I'm not used to this heat, but it's lovely to be able to swim every day."

The ladies eyed her up and down.

"Yes, you've certainly overdone the sunbathing a bit, classic novice mistake" laughed Debbie. Mel looked down at her still glowing shins.

Mel stood chatting to the group for a few minutes. None of the women she talked to seemed to have a job, unless, according to them, you count shoe collecting or striving for the perfect tan.

"Oh just look at that fresh, pink face, how old are you Melissa?" asked Mary, who had wandered over from the kitchen. Mel noticed that she looked a bit older than the other women.

Debbie began shaking her empty glass in the direction of a waitress who immediately scuttled over with a fresh one. Mel felt very self-conscious, everyone was looking at her and she was suddenly aware that she was young, very young.

"I'll be twenty one on the tenth of December,"

"Good God that is young Melissa," commented Alison, popping up from behind the group.

"Well, we'll definitely have to make sure we organise a bloody great party, twenty one, that's one to celebrate, and around here any excuse for a party is always welcome."

The women clinked their glasses.

She then turned to address the group.

"Ladies and Gentlemen," announced Alison, "can you all get your gin soaked arses sat in the dining room as we are about to dish up."

Mel noticed that Alison had let her posh accent slip slightly.

At that moment Rob appeared from the balcony and grabbed her hand, squeezed it for the third time that evening and gave her that weird smile again.

"Having fun, meeting lots of people? Try to relax, have a drink."

He was obviously excited; Mel noticed a slight shake in his hands.

They followed everyone into the dining room.

"I am relaxed and I have had a drink, in fact I've had a couple" she replied, a little irritated by his over enthusiasm.

"Good, are you hungry? Alison's a great cook and she always serves great grub."

Just how many times has he been here? she thought, feeling an irrational pang of jealousy.

"Actually I'm not that hungry, the heat really ruins my appetite."

Mel was now regretting all the toothpicks she'd nibbled on.

"Well please try to eat something, she's gone to a lot of trouble and we don't want to seem rude do we?"

He pinched her cheek in a playful manner, only it hurt.

The eight couples were sat at a huge, long dining table made from mahogany coloured rattan with a glass top and matching high backed rattan chairs covered with square cream coloured cushions.

Mel was making mental notes of every detail, she wanted an apartment just like this one.

Mel was sat next to Lizzie, a petite woman with a big smile, who introduced herself in an accent that Mel couldn't place.

Each man was sat opposite his partner, and it was at that point that she noticed it was all couples except for two men sat on each end whose names she couldn't remember, had she ever known them? She couldn't recall.

Much to her relief she noticed Malcolm had been sat three couples down, but her relief was short lived as he began to shout comments in their direction.

"So Robster, how long have you and this tender morsel been together?"

All the men laughed and turned to check out this "tender morsel." The women glanced up smiling.

"Tender morsel? Who talks like that, honestly! And in front of their wife. But as she looked in the direction of the wife she saw that she was draining the bottom of a large G and T and swaying slightly as she held it out for a refill, seemingly oblivious to her husband's inappropriate behaviour.

"About three years more or less."

"Bloody cradle snatcher! Still good on you, get 'em young, train them up 'ey!"

More laughter from the men but this comment stirred a reaction from Mary.

"You'll have to excuse my husband, he's an incurable romantic".

This time it was the women who laughed loudly. Malcolm raised his eyebrows and his glass and emptied it in one gulp.

Mary returned to her glass, smirking to herself.

Mel took the opportunity to look up and down the table trying to put names again to faces, the fact that everybody was sat opposite their partners made life a little easier.

So, she thought, starting at the far end, 'that must be Dan, nice looking in a rugged sort of way, that's Tony, that serious looking man was Mark, loud mouth we know and that... she stopped, taking in the sight for a few seconds. The man sat opposite Tess, two down from her, was very attractive, had dark hair just resting on the open collar of his pale blue shirt and the initials H.R. neatly embroidered on the pocket.

And that was Harry. He had dark eyes, almost black in this light and a slight hint of stubble on a wide, square jaw. He had a Mel Gibson air about him, sexy but not showy, good looking but not in a too obvious way.

So that's what makes Tess lucky!

His expression was serious as he listened intently and nodded as Laurel was commenting on how hard it was to get decent cleaning staff that could iron shirts without leaving train tracks on the sleeves.

He briefly looked over in Mel's direction, raised his eyes to the sky and smiled. She felt herself blush, but her already reddened face didn't give her away.

Chapter 6

The dinner party was in full swing. The starters arrived, small portions of pate on round pieces of toast, decorated with a tiny sprig of parsley and cut to perfection, Mel could just make out the marks a pastry cutter had left around the edge, genius! She made a mental note to try it, square toast was definitely out from now on.

Once she would have considered playing around with food far too time consuming but if there was one thing she had plenty of at that moment it was time on her hands. She felt herself reeling slightly from a mix of the gin, wine, heat and the constant disbelief at the situation that she found herself in.

Just a few weeks before she had been dragging the poor dog around the block in the cold, driving rain. The dog had been more reluctant to leave the house than she had and now, today, here she was in this luxurious apartment, surrounded by 'well to do' people. She was now one of those 'other halves' that her mother always talked about and she was certainly seeing how they lived. She beamed with joy; like a young child at Christmas Mel was full of excitement and anticipation.

The starter plates were carefully cleared away and each person was given a larger, white, gold rimmed one with a gold dragon painted in the centre.

After exchanging some small talk with Lizzie, she discovered she was South African and her husband worked for a large hotel chain, he was the Asian regional manager and one of the few expats here not in the banking business. This meant that got to spend the majority of time travelling around Asia with him.

How fabulous is that? thought Mel.

Mel excused herself from the table and asked one of the silent, slender waitresses to point her in the direction of the bathroom. The young girl accompanied her along the corridor and stopped outside a white door, opened a low wooden cabinet and produced a small pale pink hand towel with the word 'Guest' embroidered on it in gold thread.

Embroidering words and initials seemed to be big here, perhaps she should learn to monograph stuff, then she'd never be short of work!

The girl opened the door and Mel went inside. She looked round and saw the door closing, relieved to see that the girl wasn't going to follow her in.

The bathroom was huge, in the far corner there was a half-moon shaped bath with a single gold coloured tap at one end and bottles and bottles of various shapes and colours on a shelf behind the bath which Mel assumed contained oils or perfume. On another wall were twin marble sinks with the same gold taps and near to the sinks was a toilet with a smaller toilet next to it.

'Ah so that's a bidet!' She had never seen one before, fancy!

Whatever Tim's job was he must earn a lot more than Rob did, unless it was Alison raking in the money with her pieces of round toast! Mel concluded.

While sitting on the toilet she glanced up and saw two large, black and white sketches on the wall. They were Chinese ink drawings of two naked couples entwined together in strange sinuosities, interesting! She stared at them for a few seconds trying to understand the various positions they were in but realised that her vision was becoming blurry, the two couples were now just a fused mass of shapes and lines.

She stood in front of the mirror on the wall above the sinks, adjusted her hair and wiped a smudge of eyeliner away from under her eye.

'Everything melted in this heat!'

She stopped for a minute to admire her reddish tanned skin in the mirror, having a bit of colour suited her, finally she didn't look like death warmed up.

Mel had never been her own biggest fan and found fault in herself and her physical aspect all the time. It didn't help her self-esteem much that Rob was constantly teasing her and pointing out her faults in public but even she had to admit that that evening, in the green silk dress, she looked rather nice.

She felt a bit drunk and held onto the sink to steady herself.

'That's enough wine for you for a while,' she chastised herself in the mirror. Mel thought it best not to drink too much because her limited experience told her that she couldn't handle large amounts of alcohol without serious, messy and embarrassing consequences.

And we don't want that tonight, do we? She asked her own reflection out loud again, especially after she had been virtually threatened to make a good impression.

She opened the bathroom door, hoping that the girl wouldn't still be standing there, which luckily she wasn't. She made her way along the long corridor back into the dining room to find the majority of the men had moved outside onto the balcony and were smoking cigars. She was amazed to find Rob amongst them, since when did he smoke cigars?

As she watched him she realised that she quite liked him with a cigar in one hand and a glass of red wine in the other, he looked distinguished and grown up.

She couldn't always work out what her attraction to him was or why she had fallen so head over heels in love with him. He wasn't particularly good looking or very tall, but he made her laugh. In the beginning it was the fact that he could get her into any pub or disco and had his own car. When you're 17 these are the things that matter, not to mention that he was responsible for her first ever orgasm.

But from the moment he arrived in Singapore almost two months earlier, he had changed, he had become less attentive and his letters went from two a week to one every ten days or so. The phone calls had also become shorter and shorter and he was always too busy to chat, which is why she had almost given up hope of ever getting 'that' phone call that changed her life so dramatically.

She stood there observing him a while longer, he also looked nice with a bit of colour, he was also usually really pale, having never been out of the U.K. before it was hardly surprising. He glanced up, caught her eye and smiled.

"You okay?" He mouthed and went back to his conversation without giving her the opportunity to answer.

It may have been true that she couldn't always put her finger on why she loved him so much and was prepared to give up everything to come here to be with him, but she did, she really did love Rob and her place was here with him.

Most of the guests were now standing out on the balcony, chatting, smoking and drinking. On the record player The Beatles were doing what they did best and laughter and drunken singing began emanating from the small crowd of dinner guests.

Mel smiled again broadly then with her thumb and index finger she took hold of some skin on her upper arm and squeezed it hard, she felt the slight burning sensation and released her grip, no she wasn't dreaming.

The couples were all summoned back to the table for more artistically prepared dishes. Everything had been painstakingly transformed into a more sophisticated version of its former self with very little bearing any resemblance to its original form.

There were skewers with prawns and pieces of pineapple cut into star shapes, chicken wrapped in leaves of some sort, whole, hollowed-out pineapples filled back up with rice, a green soup with things floating in it, which Mel later discovered were wonton dumplings, and tiny, perfectly round fish cakes.

Mel had never seen so much food on a table that wasn't at a wedding.

It was a struggle to eat as the heat really had taken the edge of her appetite but she did her best.

"Is everything all right Melissa? You haven't touched the prawns." Alison looked a little worried.

"No, sorry, I'm allergic to fish, I'm afraid I can't eat the fish cakes either" Mel replied apologetically.

Alison looked horrified.

"Ah, sorry, I didn't know that, and actually Melissa they're fish medallions. Anyway, tell me," Alison continued loudly, her voice now commanding silence from the other guests who all turned to look in the direction of the new kid on the block.

"What do you think of Singapore? Isn't it just the best bloody place on Earth?"

A cheer rang out from everyone at the table and some banged on the side of their glasses with their cutlery.

"Yes, it seems wonderful," agreed Mel, now feeling quite self-conscious.

"Well," Alison continued, "that is if you can put up with the bloody mosquitoes and find yourself a decent amah, where did Rob find yours?"

Mel was embarrassed, she had no idea what that was, and this time no amount of tan or heat could cover up the fact she was blushing.

"Sorry, find a what?"

"She means a maid Melissa, someone to clean the apartment" Harry intervened and smiled kindly at her, gratefully she smiled back.

"Oh, he didn't, I mean I don't have one," she admitted shyly. "I'm not working yet so I thought I'd do the house myself."

The women all turned to look at her, and at that moment Rob quickly stepped in,

"She means we don't have one *yet*, we're still looking around."

Mel thought about that afternoon just a few hours before that she had spent sweating buckets while she got the apartment back to a hygienic state. Still looking! Since when? He hadn't mentioned one.

"Shit you need an amah" added Tess. "You can't iron and clean in this bloody heat, this is Singapore Mel. Don't worry I'll give you the number of one, my amah has a cousin who's just arrived from Indonesia and she's looking for work, it's perfect. Remind me later to give it to you, and give her a ring tomorrow, and make sure you tell her that Mrs Reese gave you the number.

"And if that doesn't work out I have a few girls who waitress for me and do cleaning also, so let me know if you need one" offered Alison.

"Okay, thank you." Mel answered politely.

'What would she do all day if the house was being cleaned by someone else? Getting a job was going to have to be a priority.

Harry, once again, glanced up from his plate and across at his wife and Alison, then shrugging his shoulders and shaking his head with a half-smile looked back over in Mel's direction and went back to his fish medallions.

Chapter 7

The next few days went by very well. On Saturday Mel and Rob had spent the day together at the pool and in the evening had eaten in the restaurant in their complex. Mel was very impressed with how well she had managed with the chopsticks. On Sunday Rob had taken her to see the zoo. She wasn't a big fan of zoos generally but the one in Singapore, she had to admit, was really lovely. The animals weren't in cages like in the London zoo she had visited as a small child, but in large open, green areas with high fences.

There had been a funny orangutan show that she had been chosen from the audience to participate in, where the orangutans had danced and clapped along to music.

Mel felt ecstatically happy as she walked around such a beautiful place with Rob by her side. When they arrived home in the evening they had showered and made love. Having worked up quite an appetite, Mel had even managed to remember a recipe and cook a romantic, and rather tasty, Thai chicken dinner which they had eaten out on the balcony in candlelight.

In those couple of days it seemed to Mel that she really was in paradise and she didn't give her home in England a second thought.

When Rob went back to work on Monday Mel spent the following days shopping, swimming and cleaning. The apartment was already transforming and filling up with ornaments and knick-knacks she found on her trips to Arab Street.

Rob spent almost every evening out with customers, leaving Mel to spend a lot of evenings alone. To pass the time she threw herself into reading and becoming an expert with chopsticks.

On Thursday morning at nine twenty Rob called from the office and woke Mel up. He had a level of excitement in his voice that you usually only hear in people who've just found out they've won the pools.

"Tim called, we've been invited back tomorrow night for dinner. Mel, go out today or tomorrow and buy yourself something nice to wear, there's some cash in my underwear drawer. If you go to the Palms Boutique here in the CBD they'll sort you out. Alison reckons it's the best."

"Oh well, if *Alison* reckons it's the best" her tone was obviously sarcastic.

"What's with the sarcasm? Don't be so childish, she's the person to know here and I need you to be nice to her!"

Rob's tone was angry and insistent.

"Okay, okay, keep your wig on" she retorted, "I'll go tomorrow morning, perhaps I'll come up at twelve thirty and you can show me your office after and then we can go for lunch together, what do you say? Rob? Rob, what do you say?"

On the other end she could hear chaos, numbers and dates being shouted around the room.

"Look I've got to go, we're busy. I'm out tonight with my boss and an important customer, so don't wait up. Bye babe."

Great, she thought another evening alone, still tomorrow we're out again together, and then we'll have all weekend, thank God!

The next day, as planned, Mel took a cab to the CBD armed with the cash from the drawer, to check out this 'best' boutique. Walking in she saw it was indeed full of beautiful things.

Mel walked over to the first rail and started looking through the clothes, almost immediately a sales assistant came over to her.

"Can I help you Miss? Do you need a dress for a special evening?"

"Yes, well just a dinner party, nothing too elaborate."

"Okay. So I think you are size ten, is it?" she asked.

Mel nodded happily.

The assistant brought her five dresses to try on, each one more beautiful than the previous. Mel looked at the price tags.

"Holy shit" she exclaimed out loud, causing the assistant to look over in surprise.

Mel then took out the wad of bank notes and quickly counted them.

Satisfied that she had enough to cover it, she settled for a light pink backless dress with a chiffon scarf sewn onto the collar which hung down her back.

Happy that she had made a good choice Mel walked over to Rob's building swinging her proud purchase back and forth in her hand.

His office was located in Raffles Place, right in the centre of the CBD. She stood looking up for a few minutes, it resembled a giant grey Toblerone and there must have been at least thirty floors.

"Please God let his office be on one near the bottom," Mel clasped her hands together in a prayer position.

On entering the building she felt the cold of the air conditioning blasting out from all sides. Mel walked over to the large panel on the wall where all the company names were listed in alphabetical order. Moving down the list, almost at the bottom, she found it, 'Rawlings and Fitch', twenty fifth floor.

Damn! That was high. She checked her watch, twenty past twelve, perfect timing.

She stepped into the lift and pressed the button marked 25. A polite English voice announced the lift doors were closing and the lift shot up at high speed. After just a few seconds it came to a stop and she nervously got out. The noise hit her like a train, people were running around shouting and arguing, calling out and slamming down phones.

How did he work in this environment all day? No wonder he needed to unwind with a drink or two.

She looked around the office and recognised Eric walking from desk to desk, he looked up and, spotting her, waved and gave a thumbs up sign, Mel waved back.

She couldn't see Rob anywhere, but she saw Harry sitting at a far desk talking busily on the phone, she waved to him also but he didn't see her.

Mel went over to the reception desk and was greeted by a very perky receptionist.

"Good morning, welcome to Rawlings and Fitch, can I help you?"

"Yes I'm Melissa Harrison, and I'm here to meet my boyfriend Robert Stevens for lunch."

The receptionist nodded, smiled and picked up a phone, after speaking for a few seconds she then replaced the receiver.

"He'll be here in just a few minutes, you can take a seat over there," She pointed in the direction of a yellow leather sofa.

"Can I get you anything to drink?"

"Yes please, cold sparkling water if you have some" she asked and the girl nodded and walked away.

Just then a rather plain woman with glasses walked across the office and headed in her direction.

"Melissa? Hi I'm Christine, H.R. department, we've spoken several times on the phone."

"Ah yes, Christine. Hello."

Mel stood and shook her hand.

"It's nice to finally meet you. I trust everything is all right with the apartment? It's one of the best in Singapore for facilities."

"Yes, no, it's lovely, really beautiful, thank you."

"Well I'm sure you'll both be very happy there."

Then, changing her tone of voice added, "Rob didn't tell me you were so attractive."

Mel smiled awkwardly but thought that that was an odd thing for a woman to say. She looked at Christine again and decided that maybe she was gay.

"Thank you," she said, looking away, embarrassed.

Just then the girl came back with a tall glass of sparkling water and Christine disappeared back into the office. Mel took the glass and drank it down in one just as Rob appeared looking flushed and ruffled.

"Hi Mel," he kissed her lightly on the cheek. "I thought this morning we agreed we were going to meet downstairs?"

"I know, but I wanted to see where you work. It's really noisy."

"Yes it is, let's get out of here, I only have half an hour."

Mel smiled, "Better than nothing I suppose."

They turned to leave as Christine walked back over.

"Going for lunch? How lovely, I'd like to join you but I have a meeting in a few minutes."

Rob led Melissa over to the lift and as Mel was walking away she turned and said goodbye to Christine who stood there watching the lift doors close.

"Rob," she said once inside. "Is Christine gay?"

"What? Why do you ask?"

"No reason she just looked at me a bit funny, that's all."

"I don't know Mel, maybe. What's in the bag?"

"My new dress for tonight, I'll show you when we get to the restaurant."

He took hold of her hand and they walked the few steps across the road to the building opposite.

"There's a small Mövenpick restaurant here, the food's really good and they're quick."

The waitress, in fact as he said, arrived immediately to take their order before Mel had even had a chance to look at the menu.

"Mel do you want to try the club sandwich? It's really good."

She nodded.

"Two clubs and two tiger beers" he instructed the waitress who scribbled it down on her note pad and left.

"So, show me what's in the bag."

She carefully took out the dress from the bag, Rob smiled.

"That's perfect, you'll look great tonight. Listen I want to talk to you about tonight, I need to talk to you about..."

Then Rob caught sight of the price tag.

"Jesus Mel, how much did you pay for it?"

"Yes I know it's a bit pricey but you did send me there."

"A bit pricey? It's just that with all the money you've been spending on crap for the apartment we're a bit over budget. I don't earn a fortune you know!"

He was clearly not happy.

"It's not crap," she protested loudly, "and besides the apartment looks nice now, and I've been using my money mostly."

Rob just commented by shrugging his shoulders.

"Look if money's a problem I'm going to get a job and..."

He cut her off in mid-sentence.

"No Mel, that's not necessary, just take it a bit easier in the future."

"But I want to work, Rob."

"We'll talk about it another time."

The food and beers arrived.

"What were you going to talk to me about before?"

Mel sensed he was tense and tried to change the subject.

"It doesn't matter, eat up, I have to get back to the office."

Chapter 8

The dinner party at Alison's was much the same as the week before, only Mel noted there were far less people, she counted only four couples. Apart from themselves and their hosts there was awful Malcolm and his wife, Mary and last but definitely not least, Harry and his wife, whose name escaped her.

They sat down to yet another fantastically elaborate dinner. Alison had prepared lobster tails for everyone and some delicious chicken and sesame kebabs especially for Mel.

After an hour or so everyone had indulged enough and the empty plates were cleared away then they sat chatting over coffee and chocolate covered mints for about another half an hour. When only a few half Melted ice cubes were left in the bottom of the whisky glasses Tim announced that it was time to begin and everyone got up from the table and trailed through to the lounge. Mel, intrigued, got up to follow behind but was held back by Rob who let everyone go past into the lounge. He was about to speak when Malcolm reached back and grabbed hold of Mel's arm and led her out of the dining room.

Mel loved their lounge, there were two huge white leather sofas and an antique chaise longue placed in between them in the centre of the room.

The incredible, unmistakable voice of Whitney Houston could be heard from every corner thanks to speakers strategically placed on shelves on every wall. In front of the chaise longue was an oval coffee table, and on each end of the sofas a large ceramic cream coloured elephant, which doubled as a drinks rest, had been strategically placed.

All the men sat down on one of the sofas and the women were on the other.

The sweet familiar notes of UB40's 'Red, Red Wine' were now oozing out of the surrounding speakers.

At that moment Alison entered holding what could only be described as a huge glass fishbowl which she carefully placed on the coffee table in the centre of the room, the large bowl contained coloured pieces of carefully folded paper.

'Great, thought Mel, charades! I love charades!'

"Have you gone through the rules of the game Rob?" Alison asked. "We wouldn't want any 'cheating' this evening."

She winked at Melissa and made her mouth into a strange pouting shape.

"God, I think I know how to play charades" Mel whispered into Rob's ear.

"Will you excuse us a minute?"

Rob grabbed Mel's hand and dragged her out into the corridor.

"How are you feeling Mel? Are you OK?" He was whispering loudly and shaking slightly.

"Yes I'm fine, ARE YOU? You look weird."

"Yes, I'm good, I need to tell you something, and I need you to listen carefully. I should have told you at lunch time but I didn't want to say it in public."

"What?" laughed Mel, looking a little puzzled. "What's going on?"

"Are you having a good time? Do you like these people? They're good fun right?"

"Well Malcolm's obnoxious, but apart from that. What's got into you anyway? How much have you had to drink?"

"I'm not pissed, well not much. Just listen, there is a reason we're here, I have only been able to come to the dinner parties before but now, with you here, we can have some real fun. We are actually going to get to join in, what do you say?"

"For Christ's sake Rob you're making no sense, what are you talking about?"

She was beginning to get really irritated. "What the hell's going on?"

Alison shouted out from the other room.

"Robert dear, are you coming back? We're ready to start in here, what's the hold up?"

"We'll be right there, Alison"

"Come on Rob, get back in here will you, we want to get the ball rolling" came the sound of Malcolm's unmistakable dulcet tones.

Rob turned to face Mel.

"Right I'm just going to say it, you know you're always moaning that we don't have exciting sex anymore, well we're going to change that, right now."

"I'm not always complaining about that Rob, I never said it wasn't exciting, just that it wasn't very often" she protested.

"Anyway, come back through to the lounge with me Mel and we'll take part in a partner exchange experience."

"A what? A fucking what?" She never used that word, she hated it, but if there was ever a situation that called for its use, this was it!

"Do you mean wife swapping? Are you talking about bloody wife swapping?

Her voice softened a little, "This is a joke right? You're winding me up, it's not funny!" She punched him quite hard on the arm and started to laugh, "Robert, you're such a git!"

But he wasn't laughing, he was staring at her with pleading eyes.

'Shit he was serious, shit, shit, shit.'

Panic surged up within her and she felt sick, physically sick. She fought back the vomit rising, coughed and cleared her throat. Without saying another word but with wild eyes screaming everything she was unable to vocalise, she walked back into the lounge just in time to see Malcolm fishing a pink piece of paper out of the bowl.

"Hello gorgeous, are you joining us then? Great stuff!"

Malcolm's eyes scanned up and down her legs from her ankles to her thighs and back again hovering slightly at her crotch area as though he had Superman X-ray vision. She glanced around the room, everyone was sitting, chatting, smiling and drinking, all seemed normal, how was that possible?

"No I'm, I'm sorry, I'm going to go, I'm not feeling too well, must be the heat."

She looked in Alison's direction, and saw her face was full of anger.

"Thank you for a lovely dinner, I'm so sorry." She repeated.

But Alison didn't reply she was too busy dragging Rob out into the direction of the kitchen closely followed by Tim.

She felt the room starting to spin, and not only from the alcohol. She perched on the arm of a sofa and tried desperately to look composed.

"That's a pity!" said Harry, smiling, and took out a cigar from his shirt pocket which he proceeded to light. His eyes fixed on her for a few seconds and Mel tried to look away but was entranced.

At that moment Rob came back into the room glaring at her.

"You can take a taxi if you're not feeling well but you're leaving on your own," his voice was icy, and his eyes were full of disgust.

He was pissed off? *He* was disgusted? That was too much, she felt the tears well up and begin to trickle down her scarlet face, tears mixing with the sweat to form a small salty river which flowed between her breasts. She stood up quickly and ran out of the room, as she reached the front door she heard the sound of laughter, and the trickle of tears turned to torrents.

She was so angry, or was it humiliated? Or both? Yes both, definitely both. How could he? How the fuck could he?

She stumbled out into the heat and ran to the gate. She stood outside on the pavement her breathing laboured and shaking with anger. The taxi arrived after just a few minutes, she turned to look in the direction of the stairs hoping to see Rob following behind her, apologetic and shamed, begging her to forgive him but there was nothing, just the long lamp lit path to "Sodom and Gomorrah ".

She climbed into the taxi. "Mandarin Towers please."

She sat in silence staring blankly out of the window for the second time that evening...

She opened the door to the apartment and without turning on the light walked over to the sink, using only the light from the refrigerator as her guide, Mel took out the glass she had used earlier, complete with lipstick marks, and poured a large quantity of gin into it. Then she took out the ice cube tray from the top shelf of the freezer and tried in vain for a while to extract the cubes. Finally in desperation she threw the tray onto the worktop and the cubes flew out violently, some finishing up on the floor. She bent down to pick them up and crumbling into a heap lay on the floor sobbing in a pathetic foetal position and cried herself to sleep.

When she woke she had no idea where she was, she saw a cockroach scuttling off under a cupboard closely followed by a small lizard. She sat up and tried to focus on the wall clock, it was a quarter to one, she'd slept for almost an hour.

Pulling herself to her feet she saw the glass of gin and the worktop covered in water dripping rhythmically onto the floor where a small puddle had accumulated. Picking up the glass she swigged it down neat, making a grimacing face and shuddering as the liquid hit the back of her throat. She stumbled into the bedroom and pulled the switch to start the fan. It turned with its usual noisy, hypnotic action.

Laying fully dressed on the bed Mel tried to focus on the situation, God it was hot, she kicked off her shoes and struggled out of her tight silk dress, she fought for a few minutes with her bra, finally undoing the clasps. 'These bloody contraptions must have been invented by a man' she thought. She tried to throw it onto the chair in the corner of the room but threw too high and it caught on the ceiling fan, spun round for a while, flew off in the general direction of the chair but missed and landed on the floor just next to it. Under any other circumstances this display would have made her laugh, but she didn't find it even vaguely amusing. She couldn't believe it, he was there now probably watching, God knows who doing God knows what to God knows who.

Tomorrow morning she would pack, she would pack up and leave. She couldn't stay here now, she'd been humiliated. He didn't want her here because he couldn't bear to be without her, he wanted her here so he could be bare with someone else - bastard! How could he have ever imagined in a million years that she would go for it, how dare he? Oh this bloody heat was unbearable.

Mel kicked the sheet off her feet and spread out across the bed feeling the cool air from the fan caressing her body. She was sweating so she brushed the sweat from her face and chest and her hand lightly brushed her nipple which stiffened at the touch. She took a deep breath and closed her eyes, as she did, Harry's face appeared in front of her and she smiled, then she stopped.

'Who was he screwing right now? Whose lips were working on his erection? She opened her eyes so full of anger, or was it?

She *was* angry, so why was she feeling so turned on right now at the thought of what Harry was doing, what Rob was doing, what they were all doing?

She closed her eyes again and allowed her hand to brush once more against her nipple, again it stiffened at her touch. This felt nice, she tried to remember the last time Rob had taken time to do a little foreplay. Lately it had been a quick cold shag followed by a long cool shower. Her hand cupped her left breast and her fingers gently tweaked her erect nipple rolling it between the index and middle finger, she sighed a deep sigh and her legs opened in an involuntary motion. She felt the cool air from the ceiling fan pass over her thighs and abdomen. Mel shuddered a little from the cool air and a little from the sensation of her soft fingers passing over to the right

90

breast, nipple already erect in anticipation. Her breathing got quicker and her heart was beating faster as her left hand slid across her abdomen lingering for a while and stroking her pubic hair, again with a will of their own, her legs parted even wider, she felt the air pass over her vagina and the blood surge into every part. Her right hand kneading her breast even harder, she moved her left hand up to her mouth and gently sucked on her fingers, with the fingers moist with saliva she caressed her vagina slowly. Her mind was ablaze, she was there, she was there with Rob, Harry, with Tim and even Malcolm, obnoxious, loud Malcolm, they all wanted her, they couldn't get enough. Her fingers slid inside her, first one then two then three, she moaned out loud. Her juices were really flowing, she began to massage herself, small, deep circular movements, slowly at first, then faster and harder, the fan turned above her head adding another dimension, the cool air made her skin tingle. Harry's wife, what's her name, Tess, was in the corner watching, watching her hot, needy husband screwing Mel as hard as he could. The imagery was too much, she felt the heat wave rise, surge through her thighs, into her buttocks and break deep inside her groin. She gasped, taking in the damp air, the backwash continued up through her abdomen and her arched back and finally into her throat. She felt her heart pounding audibly in her rapidly rising and falling chest. Releasing the grip on her breast she sunk back onto the bed, panting and glowing with sweat.

She lay there for a few minutes, legs gently trembling, trying to get her breathing back to a regular rhythm, suddenly she felt cold, the fan was now moving cool air over her sweat soaked body, every hair on end, every follicle raised.

Mel reached down and grabbed the tangled sheet entwined around her feet and pulled it up, clumsily covering herself. She needed to sleep, she was so tired now, drained emotionally, physically and mentally but her recent orgasm had her disturbed.

She shouldn't have been that turned on at the thought of participating in such a degrading orgy, she felt ashamed, really ashamed, and tears once again rolled down her cheeks and dampened the pillow her face was deeply buried in.

Tomorrow she would tell Rob that she couldn't do this anymore, that she wanted to return to the UK, to her family, her supermarket job and to the safety of her former life, where everything was normal, regular and boring...very boring... She would leave immediately, put everything back in the suitcase and leave first thing tomorrow morning or Sunday, by Monday, definitely by Monday.

Chapter 9

She woke with a start at the sound of a key in the door, through the badly drawn curtains she could see that it was getting light. She reached for the small alarm clock that was on the bedside table, the hands were positioned at five thirty five a.m. She needed to make out she was asleep, she couldn't face a discussion now, not now, so she pulled the sheet up over her face.

Damn, she needed to pee! Mel turned over trying to ignore the bursting sensation. She heard the TV go on and realised that Rob had no intention of coming in to see her. She didn't want to talk to him right now but bloody hell, he didn't know that!

Lying there tossing and turning for a while the need to go to the toilet became too great and reluctantly she got quietly out of bed and, stark naked, tip toed over to the en-suite bathroom door, still no reaction from the living room. He hadn't even checked to see if she was home, what a bastard!

She went into the bathroom, no longer tip toeing, slammed the bathroom door and sat herself down ungracefully onto the toilet sighing as she finally gave relief to an overindulged bladder. She sat slumped on the toilet, too tired to move. There was a chip in a tile on the floor, she'd never noticed that before. Struggling to her feet Mel flushed the toilet, washed her hands, brushed the hair from her moist forehead and habitually tucked it behind her ears.

Making her way back to bed Mel took a small detour over to the door, she peered through and saw the flickering lights of the TV. Peering out further she saw he was lying on the sofa fully dressed and snoring loudly, with one foot on the floor. She thought for a second about waking him and punching his pathetic little lights out but then noticing the sun coming up on the horizon decided to go back to bed.

She pulled the switch to turn off the ceiling fan, heat or no heat the noise was driving her crazy. The fan slowed to a halt and closing her eyes she slipped back into a superficial sleep.

When she awoke, for what seemed like the hundredth time that night, she saw the sun was now fully ablaze, and with the ceiling fan off the room temperature had risen to around a thousand degrees. The clock was now showing ten fifteen, and the right side of the bed was still unoccupied. She stood up and noticed a pounding sensation in her left temple. She massaged it with her fingers in a circular motion and was immediately reminded in an all too vivid flashback of the night before when the same fingers were massaging other bits of her body. She sat back onto the bed and placed her face in her hands. Mel felt ashamed, not so much for what she had done, which since her arrival in Singapore had become a fairly regular habit. She was spending so much time on her own that she felt it was a justifiable release but the fantasies which usually accompanied her exploits were generally featuring Mel Gibson naked on a beach or Kevin Costner dressed as Robin Hood and then naked in a tree house and very occasionally some naked members of Duran Duran popped by. But she had never ever thought of taking part in that kind of thing, with real people, real people she actually knew!

The anger started to build again and the pounding in her temple became stronger. She was furious, she would never forgive him for this. Rob had humiliated her in front of everyone, she would never be able to face them again so she would have to leave, him and them, and she would go right now and tell him so. She marched determinedly into the front room ready to do battle.

"Rob I'm leaving, I want to go home, coming here was a huge mistake, I'm not going to stay here with you and your pervy friends and be used by you all in some sexually depraved, sad bastards orgy anymore!" she was shouting, "and if you think I'm going to live here with you now, well you can fu…"

She stopped dead in her tracks, he wasn't on the sofa.

She stormed over to the kitchen but there was no sign. She went out onto the balcony through the opened French doors and looked down; she could just make out his bright yellow bath robe thrown onto a sun bed next to the pool seven floors below. Two figures were in the pool swimming and one of them was him.

"Wanker, stupid, idiotic, sick wanker." she blurted out, then she turned to go back inside and to her horror she noticed that her neighbours on the adjoining balcony were having breakfast, a nice quiet family breakfast.

"Good morning," she said and slunk back into the apartment, leaving the neighbours open mouthed, silver spoons with bits of fresh grapefruit held motionless in their hands.

She went back inside and picked up the phone, she was going to call her Mum to tell her that this place wasn't for her, that she missed the rain and the telly and the Saturday trips to Sainsbury's and most of all she missed her family. She started to dial, then stopped, put down the receiver and sat down hard on the over-stuffed beanbag.

She couldn't call, she couldn't say she was leaving, that would make it real. There would be questions and her Mum would never buy the "homesick" excuse after only ten days, what should she say? Perhaps she could say that Rob had become a raging alcoholic and had started hitting her. Yes, that way her Mum would then insist that she returned home immediately, and when questioned about anything Mel could well up with tears and ask to change the subject as the memories were too painful. No, she couldn't say that, she had to come up with something better than that, but what?

She decided she had time to think about it on the flight home, now she had to pack. She went into the bedroom, knelt down next to the bed and took out the suitcase that she had put under there joyfully just a few days before.

She violently threw the case onto the bed and it flew open. Stomping over to the chest of drawers she opened the top one and there in the right hand corner was the box containing the earrings that Rob had given her on Valentine's Day. Cool tears ran down her hot cheeks.

Sitting back down on the bed next to the waiting suitcase, she drew her knees up to her chest and gently rocked back and forth.

She didn't want to go, not really.

Yes she was angry, yes she was humiliated, let down and hurt, but the bottom line was she loved being there, living in an apartment with a pool, being the 'woman of the house'. She adored having the freedom to do what she wanted, go where she wanted, buy what she wanted and she loved him, yes him, Rob, the shit!

But how could she live with all this going on around her? Seeing those people at functions and parties, going shoe shopping and to brunch with people who had had carnal knowledge of each other's wives and husbands, probably even hers?

She sat thinking and rocking, back and forth, back and forth.

Eventually after a while, feeling calmer, she stood up and wiped her eyes and face on her T shirt. She caught sight of herself in the full length mirror next to the chest of drawers. She had really blossomed in the short time she had been there. She was already tanned, four pounds lighter and her arms were beginning to look more toned.

She held her breath, it wouldn't be easy but she could do it, she didn't want to leave so she would make this right. She would just tell him when he came back up that she was staying, that whatever he had done or seen in the past was to be forgotten and that they would have to find alternative evening entertainment.

Yes! She would tell him that, she would explain and it would be okay.

She would make him see reason, make him realise he didn't need to be a part of all that swapping wives thing.

Mel went out onto the balcony and saw Rob heading towards the lift.

Hurriedly she ran into the bedroom, closed the drawer, picked up the case and slid it back into its 'pre-tantrum' under the bed, position.

She grabbed the magazine next to the bed, laid herself down, propped herself up on one elbow and smoothed down her flimsy silk dressing gown which barely covered her thighs, and pretended to read. She didn't have long to wait, after three or so minutes she heard the key in the door, her heart was pounding, she grabbed her perfume bottle from her bedside table and quickly sprayed her neck, cleavage and thighs.

Rob entered the bedroom, hair and trunks still dripping from the pool and looking bronzed. He wasn't a hunk but he was nice looking, at least she thought so, especially right now.

"Rob," she began but was cut off.

"I've been thinking Mel, and it's best if you leave, you don't belong here, this place isn't right for you and after last night I see that you're not right for me. I want what they have, I want the excitement, and you're too immature to handle it, I'm sorry, I should never have brought you here. I've already spoken to Christine at the office and she's going to try to book you a flight out on Monday. I told everyone it was a family emergency so they wouldn't ask too many questions, I'm going to have a shower, it might be a good idea if you start to pack now. Oh and Chris said she'd call at some point with the flight details, so let me know if she rings while I'm in the shower."

And with that he was gone. She heard the sound of the door bolt being slid across and the water running.

Mel was in shock. *That* hadn't been an option! *He* couldn't send *her* home! *She* had to be the one to decide if she stayed or not, *she* was the one who had been upset, humiliated, who the fuck did he think he was? Sending her back like something he'd ordered from a catalogue!

She couldn't take it all in, she wanted to stay, she had to stay!

How could he be so cold and just such a bastard about it, he hadn't even looked her in the face!

The water in the bathroom was still running, masking the sound of yet more tears.

Chapter 10

The rest of Saturday she had spent aimlessly wandering around shopping centres trying to find presents to take home, something that would be great enough to take their mind of asking too many questions, but she wasn't able to concentrate on anything. When, after a few hours, she eventually plucked up the courage to go home, Rob was nowhere to be found.

She looked down at the pool but couldn't make him out among the people there.

Eventually at midnight, exhausted, drained and alone, she went to bed and cried herself to sleep.

Sunday morning she awoke, puffy eyed, to find he hadn't come home and she had no idea where he was. Now more angry than worried, she pulled out the case once again from under the bed, threw it onto the bed and began packing.

The case which had taken her about three days to pack carefully for the outbound journey; she had now almost finished in half an hour. She tore down the clothes from their recently required home in the wardrobe and shoved them untidily into the case. The contents of the chest of drawers were also thrown unceremoniously into the case and the drawers slammed shut one by one. Arriving at the bottom one she took out the bits and pieces that it contained and then she tried to slam it shut but was met with resistance. Finally, in a fit of temper, she gave the drawer a hard kick and it obediently jumped back into place. The whole chest of drawers rocked violently, unbalancing the newly framed photo of her and Rob at the zoo and causing it to fall face down on the ground. Mel picked it up and noticed a large crack in the glass right down the middle, 'ironic,' she thought sadly.

Then she looked down at her large collection of shoes neatly lined up under the once again steady piece of furniture and wondered how she had managed to amass such a large amount in such a short time. She chose three pairs at random and crammed them into the already bursting holdall which she was using as hand luggage.

Looking at the light pink dress still draped on the end of the bed, she picked it up and threw it into the wardrobe where it landed in the bottom among a pile of dropped and broken coat hangers.

She wouldn't be wearing that again, he could keep it as a souvenir.

That only left the stuff in the bathroom, Mel decided that she would wait till the last minute to pack that, that way she could make herself look and smell as great as she could for when she left. She wondered if Rob would be back to go with her to Changi but her thoughts were interrupted by the sound of the phone ringing in the lounge.

She thought about not answering it, she stood there motionless staring at it, fifth ring…

"Hello."

"Oh hi Melissa, it's Christine from the office."

Shit...

"I have the flight information Rob asked me for."

Think, think, "Hi Christine, sorry Rob's not here at the moment, he's in the pool."

"Is he? Ah, Okay. Do you have a pen? "

"There is a BA flight tomorrow, Monday the fifteenth of June, at two p.m. from Changi going to London Heathrow, there's a 3 hour stopover in Dubai, and the company will pay for an economy class ticket, not that they're happy about it, they've just paid a fortune to get you out here. Still that's Rob's bloody problem, not yours."

Mel was a bit shocked at her aggressive tone.

Christine continued, "Rob said it was urgent so I took the liberty of booking it, I hope that's all right?"

Mel sighed heavily and didn't reply.

"Are you there? I can't hear you."

"Yes I'm here, thank you, tomorrow at two, I've written it all down and I'll tell Rob when he comes up."

"Okay and I hope it isn't anything too serious, I understood it was a family emergency, anyway enjoy what's left of your weekend and make sure you let me know in plenty of time if you want me to book you a return flight, which reminds me, if you think about it, if you come back can you bring me some cheddar and Branston? I could kill for a cheese and pickle sandwich. Bye, have a good trip."

And she was gone.

Mel sighed again, now it was official, she was leaving.

She sat down on the bed staring at her open, terribly packed suitcase.

'If you return, Christine had said if!'

Finally at one o'clock Rob arrived home and without a word of explanation walked into the kitchen, Mel followed quietly behind.

'Remember Melissa, pride and dignity' she muttered to herself through gritted teeth. Mel didn't do pride and dignity usually, she had always been volatile, choosing instead screaming fits, tears and throwing things as her means of communication. This behaviour had earned her the nickname 'Vesuvius' at home.

She filled the kettle from the tap and lit the gas. She had no desire to drink tea or coffee but she needed something to do. Rob opened the fridge and took out a carton of orange juice, pried open the top and tipped the contents into his open mouth, letting just a little dribble down his chin which he then wiped away with the bottom of his T shirt.

'What a pig' she thought. She hated it when he did that and normally she would have nagged him to get a glass but right now she couldn't give a monkey's.

'All right, here goes.'

"Christine called while you were A.W.O.L.," she said in the cheeriest voice she could manage.

"She's got me on a flight out tomorrow at two o'clock in the afternoon."

"Oh good, that means I'll be able to take you to the airport in my lunch break and be back in time to watch the evening limited overs match at the Cricket Club at five."

Un-bloody-believable! He really doesn't care! And he was going to go with her to the airport, how noble.

'Probably just wants to make sure I leave!' she thought bitterly. She couldn't believe how calm he was being about the whole thing, he was acting like she had told him that she was going shopping, surely he must be feeling some regret?

'And where the hell had he been all night?'

"Malcolm reckons he can get me a game, maybe even on the team," he chirped on. "Mind you that was before your embarrassing scene at Tim's the other night."

She walked over to the kettle on the stove which was just beginning to boil, she turned off the flames before the kettle could start its terrible shrill screaming and for a brief second she fought with the urge to chuck the bloody lot over him. 'Pride and dignity Mel, pride and dignity.'

That was the first time that 'that' evening had been mentioned since his earth shattering announcement to get rid of her.

Okay, she had to be all, what's the word? Nonchalant.

"That would be good, you've always wanted to play there, I'm sure Malcolm will be able to get you in, he looks like someone who pulls strings (G strings that is!)

Right I'll go and get changed and then I'll head down to the pool, get some last minute sun while I still can."

She expected a reaction but Rob just grabbed a mug and started to make himself a cup of tea.

The tears were building up behind her eyes, if she blinked she would open the flood gates, so, wide eyed, she walked out of the kitchen and into the bedroom. Her stupid over-productive tear ducts had always betrayed her. She wondered if there existed an operation to remove the treacherous, uncontrollable things.

One tear escaped, quickly followed by another.

"Damn, stupid bloody things!" she ran into the bathroom, locked the door and turned the shower on full, the one over the bath and the one behind her eyes.

Down at the pool a large number of her neighbours had decided to take a Sunday brunch time dip, she had spent the last ten days trying to get to know people in her apartment block, chatting randomly with various people, hoping to click with a few human beings that could become friends to chat to and borrow sugar from.

'Do people do that here?' she wondered. But today she wanted to avoid everybody.

She put her towel down on a sun bed in the far corner where no other towels were currently saving places.

She dived into the pool, not as gracefully as she'd have liked, making a large splash as she hit the water and swam most of the width underwater, only surfacing when her lungs felt like they were bursting. She saw a couple of ladies just ahead of her in the water deep in conversation, leaning on the side of the pool, arms folded on the edge and legs kicking out behind them. She took a huge gulp of air and submerged once more. Touching the wall she did an awkward roly-poly and headed back under water to the other side.

This she repeated several times trying to burn off some nervous energy.

Heading for the steps she passed her neighbour's twins who were merrily trying to drown each other.

"Hello lady" they chanted in unison.

"Hello girls, having a nice swim?"

They smiled, nodded and turned to race each other clumsily to the opposite side. Mel climbed out of the pool and lay back down on her sun bed, put on her glasses and closed her sore eyes. In her hurry to leave the apartment she had forgotten her sun cream, damn! She would have to go back up soon.

'Pretend to be asleep, that'll keep people from trying to talk to you.'

She felt the hot sun on her skin, God she loved it here, this life was so great, she would miss this, and she would miss him.

Feeling sufficiently dry, and a little sunburnt, she stood up and grabbed her towel, without bothering to put her sundress back on, she passed by a row of beds where happy families and couples were enjoying the time together.

Entering the building she walked over to the lift, pressed the button and waited for it to arrive. When it did she got in and wrapped the towel around her shoulders to protect them from the air conditioning. With each floor the lift passed her heart became heavier.

She opened the door to the apartment and was immediately greeted with the sight of Harry sitting on the sofa holding a can of Tiger beer, she stopped dead in her tracks.

"Hi Melissa, how are you? Rob's just popped out to get a couple of beers from the club house, I'm surprised you didn't bump into him in the lift."

Shit, she must look such a mess, eyes all puffy and hair all over the place. She stood there slightly stunned not able to put a coherent sentence together.

He continued, unfazed.

"I just dropped by to give Rob a key, we're going away to Bali for a few days tomorrow and our amah's coming with us so I need him to water plants, feed Tess' pain in the neck cat and generally keep an eye on the place. I've got a feeling we'll come back to an empty drinks cabinet, what d'ya reckon?"

Mel forced a half smile,

'Of course the amah was going with them, otherwise Tess was going to have to wipe her own backside.'

Mel,' she castigated herself,' where did that animosity come from?'

"Yes probably, if you'll excuse me Harry I'm going to take a shower and I need to finish packing. Have a good holiday."

She took the towel from her shoulders and wrapped it around her waist so as to cover her behind as she walked past him.

As she passed by him he grabbed hold of her hand.

"Look, for what it's worth I think he was out of order to take you there the other night without giving you a heads up. You were bound to be shocked, who wouldn't be? We have rules about this kind of thing, in fact there's a rulebook, no kidding. One of the rules is that we don't talk about the club outside of our 'get togethers' so strictly speaking I'm breaking a rule by talking to you now. Everyone should be in the know and in full agreement of the situation before coming to a dinner party. I remember the first time we were approached to join the 'Singapore Swing Club' corny I know but I didn't form the group, that was Tim."

Really! She would have put good money on it being Malcolm.

"I don't want to talk about it Harry, it was humiliating. That's fine for you lot, I'm not judging you, I'm just saying it's not for me, and apparently it's impossible to stay here otherwise so I'm going home tomorrow, it's for the best."

She hoped it came across as her decision and that Rob hadn't told him the real story. Harry stood up and put a hand on her shoulder, and she shuddered noticeably.

"Don't knock it until you've tried it Mel, none of us were up for it immediately, we all took some persuading, except Tess, surprisingly she was always very keen on the idea."

Bloody hell! Thought Mel, 'if he was my husband I wouldn't want to share him with anyone.'

"Who knows," he went on, still with his hand resting gently on her shoulder, "if you'd have stuck around you might have fished my name out the bowl."

He squeezed her shoulder slightly before removing his hand, brushing gently over her arm as he did so.

She felt weird, really weird.

"I really must get on with my packing Harry. It was nice to meet you all, surreal but nice." And she started to walk out of the living room.

"Mel!"

She stopped and turned to look at him.

"If it's any consolation you were voted in unanimously. Doesn't happen often!"

She turned back and continued walking in the direction of the bedroom repeating under her breath to herself, 'pride and dignity Mel, pride and bloody dignity.'

Chapter 11

She didn't know how long Harry stayed, she remained in the bedroom all the rest of the afternoon pretending to pack. She heard Rob come back after just a few minutes and then the familiar sound of crowds cheering and chanting indicating they were watching some kind of sporting event on the television. There was the occasional outburst of 'ref!' and the odd intermittent burst of swearing and laughter. Were they laughing at her? Mocking her refusal to participate in their depraved pastime?

She laid down on the bed among the cases and coat hangers and unable to keep her red, puffy eyes open any longer, curled up and drifted off to sleep.

When she awoke she could no longer hear the TV or chatting so she emerged from the bedroom. Harry had gone and Rob was sitting out on the balcony surrounded by empty beer cans and crisp packets.

"Harry looked in on you to say goodbye, but you were snoring away like a good 'un. So he said to say goodbye and he hopes you have a good trip back."

"I don't snore!"

'At least I hope not!' she thought, 'How embarrassing!'

"Are you wanting something for dinner Rob or are you okay with crisps?"

Her tone was cold and sarcastic.

"Actually I'm starving. Let's get the Club House to send up some Thai chicken and pineapple rice, what do you think?"

'Bastard!' she despaired, 'He knows that's my favourite.'

"Actually, I'm not hungry, I'll pass."

"Come on Mel, I'll pay." He smiled at her, "Let's call it a peace offering, I know it hasn't been easy for you, this isn't how I wanted it to go, I imagined it differently. I reckon it could have been good, exciting, but I should have warned you, discussed it with you I know. I just thought you'd want to do it, that you'd be up for it. We've joked about it, about doing it in the past, remember? I should have realised that someone like you would never really go for it."

'What the hell did that mean?' she wondered angrily.

He took a long gulp of beer, belched loudly and crumpled up the beer can in his hand before chucking it onto the floor.

"But I can see now that you were right,"

He continued, now slurring quite obviously.

"I was wrong, this isn't the place for you, you need to be in a normal, regular environment. You weren't ready to fly the nest and you'll see that one day and you'll thank me."

Mel was taken aback, 'Rob never admitted he was wrong,' she thought. Harry must have said something. Good! I hope he gave him a right piece of his mind, but she doubted it.

'I was ready!' she screamed in her head. 'Just didn't expect to have been in a nest quite so high up!'

"I don't know what to say," she replied eventually, genuinely in difficulty, her pride and her fear were stopping her from backing down, from compromising.

"Except that this isn't how I imagined it to be either but it can be a normal environment, it's a beautiful, clean environment, it's just polluted with weirdoes, and just so you know, I can't imagine I'll ever thank you for any of this!"

Her voice was getting louder.

"We did joke about it Rob, but it was always just that, a joke. You've chosen this, this thing over me."

Her voice had now reached shouting level and had become more shrill. All the pent up anger she had accumulated during the past few days was spilling out all over him.

"I trusted you, you shit." She was at fever pitch. "I wanted to be here with you, I thought you wanted me here because you missed and wanted me, but it turns out you were only using me to get into your sad little club, you make me sick. Stick your Thai chicken Rob where the sun don't shine! I'm going to bed, I'll finish packing the last of my things tomorrow! GOOD NIGHT."

And she stormed off towards the bedroom.

'Vesuvius' had blown and was spewing lava everywhere.

"Mel...Mel" Rob was calling from the balcony.

She stopped and turned round. "What?"

She was imploring him, willing him with her mind. 'Ask me to stay Rob, ask me to stay.'

"What?" she asked again

"Sleep tight."

She couldn't sleep, more than an hour had passed since her dramatic withdrawal into the bedroom. She lay there tossing and turning, the fan was noisier and more annoying than usual and her pillows were part of the conspiracy to stop her slipping into the land of nod. She sat up, grabbed one of the offending items and punched it hard several times then slammed it back down onto its co-conspirator below.

She froze as she heard the door open, she closed her eyes and pretended to sleep but her eyelids were fluttering nervously, a bit of a giveaway. She heard the sound of a belt unbuckling followed by a thud as a shoe hit the wall followed by another.

Then there was a series of thuds as he caught his foot in his trouser leg and lost his balance causing him to hop around a bit as he tried to take them off.

He had been drinking and Rob always got clumsy when he drank. He sat down hard on the bed next to her and swung his legs round so he was lying down beside her. She decided to continue with the 'pretend to sleep' tactic but she was aware that she was breathing too heavily for a sleeping person.

Mel pulled the sheet up and held onto it tightly, she was banking on him being too drunk to notice the inconsistencies.

A hand reached under the sheet and roughly grabbed her left breast, she jumped and opened her eyes.

"Robert! What the hell are you doing?" she was genuinely shocked.

'Did he expect her just to lay there and let him use her once again?'

"Come on Mel, you know you want me, you can't resist me."

His hand began to move down to her stomach and quick as a flash he slid his hand inside her knickers and yanked them down. She grabbed his hand and with all her strength pulled his hand out of her pants, out from under the sheet and threw it down on the bed.

"Rob for Christ's sake, leave me alone, you've been drinking and I'm not going to sleep with you now. I have to leave tomorrow, don't I, well don't I?

She sat up pulling the sheet once again up to her chin to cover her naked breasts.

'Tell me you want me to stay' she thought, 'and everything under this sheet is yours, we'll have sex right now, just tell me!'

"Tell me I can stay," she said out loud.

"Mel you know why you have to go home, we've done that conversation. You won't fit in here, you've made that perfectly clear but I want you one last time, let's make love one more time."

His hand was under the sheet again, clumsily searching for her. She was flushed, shaking from head to toe. She did want him, she wanted to make love to him again but he showed no signs of changing his mind about her leaving or giving up this wife swapping thing and she couldn't bring herself to change hers.

Then she remembered some advice she'd been given a while back.

"If you want to get a man to do something you can either cook for him or 'hook' for him, it works every time."

Maybe if they made love, she could pull out all the stops, do all that stuff he likes and persuade him that she should stay and that he didn't need anything or anyone else.

She dropped hold of the sheet exposing her bare breasts and her nipples reacted immediately to the cool air passing over them.

'Good, all adds to the effect.'

She reached under the sheet and took hold of his waning erection.

All right Rob, if you want me I'm here and I'm all yours!"

Her voice was sexy and longing.

"Take me Rob, I'm yours, take me now...Rob? ...Rob?

She turned to see his eyes were closed and heard the first snore.

She sat bolt upright in bed, drew her knees up to her chest, rested her elbows on her knees and held her chin in her hands. Her head was swimming, she was so confused, she was feeling so many emotions that she couldn't keep track; anger, hate, love, fear and desire to name but a few.

Mel got out of bed and went out into the kitchen, she opened the lid of a biscuit tin she kept on the shelf under the clock and with shaking hands took out a packet of cigarettes and a box of matches. She hadn't smoked for such a long time but now she needed one, really needed one. She knew Rob hated her smoking in the flat but she wasn't concerned too much about what Rob hated right now. She lit the match and brought it up shakily to the cigarette dangling from her mouth, inhaling deeply she watched the cigarette end glow. She held the match under the dripping tap and it fizzled out. She took another long drag on the cigarette and felt a slight head-rush. Sitting on the stool next to the breakfast bar she continued to smoke, inhaling deeply and flicking the ash into a coffee cup, his coffee cup.

When the cigarette was finished she put it out in the same fashion as the match and chucked it into the cup.

Deciding not to return to their bedroom in case he woke up and her will power caved again she opted for the sofa, it wouldn't make any difference, sleeping was not on the agenda tonight.

She lay all night staring up at the ceiling which was gradually becoming clearer and clearer to make out as the sun rose outside the window. The room glowed orange and she sighed, time to go.

Mel got up and walked out onto the balcony, taking a mental photograph of the scene below and all the colours of the rising sun reflecting on the pond like sea. Down in the grounds some of the cleaning staff were already getting the pool ready, fishing out leaves and unfortunate insects with big fishing nets and straightening the sun beds into neat rows while others were trimming hedges and emptying rubbish bins. They were dressed in white pyjama looking outfits with white wide-brim hats. It was early to be working but later on it got too hot even for the locals. As she stood trying to take in as much as possible, a group of elderly residents emerged from one stairwell and gathered in the park area. In perfect synchronisation they began their daily Tai Chi routine. It wasn't the first time she had witnessed this scene but today it was especially beautiful, hypnotic, today she wanted to join in with them and learn how to do it, today she wanted to stay.

Returning inside she heard the sound of the shower running and quietly opened the unlocked bathroom door. The shower curtain was pulled round but there was a small gap.

Rob was upright, one hand on the wall to steady himself and the other hand was holding on tightly, rhythmically sliding up and down his erection, his eyes were firmly closed and his mouth slightly open.

She stood there for a few seconds watching, wanting desperately to drop her silk dressing gown and climb in next to him, then feeling embarrassed for spying but also a little turned on, she quickly and quietly left the room.

She went back into the kitchen and made herself a coffee and took it out onto the balcony. The Tai chi group over by the tennis courts had finished and were standing around chatting. Mel looked at her watch and decided she had time to have one last swim. Looking down from the balcony again she saw there was only one person in the pool.

She walked back into the bedroom to grab her costume and towel. Rob was lying on the bed, eyes closed with a damp towel wrapped loosely around his waist, she noticed there was still a slight bulge underneath. She stood motionless remembering the scene in the shower.

What should she do?

Then without further thought Mel walked over to the bed, she was on a mission. She slipped her dressing gown off her shoulders and it dropped to the floor. She moved over to the bed and slowly and carefully knelt down beside it. The cold marble on the floor felt really uncomfortable under her knees.

She moved down level with his calves and leaning over kissed them gently, then she moved her lips up his leg to just above his knees, his skin was still damp. He moved his head, eyes tightly closed and moaned lightly. Mel ran her tongue along the inside of his thigh until her nose brushed against his right testicle, the hairs tickled and she crinkled up her nose to stifle a sneeze. She continued to run her tongue up over his testicles, his eyes were still closed but his thighs parted slightly, again he moaned. She took one testicle in her mouth and sucked on it gently, his moaning continued, she released her lips and ran her tongue over the base of his now fully erect penis, she felt a hand on her head, he stroked her hair for a bit and then grabbed a handful gently moving her head upwards. She encircled the smooth end with her tongue deliberately allowing saliva to ooze down the length. The hand was now grabbing tighter and she felt her head being moved up and down slowly at first and then harder and faster. Her mouth was wide open, her jaws were aching, she felt him at the back of her throat and struggled with the gag reflex, she would just have to put up with it, this had to be the best blow job she'd ever given him, that anyone had ever given him and she would make him see that he needed her to stay. His hand was now pushing her head at whiplash speed, she struggled to keep up and keep her mouth in contact. She caught his foreskin on her teeth and he jumped. The moaning got louder and she felt him thrust upwards, she tried to pull back but his hand was holding her firmly. The warm salty liquid hit the back of her throat and she retched, Rob released his grip slightly and she was able to withdraw a little. Finally he released his grip completely and she pulled back, turning away from him she pinched her nose and swallowed.

Mel stood up, very pleased with herself, 'nicely done' she mentally patted herself on the back.

"Rob darling do you want a cup of tea or a coffee before you go to work? I'm making myself one."

"No that's okay, I have to go into the office early in a bit, but I'll be back by ten thirty, in plenty of time to take you to the airport."

He opened his eyes and smiled, "Oh wow, that was good Mel, really good. Have you finished packing?"

She felt sick, the taste of him was still in her throat and he still wanted her to leave, she walked out of the room and shut the door.

Chapter 12

She struggled to do up the zip on the bulging case. Eventually the two ends met and she dragged it off the bed and onto the floor, happy that everything she wanted or needed was safely crammed into that poor abused piece of luggage.

She opened her hand bag, took out her passport for the fifth time that morning, glanced at it and placed it back in the bag. Walking over to the mirror she combed her hair through with her fingers and applied some lipstick, ready to face the enemy.

When Rob arrived back from the office Mel noticed that he was dressed in a white shirt and black tailored shorts, the outfit she had bought him on a recent, time filling shopping trip to Far East Plaza. She had good taste, he looked nice. Damn! Maybe it would be easier if he stayed here.

"You don't have to come with me Rob, I'm quite capable of finding my own way to the airport."

"No, I'll come, it's the least I can do."

Mel couldn't resist commenting, "That's the understatement of the bloody year!"

"Why aren't you wearing your suit? Is it no uniform day at school?" she said sarcastically.

"No I've taken the rest of the day off work. That way I can get to the Cricket Club early. I'm having lunch with Malcolm and Ken, the captain, so I can talk to Ken and see if I can get a game. It's a public holiday in Japan today, Marine day or something, so they should be quiet."

"All the times I asked you to take a day off for me and you never did!"

"Don't start Mel. I just said it's a public holiday in Japan."

He turned away from her.

He was not in the slightest bit bothered she was leaving, or was he?

In the mirror she caught sight of his expression, it had changed, he looked sad. Rob bit on his bottom lip and took a deep breath.

He took the case from her and walked out to call the lift. Luckily it arrived immediately, the tension all the way down was overwhelming.

They didn't have to wait for a cab, one pulled up almost as soon as they stepped outside the gate.

"Changi airport please," she told the driver before Rob had the chance to.

In the taxi she found herself in her usual position of staring silently out the window. She was sure that most of the taxi drivers in the area must be convinced that she was a dumb mute.

The 'bing, bong, bing, bong' noise the cab made when it went over the speed limit was really irritating her this morning.

'Even the bloody taxi driver is in a hurry to get rid of me,' she thought.

She watched out the window as the perfectly planted trees and sparkly condos whizzed by.

The ECP (East Coast Parkway) was an incredibly straight road and mainly full of taxis, hardly anyone owned their own car here, something to do with the price of the road tax or something. Everyone they passed seemed happy and everything was clean and shiny. It all looked so lovely, and now that she was leaving, Mel could see the real beauty of this Asian Island.

The taxi passed in front of the crocodile farm, that was on her 'to do' list, along with Sentosa Island, learning to water ski and the visiting the Orchid Farm. In fact, thinking about it, she had a long 'to do' list, which she'd hardly scratched the surface of.

The taxi continued on its hurried journey and each mile that it clocked up was taking its toll. Mel started to feel unwell, her palms were sweating and her head was pounding, she felt sick and claustrophobic. Despite the air-conditioning, Mel was struggling to breathe. The taxi pulled up outside departures and Melissa quickly jumped out, leaving Rob to pay. He climbed out of the cab, seemingly oblivious to Mel's current fragile state, and went to the boot to help take out the case that the driver was struggling to extract.

She leaned against the taxi, her head was spinning and her breathing was erratic. Rob pulled her case along towards the airport door, she straightened herself up but couldn't move. She stood, eyes closed, breathing in the smells and feeling the intoxicating heat encase her body. She begged herself to get a grip and focus, mentally slapping herself across the face, painfully aware that these next five minutes could change her life.

"Come on Mel, sort yourself out, you can't miss your flight, we have to go to the desk and pick up the tickets."

She looked at Rob, she thought of getting on that plane, of losing him, she thought about her gloating sister and her doubting mother, she thought of her walks in the rain and the snow with her Mum's mangy dog. Then her thoughts turned to her pool, her view, her shoes and posh cosmetics, her feeling of independence, the smug faces of Stella and Tracey also appeared vividly before her and then, much to her surprise, she thought about Harry...

"I'll do it Rob, *We'll* do it, the swapping thing, I want to do it, all of it, I want to stay."

For a few seconds Rob didn't speak, he let go of the handle on the case and it fell over onto the pavement where it stayed.

"Mel don't be stupid, it's not what you want."

She walked towards him.

"Yes it is Rob, it is exactly what I want. Of course I was really shocked at first, you took me by surprise and I wasn't prepared. I bet anybody would have done the same thing in my position, well, any woman certainly. "

She was in full swing.

"But in these last couple of days I've had time to think about it, really go over it and get my head around the idea."

Rob looked strange, and she couldn't tell what he was thinking. She had reached the spot where he was standing and positioned herself in front of him, taking both of his hands in hers she squeezed them tightly.

"Look at me Robert,"

Her voice was calm now,

"I'm telling you I'm okay with this and I want us to do it, I think we'll have fun together."

Mel took a deep breath and studied his expression. The hint of a smile appeared on the corners of his mouth. He was buying it, he believed her. All those Amateur Dramatic classes she had taken as a child were finally paying off, Oscars had probably been presented for less convincing performances.

"You have to be sure Mel that you are totally okay with everything, I don't want another repeat of Friday, I need you to swear that you're good."

"I swear." she placed one hand over her heart and held up the other.

"I'm more than good, I'm great!"

She was oozing excitement and enthusiasm was but being careful not to go over the top. "*We'll* be great,"

Rob opened his mouth to speak but she quickly took his face in her hands and kissed him, she felt a little resistance at first but then his mouth opened slightly and she felt his tongue on hers. They were kissing deeply and several spectators had turned to watch this very public show of affection.

Rob moved his hands down and encircled her waist, yes, he was responding, he was convinced. She smiled and congratulated herself on her success.

The kiss slowly lightened and they broke contact.

"Let's go home", she said.

"Let's go home", he echoed.

They walked back over to the taxi rank and Mel permitted a single tear to fall behind the sunglasses she was wearing and then quickly brushed it away in a casual gesture before it had a chance to peek out from under the frames.

She knew now there was no going back. She would get to keep her pool, her independence and the lifestyle to which she desperately wanted to be accustomed but she was all too aware that she had just sold her soul to the devil.

In the taxi on the way home, the atmosphere was noticeably different. Rob put a hand on her thigh and squeezed it playfully. Mel turned to face him and noted that he had an expression much like the one her aunt liked to describe as the 'cat that got the cream.'

She leaned over and kissed him again, this time he responded immediately. The driver watched the couple in the rear view mirror and, probably sensing the mood, quickened the pace.

'Bing bong, bing bong' the cab sang out, but Mel wasn't the least bit irritated right now. Rob moved his hand up her thigh and under her skirt.

"I always was a sucker for a mini skirt," he whispered into her ear. "You have nice legs Mel which go all the way up to your..."

"Shush!" Mel blocked him, "He'll hear you", pointing at the driver who had put his eyes back on the road.

Rob took hold of her hand and placed it on his crotch, she felt him harden to her touch, she squeezed gently. Looking up she saw the driver staring again at the scene in the back of his vehicle.

"It's probably safer if we stop," she whispered, "otherwise we risk going off the road."

Rob looked at the driver, who quickly turned his attention to his driving. Smiling he squeezed hard and then removed his hand from her thigh.

Arriving at their building, they paid the driver.

"Keep the change" Rob insisted, a rare event indeed, Mel noted.

He grabbed her hand and literally pulled her along the path to their lift. The suitcase rocked from side to side as he dragged it with the other hand and the heavy holdall slipped down from Mel's shoulder as she struggled to keep up with him.

"Rob slow down, you'll pull my arm off."

"I just want to get you home, I am so turned on right now Mel, the thought of us and them is driving me wild."

And there it was, the first reference to 'them'. *That* was what was turning him on, the pictures in his mind not the woman in his sight. She knew that she had made a difficult decision, but now she was beginning to confront the reality and she knew she would have to act the part, go along with everything and moan and scream in all the right places.

Mel realised that she was probably going to have to learn to fake orgasms but she figured that it couldn't be that difficult, according to this month's Cosmo 80% of women did it. She, however, was convinced that it was all better than the alternative... At least she really hoped so.

Rob pressed the lift button but it was up on the 12th floor.

"We've got a minute or two to kill Mel"

Rob was shaking with excitement. He pushed her against the wall in the lobby pinning her there lightly with his left hand while he ran his right hand up her thigh.

"Now where were we?" His fingers ran along the edge of her underwear and his hand moved inside the small cotton knickers searching for her. With his foot he prised her legs open just enough to give him access. Mel glanced round desperately and looked up to check the position of the lift, it had stopped on the eleventh floor.

"Rob, stop, someone might come" she tried to remove his hand but without success.

He laughed, "Yes, you hopefully."

And with that she felt his fingers inside her, he pushed upwards in quick, rough movements. His eyes were ablaze, she'd never seen him quite so excited before. She began to feel the heat rising and her legs felt a little weak. She stretched out her arms, palms pressing against the wall to steady herself. She glanced up, the lift was moving again. His fingers were still inside her while his thumb was kneading her on the outside. The lift stopped again on the tenth floor, he quickened the pace. She had no more desire to resist or worry about the approaching lift, she gave in to the delicious sensation that was overwhelming her, his thumb pressed harder and his fingers drove deeper.

"Come on Mel, let me feel you, show me what you've got, what you want to share."

She closed her eyes and lurched, biting hard on her bottom lip to stop her from shouting out as the orgasm consumed her. Her knees almost gave way and she grabbed onto his shoulder for support. He withdrew his hand, and pulled down her skirt. She bent down and picked up the bag which had dropped to the floor. Rob put his fingers back around the handle of the case and pulled it towards him.

The 'present' light lit up on the panel and the lift door opened. An elderly couple got out and smiled at them, Mel recognised them from the Tai chi group.

"Good day." they said in unison to which the woman then added "My goodness it's hot today isn't it."

"Yes it certainly is." Rob replied politely, Mel could only manage a smile and a nod as she was still trying to get her breath back and currently unable to speak.

The couple walked off towards the door and Mel and Rob got into the lift. They heard the couple chatting.

"What did you say it was hot for? It's always hot here Cynthia."

"Yes I know Trevor, but that poor girl was obviously suffering with it, did you notice how much she was sweating?"

The lift door closed and both Mel and Rob burst out laughing, for the first time in a long time.

She leant back against the wall of the lift and sighed, she was back home and everything was going to be okay, everything was going to be just fine.

Rob opened the front door and pushed the case into the lounge.

"Can you get me a beer from the fridge?" he said, "I'm going to try and get hold of my Boss Vincent. He'll probably hit the bloody roof if they can't get their money back on the ticket."

"What will you say about why I'm not leaving now?" Mel asked, concerned.

"Leave it to me, I'll think of something." he assured her.

Mel took the case and bag through to the bedroom and returned to the kitchen, she opened the fridge door and took out a beer for Rob and the tonic water for herself. She reached over and picked up the bottle of gin from the work top and poured a generous amount into a glass, leaving a modest amount of space for the tonic.

Beer can and glass of gin in hand she walked out onto the balcony and there it was, the view. Her breathtaking view. She put his beer can down onto the table and took a large swig from her glass. She could hear him on the phone, he seemed to be arguing but she couldn't make out what he was saying, Vincent must be giving him a real telling off. Oh well, she shrugged. His problem.

It all went quiet and Rob came out onto the balcony, he walked up behind Mel and put his hands around her waist, pulling her backwards and close into him. Mel felt his erection pressing urgently against her lower back. He brushed her hair to one side with his chin and kissed her neck, biting her gently and sending shivers through her whole body.

"What did he say?"

"Don't worry about that now," he whispered into her receptive ear, "it's my turn, let's see if you can improve on this morning's performance."

Chapter 13

Mel woke after a restless night's sleep to find she was alone, she called out to Rob but there was no reply, the flat was in silence and Rob had already left for work. She rolled over and picked up the alarm clock from the bedside table, eight fifty five, under the clock she noticed a folded piece of paper. She pulled it out, unfolded it, rubbed the sleep from the corner of her eyes and read;

Dear Mel,

Didn't want to wake you. REALLY great work last night babe!!!!!

Keep that up and we'll be invited to all the dinner parties.

Gone to the office early, my Boss wants to see me about the ticket, don't worry I'll sort it. They'll take it out of my bonus or something.

Home about 8.30/9 tonight. Let's eat at the club house to celebrate.

Call Alison, she wants to chat with you, number's in the address book under Tim

Have a good day...xx

P.S. if you get a chance can you iron a couple of shirts.

Mel put the piece of paper she was holding back down on the bedside table. Hopefully Alison just wants to chat about helping her to find a cleaning lady, she thought, dreading the alternative. It was still early so Mel decided to call her later on after she'd slept another hour or so. She rolled over onto her side, closed her eyes and went back to sleep.

She woke with a start to the sound of the telephone, jumped out of bed and ran to the lounge to pick it up.

"Hello" she yawned.

"Melissa? It's Alison, is this a bad time?"

"Hi Alison, no it's okay, sorry I was sleeping."

"Do you want me to call back later Mel?"

Mel glanced down at her watch, twelve forty five! She'd slept for hours. "No that's fine Alison, go ahead"

Mel felt embarrassed, remembering the last time she saw Alison and the condition in which she had left her home. She couldn't help reflecting on the irony that it was she who felt embarrassed.

"Well we understood from Rob last night that you're staying here with us, that's good news, *if* you're sure this time." Mel detected a little frost in her tone.

"Yes I'm sure Alison, thank you."

"Good. I was wondering if Debbie, Sue and myself could pop over this afternoon, say around five for a cup of tea and a chat, will you be around?"

"Yes, I'll be at home, I was just planning a day sorting out the flat and ironing a few shirts, five will be fine"

"Oh God! Ironing shirts, you poor thing, that reminds me we have to get you fixed up with some domestic help, otherwise, well otherwise is just too awful to contemplate. See you at five-ish then...ciao for now."

Mel sank back onto the couch, so she hadn't called to organise a chat about the maid situation, crap! That means that I am probably in for some kind of lecture she thought dejectedly. Well, the least I can do is show that I am coping at home without any help from an amah. Let's get this place spotless.

Mel slipped one of Rob's T shirts on and got to work. The flat was in reasonably good condition but today that wouldn't cut it, it had to be perfect. She started in the kitchen, then stacked magazines and fluffed cushions in the lounge. She was sorry that she had thrown an old copy of Vogue out that she'd found in the bottom of the wardrobe when she arrived, It would have looked good on the top of the pile, she thought.

Happy that all cushions were resting on the sofa at the exactly the same angle she moved on to the bedroom. The biggest job there was unpacking her case, but it was done with joy. She carefully hung everything back up in the wardrobe with some difficulty as a lot of the coat hangers had been broken in her packing frenzy. That just left the bathroom, which didn't take long. She put her lotions and potions and cosmetics back in their rightful places. Mel deliberately left all the expensive stuff out on the side and relegated all the cheap stuff to the drawer. She took out her new towels from the cupboard and placed them neatly onto the rails. She looked around satisfied with a job well done.

She checked the time, it was four fifteen, just time for a quick, much needed shower before the 'Stepford Wives' arrived, laughing out loud at her comparison.

Showered, legs hurriedly shaved and dressed in a denim skirt and white v necked T shirt with flat white sandals, Mel felt she was ready for their visit. She twisted her hair round and secured it up with her trusty crocodile clip. She then went into her 'spic and span' kitchen and prepared the tea, she managed to find four matching cups, noticing that one had a small chip in it so she needed to remember to use that one herself. She searched in the back of the cupboard and to her delight spotted a small white milk jug. She rinsed it out and placed it on the tray.

"Biscuits? Biscuits?" she spoke out loud rummaging through all the cupboards and drawers. Damn, they'd run out. She glanced at her watch, ten to five.

She grabbed the keys and went down to the Club House.

She was relieved to find she was the only customer, she didn't have time for small talk today. Mel grabbed two packets of their most expensive biscuits she could find and took them over to the till.

"Can you put these on our account please?" she asked the young boy behind the counter. "Apartment 7A, Stevens."

The boy opened the account book and flicked through the pages, then stopping at one page he looked sheepishly up at Mel.

"Sorry madam, I have to talk to the boss, please wait here."

He put the book back under the counter, still open and went through the door with a sign which read, 'NO ENTRY TO CUSTOMERS.'

After a minute or two Mel nervously checked her watch, five o'clock exactly, "Come on, come on," she urged.

The young lad returned with the woman who was usually serving when Mel went in there. The woman took hold of the book under the counter and looked at the open page.

She then spoke to Melissa.

"Hello Mrs Stevens, my son told me you want this on account, is it? It seems the bill for last month is not paid yet you know, for restaurant and shop here is one hundred sixteen dollar."

Mel looked embarrassed, she remembered Rob saying he would pay this last week, she even remembered giving him a hundred dollars towards it which she'd taken out of the joint account they had.

Mel had been left ten thousand pounds by her grandma when she died last spring and when Rob had invited her to live with him in Singapore she had withdrawn almost all of it to take with her, much to the disapproval of her mother. Mel was sure her grandma would have approved and would want her to use it to travel, she always told Mel that not seeing more of the world was her biggest regret.

Luckily, before she arrived, Rob had added her to his account making it into a joint account.

Mel had been relieved that Rob had offered to do it... He was always going on about how complicated it was to get things done in Singapore and thank God for Christine who took care of all that kind of bureaucratic stuff.

Mel came from a reasonably humble background and had always helped pay her way, having had a continuous string of various part-time jobs since the age of fourteen. Even if Rob was now earning good money she saw no reason why she should become a kept woman, she valued her economic independence.

"I'm so sorry," Mel exclaimed genuinely mortified, "I'll bring it down later today, I promise. Would it be possible to just put these on the account, I've come out without my purse."

Mel took another glance at her watch, six minutes past five, the girls could be ringing on the bell.

The two spoke for a minute in Chinese then the woman walked back over to the door.

"OK now", replied the boy looking as uncomfortable as Melissa, "later you can pay."

Melissa thanked the boy profusely and then slunk out of the shop feeling like a criminal.

Mel decided not to call Rob now at the office about it, he had probably had a right telling off from his Boss already today and he hated to be disturbed at work unless it was an emergency. She decided it would be better if she spoke to Rob about it tonight calmly over dinner.

When she went back upstairs she would get the money from his underwear drawer, he always kept a couple of hundred dollars in there for emergencies and when the girls left she would take it straight down.

Walking quickly along the path to her building she saw that nobody was standing at the gate ringing buzzers. Relieved, she hurried up to the apartment.

On entering she dashed into the kitchen and emptied the biscuits onto a plate and arranged them neatly, not quite up to Alison's standards but it would have to do. Just as she was throwing the packets away, the buzzer rang, Mel went into the lounge and lifted the receiver on the wall.

"Hi Melissa, it's us."

"Hi, come up, it's the first building on the seventh floor, the door on the left."

Mel walked over to the cushions on the sofa and moved them all two centimetres to the left, *now* they were right, she smiled.

The doorbell rang and Mel opened the door with a big smile planted firmly on her face.

"Hi Alison, Debbie, Sue, nice to see you again. Come in please."

The ladies paraded in and Alison stopped to kiss Mel on both cheeks.

"Ciao, veeeery nice condominium," she enthused. "I've always loved this one but it was just a bit too far out for us, Tim loves being close to the CBD and we're so handy for the cricket club."

Mel tried not to look puzzled, she had only ever taken fifteen minutes in a taxi to get to the CBD, how can that be too far out? She wondered.

Debbie smiled at Mel, "Hello Melissa, and it's nice to see you again."

Sue stood at the back looking a little sheepish,

"We brought these." She practically whispered and held out a box with the word *Mövenpick* on the side of it.

"Cookies and brownies, to hell with the diet!" added Alison.

Mel took the box and put them on the coffee table.

"Can I get you a tea or coffee?" Mel asked looking in the group's general direction and noticed they were all still standing in a line.

"Please take a seat," she continued indicating the rather obvious sofa. The three women walked over and sat down.

"I hear Christine found you this apartment," exclaimed Debbie, "she found ours too, she's a gem, a bit strange looking but she certainly takes all the burden off the moving bit. I hate moving and loathe unpacking, thank god for removal companies."

"Yes," replied Mel, "Rob said it was all done by the time he got here, mind you it was practically already furnished which helps."

Debbie and Sue nodded in agreement but Alison pulled a 'what's that smell?' face.

"Couldn't disagree more," she said disgustedly, "living with someone else's stuff! How awful! I insisted on a shopping trip to Korea en route here and bought everything, they shipped it really quickly as well in just a few weeks."

"So," Mel continued, not really knowing how to reply to that, "tea or coffee?"

"I'll have coffee please, black one sugar." answered Alison.

"Oh me too, but no sugar, I have pills." announced Debbie producing a little box of artificial sweeteners from the depths of her purse and shaking them happily.

"Sue, what can I get you?"

"She'll have a tea, white no sugar" interrupted Alison before she had a chance to answer for herself. Sue looked up and nodded in agreement once more.

Melissa went into the kitchen to make the drinks, she picked up the kettle from the shiny cooker top and filled it from the tap. She heard voices but couldn't make out what they were saying over the noise of the running water.

"Sorry?" said Mel, turning off the tap.

"I said, mind if we have a look around the apartment?"

But Debbie was already standing up and heading towards the bedrooms closely followed by Alison and Sue trailing slightly behind. She hadn't noticed at the dinner party that Sue had seemed particularly shy but now that she thought about it, she didn't remember having had a conversation with her.

She heard doors opening and closing and voices chattering, at one point she heard Debbie comment that the apartment was a bit small. Mel was glad that she had thoroughly cleaned the whole place thoroughly.

She placed all the cups on a tray and carried them through to the lounge just as the girls came back into the room.

"Right," said Alison, in her best headmistress voice, "let's get down to business."

Chapter 14

Alison sat down, crossed her long, tanned and perfectly waxed legs and smoothed down her skirt, turning around she moved the cushions behind her five centimetres to the left and plumped up the last one, nodding smugly. Then she leaned forward slightly and fixed her eyes firmly on Mel.

"I imagine you know why we're here Melissa?"

Mel looked up and nodded timidly.

"We need to talk about what happened at my apartment the other night."

Mel swallowed hard and picked up her tea cup which was rattling slightly on the saucer in her trembling hands, she took a deep breath to try and calm her nerves.

She hadn't felt this intimidated since being sent to the headmaster's office at school, when she and Stella took it upon themselves to tack up the hem on their school uniform skirt by about five inches. Luckily her sewing was so bad that by the time she got into his office it had fallen down, hence destroying the evidence.

She took a sip of tea and placed the cup back on the table.

"Rob explained to Tim that you had a funny turn that evening on account of the heat" Alison explained, "Personally you seemed a little shell shocked to me."

"The problem is, Melissa", Debbie continued, "we can't have that kind of reaction at our little get together, it puts real dampers on things you see, spoils the whole mood."

Mel opened her mouth to reply but was interrupted.

"Now, we don't often need to hold these type of 'pow wows,'" continued Alison, "usually the person who seconds the nomination takes care of the details, but Rob had assured us that you were completely in agreement and up to speed on the situation, as it turns out he was talking crap, and I don't think you *were* fully in the know were you?

Mel once again opened her mouth to reply but was interrupted for the second time.

"So we have taken it upon ourselves to make sure that it doesn't happen again."

"Tim and Harry were both bloody furious with Rob," smiled Debbie seemingly taking great pleasure in the announcement.

"In fact Tim asked him to leave his house immediately, after giving him a right bollocking that is. He was bloody lucky not to have been chucked out the club completely, it could have been the shortest membership in history."

Bloody lucky! Damn, that would have solved all her problems, Mel thought despondently.

She picked up the plate of biscuits and offered them round, all present declined. She put the plate back on the table and then pondered, 'If Rob was sent home immediately the other night where the hell did he go until five o'clock in the morning?'

Mel forced a half grin for her audience.

"Rob explained it all to me properly when he got home," she lied, "I really wasn't feeling very well that evening and it just took me a bit by surprise that's all. He had talked to me about the club," she lied again, "but I hadn't fully understood the situation. I didn't really think he was serious I thought that he was joking, you know how Rob likes to joke around, but now that I have things clear in my mind I'm fine, really, sounds fun."

Mel gave them a wink, 'that might have been too much!' she thought.

"So why were you leaving yesterday? What was that about?" Alison asked, clearly suspicious.

"Oh that, I heard that my grandma was ill with a heart problem and I thought I needed to get back quickly, but it was a false alarm, chronic indigestion thank God."

She hoped that Rob hadn't told anyone how it really went, but she doubted it, his ego and fear of being ostracised wouldn't have allowed him to tell anyone how he had tricked her into going there that evening. Damn, why hadn't she checked with Rob to see what story he'd told in the office about her booking a ticket home to make sure she told the same? These people mustn't ever find out how she had really reacted, she was sure they would never trust her again if they did, and if this charade was going to work she needed their trust.

Alison and Debbie looked at each other, smirked and nodded, they seemed to accept her version of events, at least on the surface. Sue looked at Mel and reached for her tea, Mel noticed a slight rattle in her saucer too.

"Well, just to make sure that Rob did explain it all properly we are here to go over a few things." Alison pulled out an envelope from her bag and handed the envelope to Mel.

"Read through this and then we can go through it one point at a time together if you need to."

Mel took out a card and nervously read the first line,

'SINGAPORE SWING CLUB' RULES.

Harry was right, it was such a corny name! Under the watchful eye of everyone Mel continued to read...

RULE 1.

All couples invited to take part must attend each 'Dinner Party' voluntarily and in full knowledge of the proceedings.

'Naughty Robert, you broke rule number one!' she thought to herself sarcastically.

RULE 2

All couples must be male and female.

'That's a relief,' she thought, she wasn't ready for another leap in the dark.

RULE 3.

The 'Dinner Parties' are to take place at members' apartments only, the location of which will be decided one week before.

'Oh hell, please not here!' She couldn't bear the thought of all that going on in her house.

RULE 4

The 'Dinner parties' are to take place on the second Friday of every month and any changes to the schedule must be agreed by everybody taking part.

Mel was reading incredulously at the level of organisation of these people.

RULE 5

No 'meetings' shall take place outside the scheduled monthly one.

'Obviously not, that just wouldn't be right!' Mel's thoughts were becoming increasingly more sarcastic.

RULE 6

All potential new members must be presented and approved by a majority of current members prior to their joining.

'Like a slave auction! That explains the exaggerated interest in her at that first dinner party!'

RULE 7.

All sexual activity MUST be engaged in using the required precautions.

'Condoms and large amounts of alcohol!'

RULE 8.

Any member who attends without his or her partner may be permitted to watch a consenting couple.

'Not on your bloody life!' Mel looked up to see the girls still watching her intently, she must have looked worried.

"Is everything all right Mel? Let me know if there's anything that's not clear."

"No, really Debbie, I'm fine thanks."

RULE 9.

All sexual activity performed is at the discretion of the participants and is confined to only one hour.

'You're on a meter?! At least that meant she wouldn't have to put up with it all night.'

RULE 10.
No one must talk about or mention this club to anybody (members or non-members) outside of 'Dinner Party' hours.

'This was the rule that Harry had mentioned, there was no danger of that, who the hell would she want to tell this to!'

NB: THIS IS WITH THE UNIQUE EXCEPTION OF THE ANNUAL 'RULES COMMITTEE' MEETING.

Rules committee! You are bloody kidding me!

RULE 11.
Anybody who breaks any of these rules will be severely reprimanded and/or asked to leave the club.

Spanked severely with a rolled up copy of The Straits Times!
She fought back a smile at this last thought.

I... have read and understood the rules of this club and promise to maintain and respect all of them dated this day... in Singapore.

Mel put the card down on the coffee table and looked at her tea cup.

'I could really do with something much stronger' she thought. What the hell had she gotten into?

There were a lot of inverted commas in that document she noticed, 'Dinner parties,' 'Meetings'. She was in way over her head here, she suddenly realised the reality of the situation. There were even rules for Christ's sake, these people took this very seriously.

She looked up at the 3 women sitting on her sofa.

Sue was tapping her foot in a nervous manner,

"Can I use your bathroom Melissa please?" she asked. Mel nodded,

"Yes of course, use the one in the bedroom immediately on the left."

Sue stood up, grabbed her bag and walked into the bedroom.

Mel looked down at the card, and then up at Alison.

"Seems fine, all clear," she said feeling her mouth dry up, she licked her lips and picked up the tea cup without the saucer, her hands were now trembling even more and the saucer would have given her away. She took a large sip from the cup and put it back down.

"Good," said Debbie, "now, as you can see we expect the utmost discretion and respect for the rules."

"Your membership application was seconded by Tim", explained Alison

"He's known Rob the longest, as we said usually the 'seconder' takes care of the protocol but Rob assured Tim he had explained the rules already to you so you can imagine how pissed off Tim was to discover that he had buggered it up. You've never seen this card before have you?"

Mel shook her head.

"Mind you Alison, you have to admit that Tim was an idiot, he should have checked." Debbie went on.

Alison threw Debbie a glare.

"So, any questions Mel? Speak now or forever hold your peace."

Mel shook her head again although she had loads of questions running round in her head but none that she could ask them now, like,

"How do you sleep well at night?" And "How can you sit here being all superior?"

"No, no questions, all clear."

"I forgot to mention that if the dates of the meetings coincide with the time of your monthly there are ways of sorting it out. You can change the day you start your pill, if you take the pill that is. I would certainly recommend that you do, better safe than sorry. We all have our cycles practically synchronised, so it's a lot of fun around here in the middle of the month as you can imagine."

Debbie laughed.

Mel couldn't believe it, there was just no getting out of these meetings, all bases had been covered and she was mortified. She had problems discussing her menstrual cycle with her own Mother, she certainly wasn't comfortable discussing it with virtual strangers.

Sue came back into the room fanning herself with a handkerchief, she sat back down on the sofa and picked up her tea cup, the rattle now evident to all.

"Great", said Debbie, "that just leaves the signing of this thing and we're done. Sue, can you give Mel a pen please."

Sue dug around in her purse and pulled out a silver pen with the Singapore airlines logo on the end.

"Here," she said quietly, handing the pen to Mel, as Mel reached over to take it, it dropped to the floor, Alison and Debbie both scowled at her, 'poor thing,' Mel thought to herself, she seems more intimidated than I am.

Sue bent down and retrieved the pen from under the coffee table. When she emerged she was sweating profusely. Mel took the pen from Sue's outstretched hand and desperately trying to keep a steady hand herself scrawled her signature on the bottom of the card.

"What's the date today?" Mel asked, realising that she really had no idea.

"It's Tuesday the sixteenth of June," smiled Sue nervously.

Mel completed the card, 16-06-1987.

Alison took the card from her, put it carefully back in the envelope and popped it into her Gucci hand bag. Mel tried to ascertain if it was a real one or fake, it was almost impossible to tell at a glance, the copies here were amazingly good.

"We'll get this photocopied and give it back A.S.A.P." she announced. "Ladies, time to go."

All three stood up and started to walk towards the door.

"We're having a pool party a week on Saturday, the twenty seventh, for our fourth wedding anniversary and Tim and I would love you and Rob to come, I'm sure he's already mentioned it to Rob. Bring a costume and a towel, about two thirty, three, see you then."

Mel couldn't believe how easily they talked about and managed all this, one minute reading the rules of what to do and not to do while having sex with each other's husbands and the next minute organising an anniversary party. Mel couldn't ever imagine being that comfortable with it, but she knew she had to try, at least to pretend. If these women caught on she would be out, out of the club, out of Rob's life and out of Singapore. Mel smiled sweetly at the group.

"Thanks for coming by," she said, "we'll be there next Saturday Alison, I'm looking forward to it."

And once again Alison put her hands firmly on Mel's shoulders and kissed her on both cheeks.

"Fabulous, don't forget your costume, and remember..."

She put her index finger up to her lips and made a shushing sound.

"Oh I almost forgot, this is the number for an amah, call her tomorrow, you really need some help around here."

Then she opened the door and they all filed out just as they had filed in.

"Oh, I almost forgot," Sue stopped and faced Mel. "You're out of toilet roll," she said.

"See, I told you, you need an amah Mel dear," Alison said shaking her head disapprovingly.

Mel said goodbye and closed the door. She took a deep breath and leaned back against the closed door for a few seconds until she heard the bell which announced the arrival of the lift outside. Her heart was beating quickly in her chest and she felt a little light headed. She walked back into the lounge and lay down on the sofa, ignoring the cups of half drunken teas and coffees and the full plate of untouched biscuits.

"What the hell just happened here?" she was speaking out loud.

She stayed there for a few minutes trying to gather her thoughts up so they made some sort of sense. When the room eventually stopped turning she sat up, feeling dazed, picked up the tray and headed for the kitchen to fix a very stiff gin and tonic. Her Mum always said that there was nothing you couldn't cure with a cup of tea, Mel was developing the same philosophy about G and T's!

She wandered back into the living room, taking large gulps from the full glass as she moved.

Mel picked up the phone and dialled the number, the phone rang a few times.

"Hello," responded the voice at the other end. "Hello"

Mel struggled to keep her voice from trembling.

"Mum, Mum it's me, Mel."

"Mel, Hi love, how great to hear from you. I was just saying to your sister last night that we should call you today. We got the parcel you sent, Gillian loved the silk dressing gown and my necklace is beautiful, but you shouldn't spend your money on us. Nana wouldn't have wanted you to flutter it all away she would have wanted you to put some of it aside for a rainy day. Anyway, tell me how's it all going? How's Rob?"

Mel took another long sip from the now half empty glass and replied,

"It's great Mum, really amazing here, Rob is fine and working hard, he sends his love."

She bit down hard on her bottom lip which was beginning to tremble.

"Mel, what's wrong? You sound strange, is everything really okay?"

Mel couldn't fight back the tears anymore, she cried into the phone.

"I just miss you Mum that's all, I'm just a bit home sick, but don't worry, I'm fine."

"Mel, you'd tell me if there was something wrong wouldn't you love?"

"Of course Mum, really I'm fine, is Gill there? I'd like a chat."

"No she's gone out for lunch with Martin, but I'll tell her you called, she'll be sorry she missed you."

Martin was Gill's dopey, boring boyfriend who Mel had always taken the mickey out of but right now she quite envied her sister.

"She's got a job interview on Friday, an apprentice position in a hairdresser's in the town, fingers crossed."

"Oh that's great Mum, tell her good luck from me. I'd better go now but I'll call over the weekend, Sunday, early afternoon your time probably,"

"Okay love, if we're not home try me at your auntie's house, now don't stay on the phone it'll be costing you a fortune, love you Mel and you tell Rob to look after you from me. And be strong, you made the decision to go there now don't waste this opportunity pining for home, it'll always be here. Bye Darling and take care of yourself, oh and don't forget it's your auntie's fortieth birthday next week, I love you."

"No, I won't, bye Mum, I love you too."

Mel heard the click as her Mum put down the receiver and she clutched the phone tightly to her chest. 'I miss you so much Mum' she sobbed to herself.

She put the phone back on the receiver and wiped her eyes.

'Come on Mel', she urged herself after a few minutes, 'pull yourself together, there are shirts to iron.'

She walked into the spare room and turned on the small fan on the worktop then she took down a couple of shirts from the line and began to press them as best she could.

She hated ironing shirts, if she did have to get a maid she wouldn't miss doing shirts, that's for sure.

After a good half an hour two shirts were reasonably presentable. She took them through to their bedroom and hung them up in Rob's side of the wardrobe.

She went over to the underwear drawer and hunted around for the money to take down to the supermarket but the only thing in it was underwear.

She would have to go out to the bank and take some out the cash machine, and soon. She wanted to pay of the mini market today before it closed at eight, she'd promised the boy.

'Oh toilet roll', she remembered, she walked into the bathroom but there on the holder was the full roll she had put there earlier. Strange! 'I must have misunderstood, Sue probably meant the other bathroom.'

She turned to leave but just as she did she noticed the piece of paper sticking out from the middle of the roll.

Mel unrolled the bit of paper and read the words scribbled on it.

'Melissa, don't make the same mistake I did, it's not worth it, these people are poison, and they'll poison you.'

She stood clutching the bit of paper and looking at her reflection in the mirror, she screwed it up into a little ball, threw it into the toilet and pulled the flush.

Chapter 15

For the next few weeks Mel threw herself into trying to get fit. The thought of being naked in front of virtual strangers was a great motivator.

She swam every day, morning and evening and even visited the small gym next to the mini market. Having everything there to hand made it easier to commit and more difficult to find excuses not to do it.

She had never been very keen on exercise, deeming it to be too much like hard work, but being there with nothing much to do all day she had made up her mind to try. She even agreed to play tennis one evening with Debbie at her apartment.

"If you fancy a game come over tomorrow about six, we can knock the ball about for a while and then reward ourselves with a well-deserved swim and a drink after, what do you say? I have a spare racket you can borrow."

Mel had always been terrible at tennis, it was due to the fact, she had convinced herself, that she was left handed and her school tennis coach had refused to spend time showing her how to hold a racket left handed and instead she had insisted on Mel playing right handed like everyone else. Friday afternoons at school from March to July were consequently torture, compulsory hours and hours of swinging rackets in the vague direction of those little yellow fuzzy balls, missing and swiping air.

Not wanting to seem rude or unsociable and desperate to become a part of the group, she had agreed to give Debbie a game.

When she told Rob he was delighted.

"That's great news, Debbie's husband Mark is a valuable customer, he runs the Yen desk at his bank so make sure you let her win!"

Mel laughed out loud.

"Yes Rob, don't worry, she'll win. I've never won a game of tennis in my life."

Mel arrived punctually at the gate of their apartment, she buzzed and the gate clicked open.

"Come up, I'm just getting changed into my tennis dress, it's the second floor, apartment 2B, it's on the left as you get to the top of the stairs."

'Tennis dress!' Mel was wearing a pair of normal shorts and a Spandau Ballet tour T shirt, a decision she was now regretting. Looking down at her feet she saw her trainers had also seen better days.

Mel stepped through the open gate and saw the tennis court through an archway, it was currently occupied by two men, she checked her watch, five forty five.

She had been hoping that maybe Debbie had changed her mind about the tennis and was just going to opt for the drink, it was about eighty degrees after all.

She arrived outside the apartment and rang the bell, she seriously worried how she would cope with an actual game of tennis as just the walk up two flights of stairs had left her quite breathless and soaked in sweat.

A tiny Asian lady opened the door almost immediately, she beckoned to Mel to come inside.

Debbie shouted out from some remote room.

"Hi Mel, come in for sec, I just have to find my water bottle, do you need one?"

Mel realised that she had come totally unprepared, 'who the hell plays tennis in this heat without bringing water?'

"Yes please, if it's not too much trouble, I've just realised that I left mine in the taxi" she shouted back.

She decided it was better to be thought of as forgetful rather than stupid!

Debbie came into view looking like an ad for Wimbledon.

"Did you bring your costume and a change of clothes? We could have a shower and a quick swim before that drink, the pool is wonderful in the evening."

Mel cringed with embarrassment, damn! She didn't have those either.

"I didn't bring anything," she said timidly.

Great, now she would pass as both forgetful *and* stupid.

"Don't worry, I'll lend you something of mine, I should still have some of my clothes from last year in a drawer somewhere, I was a bit bigger then."

'Ouch!'

Mel walked further into the apartment and was suddenly hit by that dreaded odour.

"Sorry about the smell of paint, we're having the spare room decorated. My parents arrive next weekend for a few days and I want the place to look decent."

Mel was no longer listening, her heart was pounding and she felt nauseated.

"Mum, Mum?"

The little girl was banging hard on the front door of the house but there was no reply. She walked back down the path to the gate and turned onto the path of the house next door.

She knocked on the red front door.

"Linda, it's Melissa" she called through the letter box.

She waited a few seconds and then through the glass panel saw a figure coming to the door, she smiled relieved to have found her at home but as the door opened the smile faded from her face.

"Hello, who are you looking for?"

The tall rather chubby man stood at the open door. He was dressed in dirty overalls and was carrying a large paint brush.

She stared at the stranger for a while noticing he had paint in his hair and on his face but she didn't recognise him.

"I'm looking for my Mum Marion, we live next door, is she here with Linda?"

"Oh, your Mum! Marion, the lady from next door. Ah yes she's just nipped to the shops and Linda is upstairs sleeping because she doesn't feel very well."

Then lowering his voice, "Your mum'll be back in a minute, she told me to tell you to wait in here until she gets back."

Mel felt strange and slightly uncomfortable.

"It's OK, I'll wait at my house." she replied.

"No you have to come in here Melissa, she made me promise to look after you when you got home from school until she got back and you don't want me getting into trouble do you?"

Mel shook her head and stepped inside.

The smell of paint in the house was strong.

"Let's go and wait for her in the front room, you can tell me all about your day at school."

She was feeling very strange and something was telling her that she shouldn't really be there.

"I really should be going home, Mummy might be back and she'll be worried if I'm not there."

She went to stand up but the man pulled her down onto his lap and began stroking her hair.

"You've got very pretty hair Melissa", he whispered into her ear. She was now beginning to feel a little scared. He began jiggling her up and down on his knee and she felt something hard pressing against her bottom. She tried to stand up but he was holding on tightly around her waist, just then there was a knock at the door.

"Shush," whispered the man again, "let's play a game, we're going to pretend we aren't here to play a joke on the person at the door."

Mel was now really scared.

"Melissa, are you there? It's Mum, Mel?"

The man put his hand gently over Melissa's mouth. "Remember we're playing, you mustn't let her know we're here or you lose the game" he whispered.

Her Mum walked away from the door and Mel watched her sadly through the window walk back down the path.

"I want to go home, I want my Mummy, I want Linda" she was now half crying.

"I don't want to play anymore."

"How old are you Melissa?" he asked, ignoring her distress.

"Seven" she replied with a trembling voice, "and I want to go home."

"Seven? Wow, you're almost grown up."

The man began kissing her neck and stroking her leg, she felt a strange sensation down below. He reached for her hand and placed it on the hard lump in his trousers.

Mel pulled her hand back and tried once again to stand up but he was holding her even tighter.

His hand was moving further up her leg and was feeling around the elastic of her knickers at the top of her leg. His breathing was heavy and whistley, Mel thought that it sounded a bit like the way that her Grandad breathed after they had been out for a walk with the dog.

Suddenly he released his grip and stood up quickly and Mel fell to the floor.

"Now I need you to stay here a minute while I go upstairs and get Linda. Stay here Melissa, Linda will be down in just a minute and she'll take you home."

Mel felt better, she would soon be next door and away from this smell, it was beginning to make her feel a little bit dizzy.

The man disappeared upstairs and Mel stood up slowly and quietly crept out into the hall way. She heard someone moving around upstairs then she heard someone on the stairs. As she looked up expecting to see Linda rounding the corner she caught site of the man, he wasn't wearing any clothes and had just a small towel around his waist.

Without thinking she ran to the front door, turned the lock and pulled at the handle. The door sprang open and she ran out onto the path. She heard the man scrambling down the stairs and shouting something but she kept running without looking back until she reached her front door.

"Anyone for tennis!" Debbie came bounding towards her with a racket in each hand and a towel draped over each shoulder.

Mel managed a smile.

"Are you okay? You look like you've seen a ghost!"

"Yes I'm fine," she lied, "just a little allergic to paint fumes."

"Oh god, I'm so sorry, why didn't you say, let's get out of here."

Relieved, Mel followed her out into the hall breathing in the clean, paint free air as deeply as she could as she went.

The game of tennis, as predicted, was rather one sided. Mel played surprisingly well for her, she even managed to hit the ball back a few times and even won a point on a serve but the smell of the paint was still lingering in her nostrils and the images of that afternoon were dominating her thoughts.

Needless to say Debbie won, three games to nil. Mel was just glad she had survived.

They had a quick, cool and much needed shower in the small changing room next to the tennis court before putting on their costumes and diving into the pool. Mel was relieved that they didn't have to go back up to the apartment, she had only just gotten rid of the smell from her nostrils.

Debbie had been right, the pool in the evening was wonderful, the sun was setting and the pool lights flickered on, illuminating the bottom of the pool where the dark blue shape of a dolphin could now be clearly seen.

After a few token lengths of the small kidney shaped pool they sat relaxing in the Jacuzzi in the corner with a much deserved glass of Laurent Perrier in their hand, poured from a perfectly chilled bottle which Mark had kindly brought down for them during their swim.

Mel was now in heaven, she was sitting in a Jacuzzi, sipping champagne on a normal evening with nothing more to celebrate than the fact it was Wednesday. She had only previously drunk champagne at weddings, and then really it had been Spumante. The difference had always escaped her, until now! As well as the bubbles in her glass there were the bubbles in the warm water gently massaging her aching muscles.

For more than half an hour they chatted about Singapore and all the other places Debbie had visited in the last couple of years. Mel was dying to ask her how she coped with this swapping thing, how she managed to carry on with her life as usual and not get desperately jealous and so many other questions, but it wasn't allowed, the rules forbid anyone from talking about it outside the meetings and so she just went on listening to the multitude of travel stories.

With the bottle empty and the sun now completely set the girls decided it was time to get out and get dressed.

She could return to Rob with head held high, mission accomplished, Debbie had won, actually Debbie had thrashed her!

His Yen desk contact was safe and he could continue buying, selling or trading or whatever it was he did. She despaired that she didn't understand what he really did all day, still whatever it was it had brought her here, far from the UK and all its problems and nothing or no one was going to take this away from her.

Chapter 16

When she wasn't in the pool or the gym Mel kept herself busy by shopping. She had accumulated a huge collection of rattan and ceramic objects and knick knacks, ignoring Rob's insistence to take it easy on the spending. If he didn't want her working then he was going to have to accept her shopping sprees.

She read the wanted ads in the newspapers and had discreetly been to a couple of interviews mainly for bar jobs. One bar had been keen for her to start but when she had told Rob the good news he had made it quite clear that it was neither appropriate nor acceptable. He still couldn't see why she was so set on working but had reluctantly suggested she talk to Alison again to see if she had any positions in her catering company.

Mel had made up her mind however, that she didn't like Alison very much and thought they would be already be spending far too much time together. Rob, on the other hand, had made it perfectly obvious on several occasions that he would quite like to spend more time with Alison but that certainly didn't mean Mel had to!

So it was back to the newspaper ads.

Mel was drinking and smoking a bit too much for her liking but it was an 'occupational' hazard.

Her self-made rule of one cigarette after dinner and maybe one if they were out for the evening had gone out the window along with the other rule, no drinking before six p.m.!

Lunches, brunches and pool parties all consisted of drinking copious amounts of gin and tonics and Singapore slings. It was actually considered rude not to and it kept her from thinking too much about the upcoming events.

The day of the first dreaded 'party' arrived. It was being held at Debbie and Mark's apartment, their apartment was much larger than Mel's with three bedrooms and two large bathrooms.

All afternoon leading up to the dreaded event she had been in a state of panic, Rob had called three or four times from work to make sure she was okay and not thinking of backing out. He, in difference to her, was like a child on Christmas morning.

Mel arrived at the apartment with a huge knot of tension in her stomach which kept her from eating almost anything. As a result, the large glasses of wine she was downing for Dutch courage were taking their toll.

She looked around the room, there was Laurel and Tony, Harry and Tess, themselves and Debbie and Mark obviously. She was very relieved to see that neither Malcolm nor Tim were there. Malcolm she hated, he was just as she had first thought, a chauvinistic, obnoxious pig. Tim, on the other hand, she had nothing against, in fact he seemed quite sweet, but Alison intimidated the crap out of her and she reminded Mel too much of the stuck up bullies at school and it certainly didn't help matters that she could see that Rob had a bit of a thing for her. He was always far too over enthusiastic and gushingly complimentary whenever they met.

Mel had spent most of Alison and Tim's anniversary party, a few weeks earlier, just sitting pool side watching the Rob and Malcolm show.

She had to admit that some scenes had been funny and smiled as she recalled the scene in the pool with Rob precariously balanced on Malcolm's shoulders. Malcolm was chest high in the water whilst Rob, straddling his shoulders, was attempting to juggle three mangoes whilst singing 'This is my country,' the Singaporean national song.

Needless to say it finished with Rob and Malcolm almost drowning.

As he had struggled out of the pool Alison rushed over to hand him a towel and Mel winced as she recalled the moment when he playfully flicked Alison's backside with it. She was sure that Tim had also looked on unamused or was that just her imagination?

If she got jealous at that, how the hell was she going to keep it together at the dinner party?

That first night the staff were dismissed and then the names, as is always the case, were drawn out of a large glass bowl. That evening the men had put in tightly folded, white monogrammed handkerchiefs. Debbie had picked out Harry and Laurel had chosen Mark.

Mel stood there frozen to the spot when Debbie called her to the table.

"Mel would you like to do the honours? It's your turn... Melissa! Come on, mustn't keep the boys waiting."

Mel looked over in Rob's direction, he was staring at her wide-eyed, and indicated with his head towards the table.

Mel walked slowly over to the bowl where two small white squares were left inside. She swirled them round a bit. By elimination she knew one was Rob's and the other was Tony's. She picked up a tightly folded handkerchief and attempted to unfold it but her hands were shaking so much she dropped it on the floor. Debbie, obviously irritated, bent down, picked up it up and then quickly opened it out.

"Oh it's Rob!" exclaimed Debbie.

Mel sighed with relief, Rob, thank God! She would be spared this nightmare for another month.

"Forfeit!" shouted Laurel.

Everyone cheered, Rob louder than the rest.

"What does that mean?" asked Mel, directing the question at nobody in particular.

Harry obliged her with a reply.

"That means that we have to draw names again. Only one person each evening can call forfeit, and that person can't call it again the next time they attend."

Mel didn't remember reading that anywhere on the rule card.

"Come on Mel, you can't spend the first time with your own partner, where's the fun in that!" laughed Laurel.

She watched despondently as everyone put their handkerchiefs, carefully refolded, back into the bowl.

She looked over at Rob who was smiling like a Cheshire cat!

"Couldn't agree more" he replied.

Mel was asked to go first this time and reluctantly went through the same sad ritual again, only this time pulling Mark's name out of the bowl.

If it had to be someone and it wasn't Rob then she had desperately hoped the first time would be with Harry.

She wasn't sure why but she felt she would be more comfortable with him.

She didn't get a chance to find out who Rob was with, Mark took hold of her hand and led her quickly out of the room, stopping to kiss Debbie as he passed her in the hallway where she was disappearing into a room with Tony.

"Let's get the room with the en suite quick before it's snapped up" he smiled.

Mel envied how relaxed he was, they all were, she would never be relaxed about any of this and she would never ever be okay with it either.

When they walked into the room, it was bathed in candlelight. Lots of candles of various sizes had been placed on little saucers around the room. Mel found this romantic touch ironic and quite inappropriate.

The bed was covered in bright, Thai silk-covered cushions and under the cushions a simple white silk sheet covered the mattress. There was also an ice bucket with an unopened bottle in it and two glasses.

"Laurel always pushes the boat out" he smiled, noticing her surprised expression.

Mark was being quite sweet, as it was her first time he assured her he would take things slowly. He tried putting her at ease with small talk first, talking about his German shepherd dog, Jagger, who was at home being looked after by his sister. He also told her about his passion for The Rolling Stones and Dire Straits. Mel commented that Jagger was an infinitely better name for a dog than Knopfler, and they both laughed. Then, much to Mel's surprise, he confessed that he had been a bit unsure about all this at first himself, but that he had very soon got used to it.

"In fact," he confided, "it has become the highlight of the month."

He opened the bottle and filled her glass with large quantities of yet more wine.

She was just starting to think that maybe he would be happy only chatting for a while when he turned to face her and his expression changed.

"Let's not waste any more time, eh Mel? The clock's ticking."

He took the glass from her hand and put it down on the floor.

She swallowed hard trying to dislodge the lump which had formed in her throat. 'Oh God this is it!' Her hands were shaking visibly causing her to fumble with her zip.

She recalled the image of him carrying down the bottle of Champagne and the glasses to the pool a couple of weeks earlier, the doting, obliging husband!

Undressing quickly she darted under the sheet and pulled it up tightly under her chin. Mark, in contrast, undressed carefully removing every item of clothing slowly. Finally he was down to his underpants, the obvious bulge inside showing his increasing excitement. He peeled them down revealing his erection which sprang to attention obediently. Mel wanted to turn away and not look but she found herself almost hypnotised by the sight of it. She didn't have a lot of experience with men, Rob had been only her second serious boyfriend and she certainly hadn't seen many naked ones, she had to admit that Mark was surprisingly well endowed.

He slid in next to her under the sheet and tugged at it a little.

Mel released her grip slightly and it fell revealing her left breast, she instinctively reached down to pull the sheet back up to cover herself but Mark's hand blocked her move.

Her heart was beating so hard in her chest she feared it would burst right out.

Mark reached under the sheet and pulled her down to a horizontal position, squeezing her breasts hard and clumsily. Then quickly and gently he climbed on top, kicking at her ankles to move her legs apart.

Mel turned her head to the side and kept her eyes screwed tightly shut. She gasped as she felt him trying to get inside her. She was so tense that it was painful at first, she tried desperately to relax but it was impossible, she felt like she had gone back to being a virgin.

Eventually, with insistence on his part, Mel began to relax a little by trying to think of other things and the process became easier, the discomfort passed and she felt a little more at ease. Plucking up the courage to open her eyes a little she saw Mark's ecstatic expression, he also had his eyes closed but he was smiling and in full swing and working up quite a sweat. Mel lay there almost motionless, not feeling anything, she was completely numb. She wondered if she should at least make some noises to play along, so she let out a few timid moans. On hearing them he picked up speed and his face contorted into a strange mix of pain and pleasure. Mel moaned again, slightly louder and more convincingly, sensing that this would help speed up the whole process. True enough Mark thrust harder and faster a few more times and then jerking roughly, stopped and pulled out quickly.

Mel instantly felt the hot liquid running down her thigh.

Shit! She realised she had been so nervous she had forgotten to insist on a condom.

Mark climbed off her, biting on her nipple as he did so and then rolled over onto his side and rapidly fell into a deep, post orgasmic, wine induced sleep.

She dressed as quickly as she'd undressed and, quietly opening the door so as not to wake him, stepped outside. She caught a glimpse of a couple in the room opposite theirs, the door was slightly ajar and they were going at it hammer and tongs under the silk sheets. She stood transfixed on the scene for a minute or so until to her horror she heard Rob's familiar grunting. At that moment the woman turned to face the open doorway, it was Tess, and seeing Mel there watching, smiled broadly and moaning loudly she gestured for Mel to come in.

Mel, embarrassed, quickly looked away, took a deep breath and walked unsteadily towards the kitchen.

More grunts and groans could be heard coming from the living room.

So many emotions were running through her; shame, jealousy, anger and fear, but she also detected a small hint of satisfaction. She'd done it; she'd gone through with it. She hadn't run away, she'd faced her fears and survived.

She grabbed an empty glass from the side in the kitchen and finding only an almost empty bottle of whisky, tipped the remnants into the glass, shaking the last drops out. Without bothering with mixers she swigged it down and her face screwed up as the liquid burned her throat. She put the glass in the sink, grabbed a packet of cigarettes from the breakfast bar and walked out onto the balcony.

Sliding the doors closed behind her, to shut out the noises emanating from all rooms in the apartment, Mel stood looking out across the sea and saw hundreds of little lights on in the windows of the tall apartment buildings along the coast, signalling the presence of people who were still awake, watching TV, playing cards or reading a good book. Normal sane things that normal, sane people do.

She wondered if anywhere else here on this island anybody else was going through the same degrading experience she was!

Chapter 17

Mel waited out on the balcony for another fifteen minutes. With the doors closed she was at least isolated from the noises.

One by one the dishevelled figures began to emerge from their sordid dens.

Mark was the first one out, his shirt was half buttoned and untucked and he was doing up the zip on his trousers as he walked into the kitchen.

He opened the fridge door and took out a beer.

He pulled hard on the ring causing the contents to bubble out and run down the side of the can, then he thirstily drank down the contents.

Mel turned away, what the hell would she say to him now? How do you have a normal conversation with someone after doing what they had just done?

Mark spotted Mel out on the balcony, slid open the glass door and walked outside.

"Hi, are you okay? I was wondering where you'd gotten to. Sorry I fell asleep, no reflection on your performance Mel, just had a busy week."

Oh my God! How the hell do I respond to that? She thought nervously.

"I'm fine I think?" Mel replied, even managing a half smile. The situation was unbearably embarrassing and right then she just wanted to get away from them all and go home with Rob. She looked in the direction of the rooms hoping to see him coming out, but saw only Tony and Debbie in the corridor.

"How long have you been out here anyway?" Mark asked, finishing the contents of the can and resting it down on the table.

"I've been here about fifteen, twenty minutes I guess."

Tony looked around to see if anyone else was there.

"Listen, as long as nobody saw you it will probably be all right. Did anybody see you come out here?"

"I think Tess saw me leave the room before, why?"

"Shit! Well let's hope she doesn't say anything, but for now, if anyone asks, you just came out here now with me okay?"

Mel looked puzzled. "Okay, but why?"

"We're supposed to stay in the room until the hour is up, you can't go just wandering around, didn't anyone tell you that?

She shook her head, more bloody rules and regulations, Mel despaired.

"It's a privacy thing," he went on, "not everyone has four bedrooms and there are usually people all over the place. Once at Tony's, there was a mix up about the guests. Anyway, to cut a long story short, one extra couple turned up so I ended up on a Zed bed with Mary I think it was, in the laundry room!"

Mark laughed, Mel cringed.

She couldn't think of anything worse than having sex in the laundry room of a house full of people all having sex with each other. What was wrong with these people?

She sat down on the chair anxiously waiting for Rob, she checked her watch.

'Ten twenty five. The hour ran out ten minutes ago, what the hell was keeping him?' No, no, no, don't go down that street!

Mel turned her thoughts rapidly away from Rob and Tess to what Mark had said; Laundry room, laundry room, why is that familiar? And then it hit her.

"Come on Mel, we'll be late, the taxi's waiting."

Stella was at the bottom of the stairs, shouting up at the closed bathroom door. After a few more minutes Mel emerged in all her glory wearing her black and white rah-rah skirt and a white laced blouse with the most enormous shoulder pads she could find. Her fringe was sprayed straight up at the front and she had tied a black bow around her head. To complete the look she was wearing black fingerless gloves, a collection of beaded necklaces and black ankle boots.

"Blimey Mel, you look like Madonna" Stella said, looking amused.

Mel beamed with pride, thrilled that her hours of effort hadn't been in vain.

"That's the whole point you wally," she came bounding down the stairs.

"This look is so in right now."

The girls laughed, linked arms and skipped over playfully to the waiting taxi.

It was New Year's Eve, nineteen eighty three. Mel, Stella, Tracey and Clare were out on a mission.

On that occasion they had found out, through Stella's hairdresser, about a 'not to miss party' at the house of one of the boys who went to the private school up by the university, St. Something's.

The house that was to be gate crashed was out in the country near Wingham and the four of them had decided to share a taxi armed with only ten pounds sixty, ten JPS cigarettes and two bottles of Strongbow cider.

"Right," said Stella, "stick to the plan, we all told our parents that we were at Clare's house tonight, right?"

All present obediently nodded.

"And your parents are definitely not coming back until tomorrow afternoon?" She asked Clare who cheerfully nodded again. Each girl then spent the journey being interrogated by Stella and working on getting their stories straight.

Stella smiled, satisfied with her military-precise, foolproof plan.

When they arrived the party was in full swing and the music could be heard before they turned into the street.

The house was enormous and the long driveway was lit up with loads of illuminated reindeer and gnomes dressed as Father Christmas.

'Just because you've got money doesn't mean you've got taste' Mel concluded.

The taxi pulled up outside the front door of the house and the girls paid the driver and got out. Mel was still tightly clutching the carrier bag containing the bottles of cider.

"Remember," Stella had instructed, "if anyone asks, Eddie invited us."

"Who's Eddie again?" enquired Clare.

"No idea, but there's always an Eddie at these schools!"

Mel was nervous, she hated gate crashing but had to admit that without doing it her social life would be pretty quiet.

They rang on the bell and almost immediately the door was opened by a very cute, blonde boy with a very pretty, scantily clad girl draped around him.

"Yeah, can I help you?"

"Yes, we're here for the party, Eddie invited us." Stella said convincingly.

"Did he?" the boy replied suspiciously, eyeing the girls up and down.

"How do you know Eddie?"

Panic began to spread through the group.

"He's a friend of my brother," Melissa blurted out.

"Is that right, who's your brother?"

The rest of the group all turned to stare at Mel to see what she would say next.

"Come on Ryan, we're missing the party, just let them in." The girl whined, obviously cold and wanting to get back inside.

"We have cider" said Mel, holding up the carrier bag.

The boy stepped to one side and ushered them through.

"Nice one." Stella whispered in Mel's ear.

Once inside, the girls looked around, there were people everywhere, sat on the stairs, perched on every window ledge and dancing on every spare bit of carpet.

They walked through into the lounge where Mel, to her horror, saw three other 'Madonnas' dotted around the room.

"I see what you mean about it being *in* right now!" Exclaimed Tracey bitchily.

Mel saw her and Clare smirking at each other.

The house was full of young, gorgeous and very wealthy looking teenagers.

"Right," said Tracey, rubbing her hands together, "the hunt is on ladies, it's better if we spilt up, you know, divide and conquer. I'll go with Stella, Mel you go with Clare."

Mel looked over at Stella hoping she'd protest but she had already starting heading off with Tracey towards the kitchen.

Clare was also heading off in another direction.

"Wait!" cried Mel, "don't leave me."

The girls mingled for an hour or so until they found themselves cornered at one point by two, really spotty, geeky boys.

"You look just like Madonna," said one, smiling pathetically at Mel.

Mel nodded politely, she'd heard it twenty times already.

When the four girls crossed paths a while later Tracey had a bottle of Malibu in her hand.

"Look what I found! Try some, it's lovely."

Mel took the bottle and swigged some down.

"Ah, that's sweet," she said, making a face.

Tracey snatched the bottle back off her.

"No, actually it's gorgeous." she tipped up the bottle and drank more down.

After a lot more dancing and fruitless flirting, the thirty minute warning for midnight was announced.

"Where are Stella and Tracey? I haven't seen them for ages" Mel asked Clare, shouting over the noise of Dexy's Midnight Runners.

She looked at her watch realising that it had been almost an hour since she'd spotted either of them.

"I expect they're off snogging somewhere, which is probably what we should be doing" Clare shouted back, obviously fed up.

"They're going to miss midnight, I'll go and look for them, you stay here in case they come back."

She decided to start upstairs, if Clare was right that's where they'd be.

Climbing the stairs wasn't easy, every step was occupied by an amorous couple. Once at the top she systematically opened every door and consistently found every darkened room occupied by a couple having some form of sexual encounter, but none of them contained Stella or Tracey.

After opening five doors and apologising five times, she renegotiated her way back downstairs. Noticing the long queue outside the toilet she went to the front and banged on the door.

"Oy! There's a queue," said a girl in the line, most indignantly.

Mel ignored her and continued banging.

"Stella are you in there? Stella?" There was no reply.

She turned to face the queue of people, "Are you sure that there's someone in here?"

She addressed the gawping line of people who nodded or shrugged their shoulders in silence.

Mel twisted the handle and pushed open the door. Her efforts were met on the other side by resistance. She pushed harder and the door opened enough for her to squeeze through. On the other side she found Tracey passed out in a puddle of vomit on the floor.

"Tracey? Tracey? Shit! Can you hear me?" Mel shook her until she responded with a moan, she turned to see three heads appear around the door,

"Blimey, is she all right?" One of the heads asked in a drunken slur.

Mel shrugged, "I don't know. Can you find the girl who was with me, she's wearing a shocking pink shirt with a big black studded belt, ask her to come here please."

"Sorry, do I look like a policeman? Find her yourself" the head replied sharply and then disappeared followed by the other two.

Mel, with a bit of a struggle, got Tracey up off the floor and sat her down on the toilet while she cleaned her face and top. Then she helped her move the few steps over to the empty bath and climb into it and then Mel rolled up a towel and placed it under her head.

"Right, just lie down here in the bath Trace and try and sleep it off for a bit. I'm going to go and find the others and something to clean this mess up with, I'll be back in just a minute."

Mel pulled the shower curtain across to give her some privacy and left the bathroom.

"Wouldn't go in there if I were you" Mel warned the people still in the queue, pulling a disgusted face.

Mel went back to the kitchen and hunted around in the cupboards for some kind of cleaning product but found only dishwasher liquid.

"Can I help you?"

Mel turned to see Ryan, the really cute boy who had answered the door, standing over her and looking annoyed.

"I'm looking for something to clean up the bathroom with, my friend isn't very well."

"Oh great, which bathroom?"

The one down here by the room with the desk in it" Mel replied timidly.

"You mean the study?"

Mel blushed.

"Right, well the cleaning things are kept in the laundry room, I'll show you where it is."

Mel followed him sheepishly out of the kitchen and down a long corridor.

"Who are you again?"

Mel loved his accent, it was so posh.

"I'm Melissa, a friend of Eddie's brother."

"Who?"

"I mean, Eddie is a friend of my brother."

Shit, well done Mel you idiot! She chastised herself.

"Oh yes, that's right, I haven't seen you before, where do you go to school?"

Before she had a chance to answer the boy stopped in front of a door.

"This is it, the laundry room."

He pushed it open and stepped inside, it was pitch black. Mel followed him inside and he closed the door behind her.

"If you tell me where the mop is I'll clean up the mess."

"I have a better idea" Ryan answered in a strange voice.

Mel felt a hand on her breast and he leaned in and kissed her hard on the mouth.

Taken by surprise she fell back against the washing machine. He continued kissing her and she realised that she was kissing him back.

He grabbed hold of her, lifted her up and sitting her on top of the washing machine, wrapped her legs around his waist. He was a good kisser, a really good kisser and he was using his tongue. He stopped kissing her and moved his mouth over to her neck, Mel felt the sting of a love bite but didn't try to stop him, her Mum would kill her but she didn't care, she'd have a souvenir!

He moved his hand up her thigh and felt around for a way inside her underwear. Mel instinctively pushed the hand away but he was insistent and continued his search, this time he wasn't met with resistance.

Just then the room was ablaze with light, the scantily clad girl from the front door was standing in the doorway.

"What the fuck are you doing Ryan? Who is this little tart?"

"Nobody Stacey, she just needed help finding the things to clean up some mess her friend made in the bathroom."

The girl came up closer.

"Oh I remember you! Your brother is a friend of Eddie's."

She froze as she noticed the love bite on the side of Mel's neck. Mel felt the hard slap of the girl's hand across her face.

Jumping down from the washing machine Mel put her hand on her burning cheek.

Just then Stella, who'd been attracted by the crowd gathering outside, came bounding into the room.

"Leave her alone you snooty bitch!" she yelled at the girl.

Stacey and Stella went for each other, punching, biting and pulling each other's hair.

Some of the crowd that had gathered in the doorway, piled into the laundry room to try to separate them.

Mel took hold of Stella and dragged her out into the corridor where Clare was now standing talking to a tall boy.

"Guess what?" she said beaming, obviously oblivious to what was going on, "This is Eddie!"

"Quick," said Stella, grabbing hold of Clare's hand, "let's get out of here before Stacey and her posh mates come looking for us."

The girls headed towards the front door and ran out onto the drive.

"5, 4, 3, 2, 1, Happy New Year"

They ran as fast as they could down the path to the distant sound of 'Auld Lang Syne.'

When they got to the main road they stopped out of breath and began to laugh raucously.

"Shit Mel, what was that all about?" Clare asked, bemused.

"Nothing," said Mel smiling and revealing her love bite.

"Ahhhhhhh" the girls screeched. "Oh my God," they both said in unison.

The girls laughed even louder together and began walking arm in arm down the road, like a scene from the Wizard of Oz.

"Happy bloody New Year" yelled Clare."

"Happy bloody New Year" repeated Stella and Mel.

The girls stopped dead in their tracks and looked at each other.

"Tracey!"

Mel smiled to herself, that was a really crazy evening!

"Mel, I'm going to have one more drink then we'll head home, okay?"

She turned to see that Rob and Tess were standing beside her, his shirt was all untucked and unbuttoned and Tess was holding her shoes in her hand.

Mel's smile slowly disappeared.
'But not as crazy as this one' she thought sadly.

Chapter 18

When the second evening arrived Mel was even more nervous than she was at the first, she knew everybody better now, having spent most weekends at pool parties, barbecues and water skiing trips with them all. This somehow made it worse and she was all too aware of what was awaiting her. She didn't think she could go through with it so when Rob was in the shower she tried to come up with an excuse to get out of going.

"I'm getting my period Rob, I don't think I can go this evening."

Rob stopped dressing and stared at her.

"But you've just finished, about a week ago."

His voice was angry.

"I remember because you didn't want to go in swimming at the pool party because you had women's problems and you've still got seventeen pills left in the packet in the bathroom. Now finish getting dressed Mel or we'll be late."

He went back to dressing.

'He counted her pills?'

On arrival at Malcolm and Mary's place Mel stood outside amazed, staring up at their huge colonial style house. On greeting them Mary proudly gave Mel a quick tour.

Their private, single villa with extensive gardens had an enormous, rectangular shaped swimming pool with a covered bar over in the corner complete with a juke box and bar stools.

Mel entered the house behind Mary and scanned the rooms trying to see who was already there. The guest list was always kept very hush hush until the evening, apparently in an attempt to keep the level of anticipation higher. Mel found this strange as it seemed to her that the pool of guests was fairly limited, there were only eight couples in the club as far as she knew.

Sue was walking into the house from the patio, she saw Mel and waved.

Mel was then led at lightning speed through all the elaborately decorated rooms on the two floors, finishing back in the L shaped lounge.

She heard Malcolm in the other room long before she saw him.

Mary was busy dashing in and out of the kitchen, and Sue and Dan seemed to be having a heavy discussion back out on the patio.

Just then the doorbell went and Mary ran over to the door, peered through the peep hole and then opened it. Harry and Tess were standing there clutching a bottle of something that looked expensive.

Mary kissed them both.

"Everyone," she announced, "it's Harry and Tess."

Mel smiled. Harry! He really was good looking.

"Hello, Mary, Stuart and Lizzie couldn't make it this evening, there's been a problem, some last minute emergency with an opening of a new hotel in Dubai so they've had to go there for a few days" announced Tess, "so we're here instead."

Harry's presence calmed Mel down a little and this time she even managed to eat a little something. She knocked back three large glasses of white wine and a glass of Harry's offering that turned out to be a bottle of Moët. A French bottle of Dutch courage, she consoled herself.

At nine fifteen precisely the group moved ceremoniously into the lounge and took positions.

Sue was asked to draw the first name.

She walked slowly over to the bowl and stood for a few seconds fixed on the large glass object containing the embroidered handkerchiefs.

"Sue, we're waiting" snapped Dan. Sue put her hand in the bowl and closing her eyes she fished one out.

Malcolm's name was read out much to Mel's relief and even Tess looked a little relieved.

"Forfeit" shouted Sue.

"You can't call forfeit Sue, you called it at the last party we went to" said Dan, now noticeably irritated.

"Does anyone else want to call forfeit this evening?" Sue asked the small group gathered in the room. Everyone shook their head.

Sue filled her glass up to the brim and followed Malcolm out of the room. Mel noticed that Sue looked desperately unhappy and also a little scared, she felt sorry for her but was too relieved that it wasn't her to feel too badly.

It was down to Harry, Rob and Dan. She crossed her fingers behind her back; she desperately wanted it to be Harry.

Since that evening when they had met at the first, fateful dinner party, she had liked him. He had a nice, kind smile and didn't make her feel uncomfortable like the others did. Dan, on the other hand, gave Mel the impression of being a bit of a bully.

Mel pulled out the next hanky and carefully unfolded it. Tess, who was hovering nearby, snatched the hanky from her hand.

"Well, well Mel, you've got Harry. Have fun and try to give him back in one piece!"

Mel, embarrassed but relieved, smiled awkwardly.

'How could Tess be so unbothered by all this? Mel was extremely bothered about who Rob was going to end up with. She crossed her fingers again as Tess pulled out a hanky.

'Please let it be Dan!'

"Oh! I've got Rob again this evening," Tess smiled over at Mel. "Don't worry, you'll get him back in one piece as well... eventually."

Mel felt a wave of jealousy well up in her and she desperately wanted to slap her perfect, smirking face. The image of Tess grinning and moaning in that bedroom with the door ajar flashed vividly into her mind.

Harry, maybe sensing the tension, took hold of Mel's hand and led her quickly out of the room and up the stairs.

They entered a room at the far end of the first floor corridor, which was in total darkness. Harry let go of her hand and walked over to the corner of the room and without any fumbling around he found the lamp. He knew exactly where to look, no need to guess how he knew where to find it.

The room lit up unveiling a small simple double bed covered with a plain pink sheet and matching pillows. The lamp, made of a brightly coloured vase and pink shade, was sitting on a low chest of drawers. Above the bed was a large rectangular mirror in a garish ornate gold and green frame.

Looking quickly around the room Mel noticed there was no other furniture, no candles and there were also no bottles or glasses. The only accessory that was visible was a large box of condoms half hidden behind the lamp.

Harry sat down on the bed and patted the space next to him signalling for Mel to join him.

She walked slowly over to where he was sat kicking off his shoes.

"There's nothing to drink," she said in a disappointed voice.

"Good! I prefer not to be drunk, it interferes with my performance. Do you mind?"

"No, not at all" she lied.

Mel began feeling something other than dread and fear, Mel began to feel excitement.

She sat down next to him on the bed and he started to undo his top shirt buttons. Spontaneously she leaned over, brushed his hand to one side and began slowly undoing them herself. Each open button revealed a mass of dark chest hair, she paused after the third and slipped her hand inside the shirt caressing the silky strands, he smelled nice.

She was no longer thinking about Rob or Tess or even about how really sordid this situation actually was. She was aroused by this man, by the thought of what was going to happen.

He responded by taking hold of her hands, raising her arms upwards and pulling her top up slowly over her head. As her head broke free from the top her hair fell back into place covering her face slightly, she quickly blew it to one side.

Harry bent forward and kissed her neck and shoulders. In a single movement he reached behind and undid her bra, releasing her small but perfectly round breasts and Mel shuddered. Harry then undid the last of his own buttons and took off his shirt which he threw onto the floor. Gently but firmly Harry pushed her down into a horizontal position. He pulled down her skirt and then very slowly peeled off her black, lace and very skimpy knickers, which she was very happy she had decided to wear.

She reflected on the irony that her mother had picked them out and would never had imagined in a million years that they would be used in a situation like this.

Harry stood up, looked Mel up and down and smiled. Then he took off his trousers and let his boxer shorts fall to the ground.

He was standing there naked and Harry was every bit as good as he looked. He grabbed a condom from the box and opening the packet with his teeth slid it on expertly. Mel was really relieved he hadn't asked her to do it, she had never got the hang of them.

'Was she going to have to start training with those now as well as chopsticks?'

'The perfect scenario', she smiled to herself, 'being able to put a condom on with chopsticks!' she laughed out loud at the image.

"Is everything all right?" Harry looked a bit concerned.

"Yes sorry, nervous laughter." she apologised, feeling angry with herself for her childish outburst.

Holding her expertly in her arms he grabbed her and moved her around the bed, Mel was trembling from head to toe.

He began caressing and kissing every inch of her body, then flipping her onto her stomach he raised her up onto all fours and he was inside her but this time there was no resistance or discomfort.

As she watched him behind her in the mirror cupping her breasts she was overcome by this new, voyeuristic experience which she was finding totally electrifying. Watching the image of the two of them together in the mirror was driving her to delicious distraction and soon she felt the indescribable, unmistakable surge of an orgasm.

A moment of guilt at the intense pleasure she was feeling crept into her head for just a second but it was quickly kicked back out again.

Rolling her over onto her back he pulled her down into a half sitting position and he took her again. She gasped as he swung her around and lifted her up off the bed as though she weighed nothing. She wrapped her arms around his neck as he reached down, took hold of each ankle and pulled her legs around his waist. Walking across the room Harry pushed her against the opposite wall where he was in the fully upright position. He had remained deeply inside her during the whole manoeuvre and had never faltered.

After about another half an hour and two further mind-blowing orgasms, Mel was crudely brought back down to earth by the sound of a small watch alarm signalling that their 'time' was up.

Harry moved her gently away, kissed her long and hard on the mouth and then silently dressed and walked out of the room leaving her panting there on the bed, covered in only a glow.

Chapter 19

The following morning she was woken early by the phone.

She struggled out of bed and saw Rob was still out for the count and oblivious to the continuous ringing.

She'd slept really well for the first time in ages, she stretched and smiled as she remembered her time with Harry, just maybe she was beginning to see the attraction in this alternative pastime.

"Hello," she yawned into the phone.

"Hello Mel, it's Tess."

Tess' voice was like a bucket of ice cold water, she was now wide awake and attentive.

Her first thought was that Harry had said something to Tess about their evening, maybe he had felt the same twinge of passion, the same connection as she had and had felt the need to confess all!

She braced herself for what was coming next.

"Good morning Tess, how are you?"

"Yeah, good thanks, listen I'm calling about the dinner dance on the twenty ninth."

Mel felt a pang of relief and disappointment, so he hadn't felt anything worth confessing, it had been just another game to him.

Mel mentally chastised herself, she was really going to have to grow up and, more importantly, toughen up. She would have to take it for what it was and not let feelings creep into the equation, negative or positive, she would have to learn to switch off, and fast. This was going to be yet another problem in this already arduous situation.

Tess continued. "Some of us girls are meeting up this morning at the Plaza Centre, there's a tailor's there and we're going to get our evening dresses sorted out. I'll warn you, it's a bit expensive but they're very good and quick and it is for *the* social event of the year after all. So we were wondering if you'd like to join us there, say ten o'clock?"

Mel looked over at the wall clock, eight fifty.

"Yes, that would be good, thanks Tess, I'll see you there."

"Ok great, give Debbie a ring, she was thinking that you could get a cab in together. See you later."

Yes! Mel smiled, she had been invited to go shopping with them, she was in!

Mel's hope of finding a job had been fading fast. She had applied for many various positions from shop assistant to personal assistant but the problem was she had no experience in most of the jobs she went for and her C.V. was a little pathetic to say the least. She had also had a number of heavy discussions about it with Rob because he seemed to think it was some kind of shameful behaviour for a woman to work here in Singapore, an expat woman that is!

"But Alison has a job and Tim doesn't seem to mind" she had argued.

"She doesn't have a job, she has a company! She doesn't actually do the catering, she just uses Tim's contacts to organise her team who, once or twice a month, do the cooking and waiting tables."

"But Rob that's still a job, she still…"

She was cut off.

"Mel leave it, can't you just enjoy being a woman of leisure like the others? Go shopping, buy stuff, have lunch."

After showering and dressing Mel called Debbie to organise the trip into town and then went out onto the balcony to get some air and drink her coffee.

She looked down at the hustle and bustle below, the pool was really busy this morning. She rarely went down on Saturdays; there were always loads of noisy kids jumping, splashing, spitting, screaming and weeing in the pool.

She began to wonder when her maternal instincts would kick in!

There were also a lot of people in and out of the mini market.

She had never spoken to Rob about the unpaid account, choosing instead to pay it herself and not mention it, it was strange though, they always kept at least a couple of hundred there in the drawer for emergencies, but she had decided they had enough on their plates right now.

Since that embarrassing episode she had always paid for things as she got them and didn't put stuff on account any more as it made keeping track of what she spent easier.

Not wanting to wake the still snoring Rob, she hunted through the kitchen drawers for some paper but not finding any blank pages tore off the corner of an old bank statement that she found at the back and scribbled a note explaining where she'd gone and that she would be back some time mid-afternoon, then she propped the note up against a Singapore cricket club coffee cup on the side.

Noticing that she was late she headed for the door, quickly folded the remains of the bank statement and put it in her bag.

When the taxi pulled up outside Debbie's apartment building, Debbie was already there waiting for her. She was always so glamorous, she could throw on a T shirt and a pair of jeans and look like a million dollars. Mel on the other hand spent hours getting ready and always managed to look, at best, reasonably presentable. She decided it was a question of DNA and useless to fight it.

"Good morning Mel, how are you doing today?"

"I'm good thanks, a bit tired, we had quite a late night."

Debbie turned to look at Mel. She put her finger to her lips and made a shush sound.

"Uh uh, not a word remember!"

"Yes right, of course." Mel sighed, she wasn't actually going to say anything, just that she was tired.

These people were worse than the FBI!

The taxi soon pulled up outside Orchard Plaza and the girls got out. Mel reached for her purse but Debbie insisted on paying the fare.

"You can get lunch," she said graciously.

They walked through the sliding doors and into the cool shopping centre. The other girls were already gathered together near the bottom of the escalator busily chatting.

Alison turned and beamed at them. "Hello darling" she hugged Debbie and then turned to kiss Mel on the cheek.

Mel turned to look at the small group of women, "Hi" she smiled.

Aside from Alison and Debbie there was Mary, who was looking even more tired than usual and shook a couple of pills from a small box into her open hand which she then threw into her mouth and swallowed. There was Tess, looking as lovely as ever, she was feeling a definite touch of animosity towards her and also a little envious that she had Harry whenever she wanted him.

Look at her, all perfect! Why on earth would he want anyone else?

She would never understand this need to have sex with other people.

Then there was Sue, quiet, shy Sue. Mel noticed that she was looking rather unhappy so, smiling, she walked over to her.

"Good morning Sue, how are you? Is everything okay?"

Before Sue had a chance to reply Alison had slipped her arm through Sue's and was walking her over to the escalator.

"She's fine, aren't you lovely?" she said rhetorically.

Sue nodded timidly.

"Yes thank you, I'm fine."

The group rode the escalator to the first floor where they headed in the direction of a large open fronted shop full of rolls and rolls of badly stacked brightly coloured material. Mel thought that it looked more like a market stall than an expensive tailor's.

"Ok ladies, let's shop."

A small man with a worn out tape measure draped around his neck greeted Alison as she walked into the premises.

"Oh hello again Mrs. Phillips, so lovely to see you, you are splendid as always you know. And look at all these beautiful ladies today, hello ladies, come, come."

He ushered them towards the back of the shop where two women were waiting eagerly with tape measures in hand.

The man began shouting instructions at the women who ran around the shop grabbing enormous and very heavy looking rolls of fabric which he then proceeded to lay out before them.

Oh I love this bit!" exclaimed Tess excitedly.

She began feeling the various cloths and running her hand over the smoothed out fabric, the rest of the group all did the same.

Mel joined in, beginning to feel rather excited herself although not really sure why!

An hour and two cups of jasmine tea later, all the measurements had been taken and the materials had been chosen. The man handed the girls a large book with pictures of many different styles of dresses and the discussions began.

After another hour and yet more tea it was all decided. Mel had opted for a long plain, off the shoulder design in a Thai silk material that looked blue from some angles and green from others. The majority of the other girls had gone for much more elaborate and expensive designs.

Sue had seemed quite unenthusiastic about the whole thing in the beginning, she had sat in the corner of the shop flicking aimlessly through the style book. Mel felt a need to try to help her out and cheer her up, as she walked over in her direction, Mel remembered the note she had left in her bathroom and was grateful to Sue for the advice but like Sue herself, was still here.

After some gentle persuasion Mel convinced her to try out some fabrics and to go for a similar design to hers only shorter. Mel then grabbed a roll of pinky-orange Thai silk and Sue smiled broadly as she draped the cloth around her, noting how well it went with her strawberry blonde hair.

She picked up the roll of fabric and brushed past Mel on her way to the waiting tailor.

"We'll look like a dream," Sue whispered, "but we'll still be living a nightmare!"

Mel looked up, Sue's eyes were closed as she held her arms out to the sides while the woman ran the tape measure expertly down from her armpit to her knees, her forehead was visibly creased in thought.

When all their measurements had been taken, all the decisions had been made and all the tea had been drunk, the man took deposits of fifty dollars from each of the women and told them to return the following Saturday to pick them up, and that was that, done.

Mel had enjoyed her first experience at a tailor's, she felt like she was really beginning to fit in and she tried hard not to think about the two hundred dollars the dress was going to cost her. She had never spent that much on anything in her life, in fact that had probably been more than her total annual clothing budget when she was at home. She decided it would be better not to mention the cost to her mother; she would be very disapproving of such extravagance.

Mel checked her watch, twelve twenty, she was starting to feel hungry, and was just about to suggest lunch when,

"Right ladies, shoes!"

Debbie raised her right arm and in an exaggerated gesture swung around and pointed to a shop on the other side of the gallery. All present started chattering excitedly.

Shoe shopping here really *was* the number one pastime.

The rest of the afternoon was spent in and out of different shoe and accessory shops with a brief pit stop at the Mövenpick for a bite of lunch. Mel checked her watch again, four fifteen. She wanted to go home and take a swim, now she really needed to cool off, her feet were swollen and her purse was empty.

Much to her relief Alison announced that the day's hunt was over. Each woman held a handful of assorted bags which they cheerfully swung back and forth as they waited in the queue for a taxi.

As the first one drew up Alison and Tess got in blowing kisses in the direction of the other three.

Mel didn't have long to wait for hers.

"Debbie, are you coming back with me?" she asked.

Debbie shook her head.

"No, I'm going to go for a sling at Raffles with Sue thanks, we'll see you soon."

A sling! That sounded good, but their taxi pulled up at the rank and they jumped in before Mel had a chance to ask if she could tag along.

She was going to have to wait a while longer before being a real part of the gang, she sadly thought to herself as she watched their cab drive off in the direction of Raffles.

Chapter 20

Finally the evening that had been the source of much excitement, primping, preening and not to mention expense, arrived. Mel had spent practically all day down in the beauty salon having hairs waxed off from virtually everywhere on her body and any that were lucky enough to have escaped removal were painstakingly trimmed, plucked or curled. She had decided to do her own toenails in a vain attempt to save some money, and now, looking down at what a poor job she had done, was deeply regretting it.

Rob, on the other hand, had been out at the cricket club practically all day and had come home just in time for a shower and a quick shave. Men!

When she walked into the bathroom wearing her dressing gown, Rob was covered in shaving foam and had a small towel wrapped around his waist.

"You look nice," he smiled as he grabbed hold of Mel and tried to kiss her.

She recoiled in disgust.

"Don't even think of coming anywhere near me with all that foam on your face. This hair and makeup took all afternoon to put on, and cost me a week's wages, your wages that is."

He grabbed her again.

"Well it was worth every penny, you look good enough to eat! Come on Mel, just a quickie, what do you say?" He dropped his towel and Mel saw his erection in full glory.

He picked up the towel and draped it over his penis.

"Mel look, I'm a towel rack!"

"Rob stop being an idiot! We don't have time for sex and I'm really not going to risk messing my hair up and getting even more sweaty!"

"Suit yourself Melissa, I'm not going to beg you for it, I don't need to!" he said coldly, throwing the towel onto the floor.

She glared at him, 'What the hell did that mean?' Never mind, it was obvious.

Mel felt tears welling up in her eyes.

'Don't you bloody dare,' she said to herself. 'You'll spoil your make up!'

She left him standing there naked except for the shaving foam and stomped off into the bedroom.

Her tailored dress was hanging there on the wardrobe door. It really was beautiful, and as to be expected, after paying so much. It fitted her perfectly. She had tried it on three times that week already.

Placed neatly under the dress, on the floor, were the handmade shoes. They were made of the same colour silk as the dress and were sling backed and open-toed. They were also much higher than she was used to but Alison and Debbie had insisted that such an occasion merited stiletto heels. They had cost almost as much as the dress in the end.

She shook her head to pull herself out of her irritated state.

'Tonight,' she beamed, 'tonight I'm Cinder-bloody-rella!"

She stepped into the dress, pulled it up and slipped her arms into the short, elasticated sleeves, which she then adjusted to their off the shoulder position. In front of the mirror she smoothed it down and adjusted her boobs inside the dress by leaning slightly forward and giving them a little shake, then she reached behind and pulled up the zip to her bra line.

'Damn', she couldn't reach any further, she was going to have to ask Rob for help.

Just at that moment he walked into the bedroom.

"Wow, you look fabulous Mel, really fabulous."

His mood had changed again, the previous acidic tone gone from his voice.

Mel blushed, she wasn't used to compliments.

Rob pulled up her zip to the top and gently brushing her hair to one side kissed the back of her neck. She shuddered, it was her weak spot.

The cab ride was short, just ten minutes. They sat quietly holding hands in the cab and Mel admired her man in his tuxedo and dicky bow.

"You look like James Bond," she said proudly.

He didn't reply. "You're quiet Rob, is everything ok?"

Rob nodded." Yes, sorry I'm fine, I'm just going over my speech in my head."

Mel looked puzzled.

"What speech?" she asked abruptly.

"Malcolm has asked me to do a quick speech before announcing the raffle prizes tonight. I got the job as I'm the newest recruit apparently."

Mel smiled, her boyfriend was making the speech and announcing the raffle. That was status!

The evening was going well. They had been sat on a large table with some of the usual couples. Mel had hoped that she would have the chance to meet some new normal people who at worst could undress her from imagination not memory!

The food had been wonderful, and everyone had eaten every dish wholeheartedly. Everyone except one, Sue had pushed the food around her plate without eating very much. Mel felt really sorry for her, poor girl obviously wasn't very happy.

Malcolm was telling obscene jokes and making even more obscene comments about the women in the room. Mary was already drunk when she arrived and was her usual quiet self. The other women all looked stunning, of course.

Tess and Debbie were looking stunning in their elaborate creations and Debbie was wearing a fresh red rose in her long, straightened hair.

Sue was looking gorgeous in her dress, the colour, as predicted, looked amazing with her blonde hair, which had been expertly pulled up into a perfect chignon. Mel couldn't help feeling proud as she'd help her to choose it.

"You look great Sue, that dress really suits you."

"Thanks" she replied apathetically.

Sue's eyes were glazed and she looked very tired.

Counting the empty glasses lined up in front of her, Mel saw that she was on her fourth Singapore sling and she wasn't the only one to notice.

"Take it easy Sue," Dan commented sharply as he sat back down at the table and called over a waiter to clear away the evidence.

Sue didn't reply but raised her glass up as though toasting with it and took a large sip.

A lot of people had commented on how lovely Mel looked, and how nice it was to see her out of denim skirts, to which Malcolm replied that he was very much looking forward to seeing her out of her everything. Mel blushed crimson.

This comment visibly angered Alison who glared long and hard at him. Malcolm, sensing her anger and feeling obviously uncomfortable, then got up from the table and walked out to the bar.

Alison turned to Tim and gestured to him to follow her over to the corner of the room. There, quite in sight of everyone, they began to have a heated discussion, Alison was pointing in the direction of Malcolm and her head was bobbing up and down, even from the back you could see she was furious.

The music began playing loudly and couples started drifting onto the dance floor which soon became crowded. Everyone started moving, jumping, contorting and spinning around to the tunes of Spandau Ballet and Rick Astley.

Tess and Laurel came over and grabbed Mel.

"Come on, let's dance."

She was pulled onto the centre of the dance floor and began to move the top half of her body to the music, thanks to the stilettos the bottom half was proving impossible to manage.

Mel's feet were killing her already. Why had she allowed Alison and Debbie to convince her to get such ridiculously impractical shoes for dancing in?

The music was good, a lot of her favourites were playing and she began to really get into it. She was the dancing queen, she had Saturday night fever and Grease was definitely the word.

The music faded down and Harry was at the mike. Mel couldn't take her eyes off him, in that tuxedo he looked even sexier than usual.

'Now *that's* James Bond!'

She closed her eyes to bring back the images of their brief night together and sighed deeply. When she opened them Rob was walking up to the mike to take his place next to Harry.

"Ladies and gentlemen, we hope you are enjoying your evening and the meal was to your satisfaction. We thought we'd stop the music before some of you do yourself a mischief" Harry grinned.

Mel pushed through some of the crowd until she was standing just a few feet from them. She was having trouble taking her eyes of Harry.

'Look at me, look at me' she was willing him, but he was scanning the crowd and winked at Tess when he spotted her.

Mel sighed again, she really had to let this go. He was 'a professional' at this swapping thing, he wouldn't let himself get involved, he really had no reason to. Tess was gorgeous!

'Look at her' thought Mel, 'not a hair out of place, figure to die for and oozing charm!'

In fact, scanning the room she was incredulous of all these men, all their wives were really attractive, even Mary in her own, simple way.

"So tonight ladies and gentlemen, well more ladies really, unless you believe the rumours!"

The room tittered. "For your pleasure, we've asked our newest member of the cricket club and a half decent bowler, to draw the famous raffle this evening. So without further ado and because I need a drink, please give a big round of applause to Mr... Robert...Steeeeveeennnns!"

All present gave a loud cheer and there were a few wolf whistles.

Mel felt a surge of pride and turned her attention back to Rob. She was wishing though that he wasn't standing next to Harry, it made it difficult to concentrate on him. She felt a hand squeeze her shoulder and when she turned around Alison, Debbie, Tess and Sue were standing behind her.

"He looks cute all dressed up" smirked Alison.

Sue was still holding a glass tightly in both her hands which were still shaking quite noticeably.

Debbie put an arm on Sue's back and rubbed and patted it like she was trying to get her to burp.

"How are you enjoying your first dinner dance Melissa? You know that dress does wonders for you, you look lovely."

Mel thanked Debbie for the unexpected compliment and turned back round to face Rob.

'Praise indeed.'

"Now don't we all look nice this evening?" Rob began, and there was another round of cheers and whistles.

"I hope you tight arses have bought hundreds of raffle tickets, it's for a very good cause, 'Help the Typhoon Betty victims in the Philippines and Vietnam.'

A huge cheer and clapping could be heard in the entire room.

"Now wave your tickets in the air, wave them high like you just don't care!"

Rob was doing a poor job at rapping, but the crowd, gathered on the dance floor, were loving it.

"And wait to throw them in the bin, 'cause you know that you just might win."

Everyone was clapping in time to the rap and Rob began to make strange noises with his mouth into the microphone.

"Now if you haven't heard it yet, I'll tell ya what ya gonna get!"

The crowd roared, it was so bad that they were loving it. Mel was beaming and clapping along with everyone else.

Rob signalled to everyone with his arms to quieten down and the crowd obediently went silent.

"Now, this evening guys and gals, we have some fantastic prizes for you.

First prize has been very generously donated by the Hotel Palace, in Penang, it's a three night, long weekend break for two, flights and food included!"

That announcement was met by an enormous, raucous cheering.

"Second prize iiiiiiiis a night with my girlfriend, and third prize, of course, is two nights!"

The men in the room laughed, some of the women laughed politely but from the majority of the women there was complete silence and many were now staring straight at Mel.

Mel looked down at the ground willing it to open up and swallow her whole but the marble floor just stared back without so much as a crack.

From somewhere behind she heard a woman speak,

"Shit! What a horrible thing to say, I pity his poor girlfriend, do you know who she is?"

Mel sighed heavily.

"Just ignore them Melissa, they don't know Rob, he's a kidder" Tess said, squeezing her shoulder and trying to comfort her.

"If I was her I'd rip his heart out" Alison whispered, much too loudly.

"Bloody right," agreed Debbie and Mel sighed again.

Rob, sensing the change of atmosphere in the room, continued quickly.

"Just kidding of course, second prize is a dinner for two courtesy of the Shangri-La hotel and a night's stay in the Honeymoon Suite!"

The crowd 'woo wooed.'

"And last but not least, third prize tonight is a one hundred dollar voucher to spend at Lim's tailor's and shoe designers in Orchard Plaza."

More enthusiastic clapping.

"So let's draw these numbers."

The gathered dinner guests cheered again loudly, the atmosphere changed and the incident forgotten, by *almost* everyone.

"They're all the bloody same these men, pigs, bloody pigs. I told you to get out and go home but did you listen?"

Sue was standing next to Mel and speaking loudly into her ear in a drunk and bitter voice. Mel went to reply but Dan grabbed hold of Sue's arm tightly and began pulling her off the dance floor.

Sue could be heard shouting as she was led through the crowd to the doorway of the ballroom.

"Hecklers!" exclaimed Rob, looking over at the direction of the noise. "Every great comic gets them."

The people turned their attention back to him and away from the scene at the door. Mel watched as Alison,

Debbie and Tess headed off quickly in the direction of Sue and Dan. A small crowd had gathered in the bar area on the other side to watch the scene unfold. She wondered if she should have gone too but decided that her presence was neither needed nor appropriate. She hadn't known everyone long enough to be involved and she should really stay with Rob, but she decided it would be okay if she moved a little closer to the doorway to get a better look at what was going on.

Meanwhile Rob was telling more jokes and making comments on something but Mel's attention was now focused on the group of people surrounding Sue.

She watched as Dan spoke to the girls who then led Sue out of the main door into the garden at the front of the building.

Tim starting walking over to where Dan was standing but he gestured for him to stay away so Tim changed direction and headed for the bar instead. Dan then followed the girls outside and handed Debbie a packet of cigarettes.

Mel moved even closer. He was shouting angrily at the crying Sue who was being held on either side by Alison and Tess while Debbie was lighting two cigarettes simultaneously, one of which she handed to Sue.

Alison and Debbie then began shouting back at Dan but Mel couldn't make out what was being said.

Cheering went up from the crowd in the main ball room as Rob announced it was time to draw the numbers.

Tess was now talking calmly to Dan, who then turned and walked back into the Club closely followed by Alison. They all sat for a while at the bar and Dan was resting his head in his hands. From where Mel was standing it seemed that Alison was succeeding in calming him down.

More cheering came from the ballroom.

"And now the moment you've all been waiting for..,"

Mel, feeling guilty for abandoning him, went back over to the table and looked down at her tickets.

"The third prize this evening goes to ticket number one hundred and twelve. That's ticket number one one two."

There was a buzz of excitement around the room. Suddenly a man in the corner stood up waving a ticket in the air. Mel recognised him from Alison's anniversary party.

"John Adams, congratulations, you are the proud owner of a one hundred dollar voucher for Lim's tailor's and shoe designers in Orchard Plaza."

"Damn," exclaimed Laurel, who was sitting calmly at the table, seemingly oblivious to the Sue situation. "I could have done with some new shoes."

"Says the woman who could give Imelda Marcos a run for her money" retorted Tony. Laurel gave him a playful punch on the arm.

"Now, eyes down for second prize," continued Rob, "the dinner for two and honeymoon suite at the Shangri-La hotel. Ticket number sixty two, that's six two."

Immediately there was a yell from the table behind Mel's.

"Rob, it's mine, ahhh, it's mine, here!"

Mary was standing and waving her ticket excitedly in the air.

"Mary, come up here and get your prize and bring that no good husband with you."

Just at that moment Malcolm, sweating heavily, came in from the bar, he had a drink in each hand and was swaying.

'Great, couldn't have happened to a nicer guy' Mel thought sarcastically.

"This is it, the first prize of a weekend in Penang goes to..."

There was a long pause as he put his hand in and swirled it around before he picked the ticket out of the large glass bowl.

Mel winced as she remembered when she had witnessed a similar scene before.

"Wait for it, wait for it." He slowly opened the ticket up.

"Ticket number twenty one, which lucky sod out there has got ticket number twenty one?"

There was another much louder buzz of excitement as everyone looked desperately through their tickets.

A shrill scream came from the table in the corner.

"Me... It's mine... Number twenty one... Oh, here, I've got it."

All eyes turned to face the shrieking woman, Mel recognised the voice.

"Christine Weaver, H.R. extraordinaire, well, well, well, congratulations Christine, come up here and collect your prize."

She raced up to where Rob was standing waving her ticket.

"So who's the lucky man going with you Christine?" Rob asked her.

She shrugged her shoulders in silence and Rob, congratulating her with a kiss on the cheek, handed over the envelope.

Just then the girls came back into the room and Mel saw Dan in the distance heading off with Sue towards the car park.

"God, I need a drink," exclaimed Tess as she got back to the table.

"You and me both!" remarked Debbie.

"Bloody good idea!" added Alison.

They beckoned to a waiter who arrived quickly.

"Three G and T's, Mel do you want one?"

But before she had time to answer,

"Make that four."

"I can't believe bloody Christine won the first prize, only single woman in Singapore!" complained Laurel, "it wouldn't surprise me if she's gay you know!"

"Yes I thought that as well, she looked at me funny when I went into the office once" said Mel, desperate to get in on the conversation.

"No she's not, I heard she's shagging someone at the office" smiled Debbie, revelling in being the gossipmonger.

"How's Sue?" asked Mary, tottering over on her extremely high heels from the next table.

"Dan's taking her home, she just needs to sleep" said Debbie, looking quickly over at Tess.

"A night in the honeymoon suite at the Shangri-La with Malcolm, how lucky are you?" joked Debbie.

Mary smiled and raised her eyebrows.

With the raffle finished Rob returned to the table to a round of applause.

Mel glared at him furiously as he walked over to kiss her.

"How could you have said such a thing? And in front of everyone! Offering me as a raffle prize!"

"Yes and not even first prize Rob!" laughed Harry. "She should have been first prize at least, Rob mate!"

Mel tried not to smile at his comment, she was trying to be serious and angry!

"Come on, where's your sense of humour? It was just a bloody joke!"

"Well I didn't find it funny, I thought it was downgrading and OTT."

"Thank you Laurel" said Mel, genuinely grateful for some support.

"Ladies and gentlemen, we would like to invite you all to take your seats for the President's speech."

"Oh God no! Wake me up when he's finished please!" joked Alison, "if it's anything like last year..."

Just then a loud bang was heard outside followed by screaming and a lot of shouting.

Everyone jumped up from their tables and rushed to the doorway.

Chapter 21

Almost the entire contents of the room were trying to squeeze through the narrow doorway to see what was going on outside.

Mel was one of the first through and stood staring at the surreal scene before her.

A white BMW convertible was part of a bizarre still life picture that resembled a scene from a film. The front part of the car was a crumpled mess and had moulded into the trunk of the palm tree that it had collided with shortly before.

Judging by the angle the tree was now at, the car had been moving at quite a speed. Steam was rising from the bonnet and the windscreen was badly cracked. The roof of the car was down and the still figure of a woman slumped over the steering wheel could be clearly seen.

A few people rushed over to the car to check the driver while Mel, uselessly, stood frozen to the spot.

The first man to arrive yanked open the car door and Mel caught a glimpse of the orangey pink dress that the driver was wearing, the orangey pink dress that she had helped to choose.

"Sue!" she gasped, just as a group of women broke away from the crowd and ran towards the damaged car.

Mel, finally overcoming her fear, also tried running over towards the car, but her stiletto heels sank into the ground with every step. Half hopping, half running, she reached for the shoes one at a time, wrenched them from her feet and threw them into the distance. She watched to see where they landed so she could go and retrieve them later, at that moment she caught sight of the dark figure lying face down and still, twenty or so feet away on the grass.

Bare foot, she slowly walked over to the figure, Mel stopped in her tracks, she felt a surge of panic rising, he looked dead. She took a few more unsteady steps towards him and when she was just a few feet away Mel knelt down and saw to her relief that he was breathing, all be it barely. She recognised the large silver ring he had on the little finger of his outstretched hand.

'Dan!'

She was about to call for help when two men came running over and knelt down on the ground beside her. The one to her right bent down and put his ear close to Dan's mouth to listen to his breathing. The man on her left put his arm around Mel's shoulder and pulled her towards him, she stayed there a few seconds taking comfort in the gesture then the scent of a familiar aftershave arrived at her nostrils and looking up she saw the worried face of Harry. She took a big breath inwards to take in more of his aftershave as he gently stroked her bare arm. Feeling unnervingly good there snuggled into him, Mel broke free of his arm and stood up.

"Dan? Dan mate, can you hear me?"

The man to her right she recognised as Eric, one of Rob's colleagues, he lifted Dan's hand and felt his wrist to check his pulse, Dan groaned softly.

"Dan, don't try and move, we've called for an ambulance and it'll be here any minute."

Harry took off his dinner jacket and laid it over him.

Mel suddenly felt she was in the way and deciding that Dan was being well cared for, stood up to leave. As she turned Harry caught hold of her hand and squeezed it gently.

"Melissa, go and see if Sue's all right, we'll wait here with him" he whispered.

Mel returned to the scene of the crash to see what was happening.

The crowd had gathered tightly around the car, stopping Mel from getting closer and completely blocking her view. Steam was still rising from the front of the wrecked vehicle and everyone in the crowd was chatting excitedly. People were pointing to the car and over to where Dan was still lying and some of them had broken off from the main crowd to gather around him now groaning loudly on the ground.

What was it about scenes of damage, death and destruction that fascinated people so much?

A siren was heard in the distance which grew quickly louder and louder. The police car, with its flashing blue lights, drove rapidly up the driveway. Sounding the siren twice in quick succession it signalled for the crowd to move aside.

The gathered group complied by parting quickly down the middle, as if Moses himself was in charge of crowd control. At that moment Mel was able to clearly see Sue in the driver's seat, now upright and seemingly unharmed except for a cut to her forehead from which a small trickle of blood was flowing, and her chignon, which was showing obvious signs of trauma. From the short distance away Mel could see Sue was crying and shaking violently.

Alison had gotten into the car and was now sitting beside her in the passenger seat dabbing at her forehead with a handkerchief and holding her hand.

Debbie and Tess were standing next to the car silently smoking cigarettes and taking large swigs from their glasses.

The two police officers got out of their car and walked over towards Sue, putting their hats on as they moved.

Just at that moment a speeding ambulance arrived and drove straight across the manicured lawn to where Dan was still lying motionless.

The staff too were now gathered at the main door to see what was going on. Some of the crowd were gossiping, pointing and speculating as to the cause of all this chaos while others of them were silent and had their hands up covering their mouths, visibly shocked.

Mel got closer to the car and was met by Laurel.

"Oh my God Mel, what the hell! I knew she was drunk, but I didn't think she was that drunk! What happened to Dan?"

Mel shook her head and raised her shoulders unable to speak.

A woman, standing away from the rest of the crowd, was crying while she was talking to the police and pointing at the car and then at Dan with a trembling finger, who were scribbling down notes on a pad and nodding enthusiastically.

Debbie and Tess walked over to where Mel and Laurel were standing.

"Shit, what a mess. Alison is just trying to explain to the cops that she wasn't actually in the car at the time of the accident. They want to talk to anyone who saw anything."

Tess was lighting her third consecutive cigarette.

"Can I have one?" Mel asked timidly, "I left mine on the table."

Tess handed her the packet and she struggled to extract one as her hands were shaking so much.

Debbie leaned across and, holding up a lighter, began striking the little wheel with her thumb trying to get it to work. After quite a few failed attempts the lighter finally cooperated and a large flame leapt from it, Mel leaned in and took a long hard drag.

"Well we didn't see anything, we were all inside" exclaimed Debbie. "What the hell happened anyway? Sue told me she wasn't feeling well so I suggested that Dan take her home. I thought that's what she was doing! Give me a ciggy too please Tess."

It was the first time Mel had seen Debbie ruffled.

"Has anyone seen Harry?" Tess asked, looking around the crowd.

"I saw him over with Dan by the ambulance a few minutes ago" Laurel replied.

"Oh God, Dan! How is he?"

Everybody shook their heads and shrugged their shoulders.

"Alive I think" Mel said quietly.

At that moment the ambulance with sirens screaming, drove off back across the grass, passed the girls and went out towards the gate.

At the sight of the leaving ambulance a large number of the crowd turned and went back inside the club. A small number were still hanging around the car but most were losing interest in the whole thing.

'Where's Rob? I need him here!' Mel wondered angrily.

"Does anyone know where Rob is? I haven't seen him for a while."

"Last time I saw him he was propping up the bar with Malcolm, he's probably still inside" replied Alison, who had joined the group of women in time to overhear Mel's question.

Mel ran inside the club and immediately saw Rob standing talking with a group of men and Christine.

"There you are! Christ Rob, what are you doing in here? Haven't you seen what's going on outside?"

"Mel everyone, everyone Mel." He indicated the group of men with his outstretched arm and the group fell momentarily silent.

"And you remember Christine."

"Hello, yes of course, congratulations on your win. Rob why are you still in here?" she repeated, "haven't you see what happened to Sue?"

"Of course I saw it!" he barked. "When I saw that the police and ambulance had arrived and that everything was under control I came back in here. The last thing they need are drunken idiots standing around gawping at them. Where are your shoes?"

Mel looked down at her bare, grass covered feet and felt a surge of embarrassment.

He put down his drink and came over to where she was standing, trembling like a leaf, and then more gently he continued,

"Don't worry about it too much, it's not our problem. Dan and Sue have been having problems for years apparently."

"She's just had some kind of meltdown, obviously" added Christine.

"Now Mel, what are you drinking?"

The people began drifting back into the ballroom attracted by the familiar music of Madonna that the DJ was blasting out in an obvious attempt to get the people back in a party mood and distract them from what was happening outside.

Mel was not in the mood to dance and quite frankly couldn't understand anyone who was. She took hold of her freshly poured large gin and tonic and gulped down almost the entire contents of the glass then she walked back over to the door and stepped out into the hot night air.

Sue was being handcuffed and led, by the two police officers, to the waiting police car. Her head was hanging down and her long blonde hair was covering her face. As they arrived at the car she flicked back her head revealing her blank, unrepentant expression, then as she turned her head she caught sight of Mel standing by the doorway and stared icily at her.

A chill ran down the full length of Mel's spine. She closed her eyes and counted to ten to try and calm herself, when she opened them again the police car with Sue inside had gone.

'Now where did I throw those shoes?'

Chapter 22

There had been rumours of postponing this month's meeting after what happened to Sue and Dan but in the end, and as Malcolm indelicately put it,

"Why should the rest of us suffer because of that deranged bitch?"

Sue, according now to everyone who did and didn't know her, had always been unstable, had a drinking problem and took antidepressant tablets regularly.

She had apparently simply snapped under the pressure of the move to Singapore and the heat had pushed her over the edge.

At least this had become the official story.

The news of the dramatic event was soon all over the island, and people were happily lining up to say 'I was there!'

It made front page news in the Straits Times.

"Mrs Susan Chapman, a twenty eight year old housewife from Great Britain, who currently resides on East Coast road, attended a Gala dinner dance organised by the Singapore Cricket Club on Saturday evening with her husband Daniel Chapman, a twenty nine year old bank employee, and eighty eight other guests. The annual event is held to raise money for various charitable organisations.

According to eye witnesses, during the dinner she had rowed heatedly with her husband and several people saw Mrs Chapman drinking heavily throughout the course of the evening.

A police spokesman told us that several people had seen them move their argument outside the club into the grounds, and that there, Mrs Chapman had been able to obtain the car keys from her husband Daniel.

She was then seen running to their family car, a 325i white BMW convertible, which had been left in the cricket club car park. She then attempted to drive off in the vehicle.

Her husband Daniel, concerned for her safety, had tried to stop her from leaving by putting himself in the vehicle's path. Mrs Chapman, according to three separate eye witnesses, on seeing her husband in front of vehicle, had accelerated and driven her BMW straight into him, knocking Mr. Chapman an estimated ten feet into the air.

Each eyewitness that gave a statement to the police said that she hadn't made any attempt to brake, and that after the impact with her husband, had steered the BMW at high speed into the palm tree.

Mrs Susan Chapman escaped any serious injury, suffering only cuts and bruises to her face and neck.

She is now being held in police custody at the Tanglin Police Division Headquarters, where she is being questioned in the presence of a lawyer.

Mr Daniel Chapman has been taken to the Gleneagles Hospital and Medical Centre in a critical condition."

So the evening at Harry and Tess's, much to Mel's dismay, went on as planned.

Mel couldn't get the image of Sue being taken away in handcuffs, out of her mind. She had looked directly over at Mel with eyes so cold, empty and unemotional fixed firmly on her. She never once shifted her glance even when the police were pushing her down into the car.

Mel shuddered as she relived the moment.

Sue was now sitting in prison awaiting her fate and was probably scared, terrified even, desperate and alone, but in a strange and terrible way Mel almost envied her for being out of this situation.

"Mesdames et Messieurs, eyes down for a full house" shouted Malcolm, grabbing hold of the fish bowl.

Alison glared at him and snatched it back.

"One moment Malcolm, there's an important thing to add this evening before we start. The general forfeit rule, which was suggested by the unfortunate Sue and implemented experimentally, has been withdrawn and we will no longer be using it at our meetings. Only in the case that you choose the name of your actual partner will you have the choice of keeping them or exchanging them, is that all clear?"

Everyone nodded.

"Good, so Mel, with the formalities out of the way, would you like to go first this evening?"

Alison nodded in the direction of the table.

Mel walked slowly over to the bowl and pulled up her sleeve a little as if expecting to find water inside and swirled the handkerchiefs around. She desperately tried to make out some initials but, as usual, they were folded too tightly.

Finally after a few seconds she grabbed hold of one and pulled it out, her heart was once again racing so fast and beating so loudly in her heaving chest that she was sure everyone in the room could hear it.

Handing it over to Alison with a sweaty, trembling hand she took a step back. Alison took hold of it and slowly unfolded the handkerchief.

Mel glanced over at Harry, he made a quick fingers crossed sign and smiled. Mel felt the fear and trepidation fading a little and excitement beginning to rise, another evening with Harry would be bearable, but all too quickly she was back to fear, the initials were there in big red letters. 'M.A'.

Alison happily announced to the room that Mel was paired with Malcolm.

Mel's stomach came up into her throat and she stifled a shocked gasp.

'Why the hell did the forfeit rule have to be taken out today of all days!'

"Result!" shouted Malcolm, "'Bout bloody time I had a ride on this filly. I knew we did the right thing not cancelling tonight!"

He held out an outstretched arm indicating the door. "Shall we, my dear?"

Mel felt sick, physically, overwhelmingly sick. She looked over in the direction of Rob but he wasn't even looking, he was chatting to Tony and shuffling from one foot to another in excitement, waiting impatiently for his turn like a child in a pass the parcel game, Harry too had turned away.

Once in the hallway Malcolm lunged forward and grabbed her right breast causing her to lose her balance slightly and topple backwards against the wall. His lips moved in towards her face and pouted for a kiss, Mel quickly ducked to one side.

"Why don't you go through to the bedroom, I'll go and freshen up and be right there," she said in a voice so calm and seductive that even she was taken by surprise.

Malcolm grabbed a large piece of backside, winked with his tongue slightly protruding from the left corner of his mouth, and staggered off into the room opposite. Mel felt her legs begin to buckle underneath her, she turned to face the wall and felt her way along in the direction of the bathroom like a blind woman. She turned the handle and opened the door then immediately closed it and bolted it quickly behind her, momentarily safe.

She sat on the edge of the bath and tried to gather up her thoughts.

'Pull yourself together Mel,' she spoke out loud staring at herself sternly in the mirror opposite. 'This is no different to the other times, it's an hour of your life and it's all just a means to an end, Keep your eyes on the prize Melissa, you can do this this!'

Her thoughts turned to Rob, who had he got in tonight's sordid lucky dip? And Harry?

She splashed on some cool water to tone her bright red face and neck down to an acceptable shade of pink. Then she combed her hair through with her fingers and checking her face once more in the mirror, reluctantly slid the bolt across and opened the door.

As she did so she saw two figures were entering the room next to theirs, she recognised the back of Alison's dress and saw, to her dismay, it was Harry who was holding the door open.

As Alison went into the room Harry turned and caught Mel's eye, his expression changed and he opened his mouth as if to speak but just as he did so Alison's hand reached out, grabbed his arm and dragged him into her lair.

She stood motionless for a second, shit, Alison! Why bloody Alison? Tonight of all nights, the night she got the fat, obnoxious pig and where the hell was Rob? He must have gotten Mary or Tess again!!

She sighed heavily and headed, lead footed, towards the room.

'Maybe he's fallen asleep and is now drunkenly snoring away,' she hoped as she arrived at their room, but as she quietly pushed open the door she was greeted by the sight of Malcolm lying naked on the bed except for his badly tied dicky bow. He was propped up on one elbow and swigging from a champagne bottle which he held out for Mel.

"Finally you little minx, keep me waiting at your peril!"

He gave a smile which looked more threatening than sexy.

Mel sat on the bed and took hold of the bottle taking two large gulps of the much needed liquid.

'Okay, let's do this. Just lie back and think of England' she thought nervously.

"So tonight's your lucky night Melissa," he grinned, "you haven't lived until you've been had by 'big Mal' ...Come." He winked exaggeratedly.

Mel grimaced at his tacky play on words.

He grasped hold of her arm, pulled her down sharply onto the bed and began very clumsily to pull at her zip; struggling unsuccessfully to get it down he quickly became irritated.

"Take it off, take this fucking thing off, it's bloody well broken" he shouted.

Mel began to feel very uneasy, then she remembered Laurel's advice at the last dinner party.

"If you ever pick Malcolm you should know that he can get a bit rough, but if you don't fight him he'll be finished in a flash, in fact you may not even notice he's started!" she had concluded with a smile.

Okay... No resistance. She unzipped her dress, without difficulty, and lay down on the bed next to him, the smell of Cognac and cigars was strong on his breath. The next thing she knew he was on top of her, heavy, sweating and awkward. He fumbled around until finally he found what he was looking for, and like a teenage boy trying to do it for the first time, put his half limp organ just inside and began grunting like a crazed animal.

Mel lay there for a few minutes trying to decide if it was in fact in or not, she began to smile to herself at the ridiculous nature of the situation.

No sooner had she began to relax, thinking that soon it would all be over and in fact she wasn't actually having sex with Malcolm at all because penetration had not actually been achieved, her lightened mood changed dramatically.

Malcolm had propped himself up on his elbows and now had his hands firmly around her throat, the majority of his weight pressing down on her chest.

She tried to scream but the sound was blocked by the squeezing.

"Shush," spat Malcolm. "Don't panic Melissa dear, I'm not going to kill you, but your body doesn't know that... any minute now your brain will release a chemical, which, when mixed with the elevated level of carbon dioxide will give you the best bloody orgasm you've ever had."

Mel began to feel the veins in her head pulsating violently and her vision began to blur.

She was now in a state of complete panic and tried desperately to push him off but he was heavy and her strength was fading.

Malcolm was in full swing, panting excitedly, and she could feel his full erection now inside her, he was still grunting and squeezing with every thrust.

She couldn't believe she was going to die like this, in a house full of people! She tried once more to scream for help but still the scream was blocked by his hands.

"Can you feel it? Don't fight it, just relax and give in to it."

In desperation, Mel stretched out her arm trying to find something to make a noise with, she brushed against the bedside lamp and grabbed it, then with all her remaining strength she brought it down on Malcolm's head.

The Chinese vase lamp broke into pieces and Malcolm slumped into silence. His hands released the pressure on her throat and his full body weight pinned her to the bed.

Mel lay there for a few seconds in the darkened room, gasping for breath, trying to re-oxygenate her body. She managed to struggle from underneath him, pushing and kicking her way out of her obscene trap. Finally she managed to roll him over, his motionless body lay face up on the bed and she was free.

She looked down at him, in the dark room she could just make out a stream of blood trickling down his temple and into his ear. She put her ear to his chest but couldn't hear a heartbeat and she couldn't see his chest moving up and down. She jumped up off the bed.

'He's dead, oh shit, he's dead' she repeated, quietly panicking to herself.

She began to shake and dropped to her knees where she vomited onto the silk rug.

'What should she do?'

Her first instinct was to run away, but should she run or should she go and tell somebody?

There were no witnesses and she was sure nobody there would testify on her behalf, they would all deny everything.

The others would never admit to their activities and knowledge of Malcolm's rough behaviour, the club had to remain a secret.

'Rob!' Surely Rob would help her. No, right now she couldn't be sure of him either. No, she had no choice but to go with her first instinct, she hunted around for her shoes, but able to find only one, abandoned the search. She grabbed her dress, pulled it over her head and tugged at the zip, pulling it up to half way.

Slowly she opened the door and heard the sound of music and loud grunting noises coming from the direction of the lounge, Rob's grunting noises.

She crept along the hallway and slowly twisted the key in the door, her hand was shaking violently. The door opened and she slipped outside closing it quietly behind her.

She looked at the lift, it was on the ground floor and she didn't want to waste precious time waiting, so she decided to take the stairs.

She half ran, half walked down the steps, the marble felt cold under her bare feet. She began to feel faint, becoming dizzier with each flight.

She was weak and shaken from the experience, her heart was racing and her head was throbbing, suddenly everything went dark.

Chapter 23

"She's waking up, please step back from the bed."

Melissa opened her eyes and then quickly shut them again, reacting to the bright ceiling lights.

"I'm going to have to ask you all to wait outside while I examine her, thank you. Nurse, show them out please."

Mel blinked and then felt her eyelid pulled upwards. A bright light was shone into her left eye and then the process was repeated with the right.

"Can you hear me? Can you tell me your name and what day it is?"

"Mel, Melissa Harrison, it's the eleventh of September. Where am I?"

"Parkway East Hospital, I'm Doctor Timothy Tan, actually it's the twelfth of September but that's close enough. You were brought in just before midnight yesterday after a fall down the stairs. You've got a slight concussion and a distal radius fracture .We set it for you under anaesthetic so you'll feel a bit light headed and sleepy for a while. You'll have to keep it in plaster for about seven or eight weeks I'm afraid."

Mel looked down at her right forearm in plaster to the elbow.

The events of the previous evening came flooding into her mind.

Malcolm, oh shit, she'd killed him! She remembered hitting him with the lamp to stop him from strangling her.

She began to shake.

"Miss Harrison, Melissa, are you okay?"

The doctor put his index and middle fingers on her wrist and glanced at his watch.

"One twenty, you need to breathe Melissa, calm and deep, in and out, in and out, that's it.."

She followed his breathing pattern and felt herself calm slightly.

"I need to speak to a policeman, please, please get me a policeman."

"A policeman? Your friends said you fell down the stairs, were you pushed?"

"No, no… Just please get me a policeman."

She was there, she was trapped so she had to at least try to explain it was self-defence, she had to make them understand.

The doctor walked out of the room and stopped to speak to the group of people who were gathered outside her hospital room.

She then saw the group, through the patterned glass door, turn to look in her direction. One of them, a man it seemed - her vision was blurry - shook the doctor's hand and she watched the white coated figure walking away. Just then Alison and Rob came into the room.

"Bloody hell Melissa, you gave us quite a fright!" Alison took hold of her left hand, "You really should ease up on those G and T's Mel. You must have taken quite a tumble down the stairs, you're lucky to have only broken your wrist and bumped your head a bit."

"Personally I've had worse hangovers" Rob laughed, "but seriously darling, where the hell were you going anyway? It took us ages to find you on the stairs. You could have told me you were leaving, what's wrong with you?"

Mel looked down again at her lower arm in plaster and for the first time felt the painful throbbing, at least it was the right one, luckily she was left handed.

She looked up at them both, why was nobody mentioning Malcolm?

They must have discovered his body by now.

"I need to speak to the police, I need to explain what happened to Malcolm... I..."

"Malcolm?" interrupted Alison, "What on earth for? What has the drunken sod been up to this time?"

"It went too far, I didn't mean to kill him, I just couldn't make him stop and I thought I was going to die. I'm so sorry Rob, I didn't mean to kill him" she repeated, now crying and trembling from head to toe.

"Kill who? Who are you talking about?

Mel recognised the voice and looked up to see Malcolm entering the room. She stared in disbelief, searching for signs of an injury but he was wearing a dark green baseball cap, pulled down and covering his head.

"Thank God you're all right young lady!"

He bent down and kissed her on the cheek, she flinched visibly, the vision of him lying there not breathing was still vivid in her mind.

"But... but I... I thought you were..."

Malcolm interrupted her.

"Poor girl, you took quite a fall, drunk as a skunk last night, it happens to us all, a lethal mix of Gin and humidity. Pity about the wrist, still you're used to being plastered!"

Malcolm laughed out loud at his own joke.

"I just wanted to check you were all right. We'll go now and leave you to rest, Rob take *good* care of her, I'd like a quick word outside if I may."

Rob nodded sheepishly.

"Goodbye Melissa, see you around."

Alison and Malcolm left the hospital room, Alison blowing a kiss as they went.

"I'll be back in just a sec."

Mel was disorientated, she could no longer work out what was real.

Rob left the room and walked over to the waiting Malcolm.

She could see they were talking and Malcolm was waving his arms in the air.

'What the hell was he telling him?'

After about five minutes Mel saw Malcolm hand something to Rob, which he took, put in his pocket then Malcolm walked away.

Rob came back in the room smiling and sat on the edge of the bed.

"Rob, I'm so sorry," Melissa began immediately, desperate to get her side across. "I really believed I'd killed him, I thought he was going to choke me to death, his hands were around my throat and he was squeezing..."

Rob plumped up the pillows and helped Mel to get into a more upright position and then he took hold of her hand gently.

"Listen darling you've had a fall, you hit your head and you're confused."

Mel went to speak but Rob continued,

"It doesn't matter anymore, Vincent called me earlier and told me that I'm being transferred to the Sydney office. We're finished here, it's over and you don't have to worry about anything. We'll leave in about a month, isn't that great?"

He was grinning from ear to ear.

"And that's not all", he added, "I've been given a promotion, that means more money, a bloody great big apartment, first class flights home and a six monthly bonus. How good is all that?"

Mel sat in disbelief, that was a lot of information to take in, she was overwhelmed.

'We're leaving here? Sydney? As in Australia?"

Rob nodded, smiling.

"Rob, I really need to finish telling you something."

His face changed into an angry expression.

"No," he squeezed her hand, "you don't need to tell anyone anything *ever*! Is that clear Mel?"

He squeezed it again, this time harder.

Mel nodded, he was hurting her.

Just then Doctor Tan came back into the room.

Rob released his grip.

"Okay, we'll keep her in tonight under observation just to make sure, she still has a slight concussion and a bit of confusion."

"Don't worry doctor, I'm sure she's fine, really, I'd like to take her home."

"I really feel it's best if she stays here tonight, she is still very woozy."

"We live very close to the hospital, I'll bring her straight back if there are any problems, I'm sure she'll be happier at home in her own bed, won't you babe?"

Mel didn't reply, she had absolutely no idea what was going on right then and she certainly couldn't say what was best for her in that moment.

"All right," agreed the doctor, "but if she vomits or her dizziness gets worse please bring her straight back. Now, I need you to sign some forms to say you're taking her home without my approval so follow me please. By the way Miss, do you still need to speak to the police?"

"No, no thank you doc that won't be necessary, will it darling?" Rob replied for her, squeezing her hand hard once again.

"No," agreed Mel, still unable to fully comprehend anything that was being said.

Her head was pounding terribly. "It doesn't matter."

Rob stood up and left the room with the doctor.

"I'll be back soon darling, I'll just sign these papers and pop home to get you some clean clothes." He smiled at her.

Then when the doctor had distanced himself slightly he added in a more serious tone and without the smile.

"*Don't* go anywhere."

Mel noted that he had called her darling at least three times in the last five minutes.

That was more than in the last five months, she thought.

She lay there for a few minutes trying to take in everything that had happened in the last 24 hours, but tiredness overwhelmed her and she drifted into a deep sleep.

She woke some time later with the urge to pee and scanned the room, Rob still wasn't back. 'How long had she been asleep? In fact what time was it?' Mel realised that had no idea… morning, afternoon, evening?

She sat up and pulled the sheet to one side, swung her legs over the edge of the bed and stood up. Everything ached. Her head began to spin and she sat back down quickly on the bed placing a hand on the bedside table and her feet on the floor in an attempt to slow down the merry go round.

'Where was Rob? She desperately needed to pee and needed a hand getting to the bathroom.

She looked around for a buzzer or bell of some description but just then a nurse passed by the room,

"Excuse me, nurse!"

The small, thin woman in a dark blue uniform shuffled into the room.

"Yes, you need something is it?" she asked in a heavy accent.

"Can you give me a hand please getting to the bathroom? I still feel a bit dizzy."

The deceptively small and fragile looking woman practically lifted Mel off the bed and, taking almost her full weight, accompanied her into the bathroom.

"You should stay here now, not go home, you don't look so good to me."

The nurse scolded Mel.

"I'm fine," she said, not very convincingly.

In the bathroom Mel looked at her face in the mirror, she resembled a train wreck. There was a large purple bruise on her right cheek, a small cut above her right eye and large mascara smudges under both her puffy eyes.

She turned on the cold tap and put a handful of toilet paper under the running water, carefully she wiped the mascara away.

Her face hurt, her wrist hurt and her pride hurt.

How did she let herself get caught up in this world? How could Rob have dragged her into all this?

She suddenly had a desperate urge to speak to her Mum, she always knew exactly what to say to make her feel better, even if Mel didn't often admit that to her!

She would call her as soon as she got home, she decided, she would tell her about the promotion and the move, she wouldn't and she couldn't tell her anything else.

The nurse and Rob were waiting for her when she came out of the bathroom.

Rob took her by the arm and helped her over to the bed where he had laid out her clothes. He had brought a white vest top and her favourite denim mini skirt.

"I thought if you were wearing this people wouldn't notice your face so much!"

He was laughing and Mel managed a half smile... ouch!

While the nurse was helping her with her shoes the doctor popped his head around the door.

"I've given all your medication and instructions to your husband. Remember if there are any problems, if your headache worsens or your eyesight becomes compromised further you must come straight back, okay? Goodbye and take it easy on the alcohol."

Great, she had been passed off as an alcoholic, still it was a damn sight better than the truth!

In the past hearing Rob referred to as her husband would have brought a huge smile to her face, but at that moment she just felt numb.

"Right beautiful, let's get you home."

'Beautiful'? He had never called her that before, maybe she wasn't the only one who had bumped their head!'

Chapter 24

On Monday morning Mel woke up feeling a little better. She had slept from the moment she had gotten home from the hospital Saturday and virtually all day Sunday, thanks to the mixed effects of the anaesthetic, the strong painkillers she had taken and just sheer emotional draining.

Rob, strangely, had been very attentive and had always been there by her side when she woke up for fetching and carrying.

"Good morning sunshine, how are you feeling today?"

Rob came into the room, he was already dressed for work and he looked very smart in his suit, an M&S special, dark grey with light grey stripes.

He was carrying a tray and on it Mel could see a glass of orange juice, a flower, which had been extracted from the beautiful bouquet that was awaiting her when she got home, a bottle of pills and a small square box.

"I'll never understand which sadistic bastard decided that we should all wear ties to the office in this bloody heat! Still at least the temperature in Sydney is a little more bearable, not this humid."

He placed the tray on the bedside locker and sat down on the bed next to her and handed her the bottle of pills and the glass of juice.

Mel shook two pills from the bottle, drank from the glass and with the orange juice in her mouth, threw in the pills to the back if her throat and swallowed down the lot.

"Now, I know things haven't been easy for you here and you haven't been as happy as you could have been," Rob said, his expression now serious, "but seeing you lying there in that hospital bed, all battered and bruised after your drunken mishap on the stairs made me realise how much I love you and, how much I want to take care of you, so..."

He slipped off the bed and knelt down on one knee on the floor next to her and reached for the little square box on the tray.

Mel, not believing her own eyes or ears, sat herself up and glanced over at him. When she moved she noticed that her head was still throbbing and her neck was very stiff.

Rob opened the box slowly and there inside was a beautiful gold ring with an inset of three quite large, round diamonds mounted closely together.

"So," he repeated, clearing his throat nervously, "Melissa Marie Harrison, will you do me the honour of becoming my trouble and strife?"

Mel sat there for a few seconds unable to speak. She was desperately trying to ascertain if she was having some kind of painkiller induced hallucination or if the scene unfolding before her was real.

"Mel? Mel, did you hear what I said?"

Mel looked down at the open box, up at Rob, down at her aching wrist and then out of the window of their room at the sparkling sea in the distance where she remained transfixed for a few seconds, then finally but without taking her eyes off the sea she spoke.

"This is really unexpected Rob."

He took hold of her left hand,

"Well?" he asked again.

This was not the romantic proposal she had dreamed of, with the candlelit dinner, the violinist and the ring in the bottom of the champagne glass but it was a proposal, a real proposal. Mel looked into his puzzled eyes. She had been waiting impatiently for this moment for a long time and had dreamed of getting married ever since she was ten and had draped a net curtain over her head and waked down the path in the back garden holding a bunch of dandelions in one hand and a two foot poster of David Cassidy in the other, but she had never envisaged it like this.

His puzzled look was rapidly turning into a worried one.

"Melissa look at me," she turned her head slowly, wincing at the pain the simple manoeuvre caused.

"I know things haven't gone like you thought they would but it's all just made me realise how much I want to be with you. We're leaving Mel, we're putting this all behind us to start a new life together, so I'll ask you one more time, Melissa Harrison will you marry me?"

They were leaving and soon this nightmare would be at an end and she would have a normal life again. No more sordid clubs, no more sharing anything or anyone, finally just her and Rob, alone, together.

"Yes Rob, yes I'll marry you!"

He smiled a relieved smile, and standing up, kissed her playfully and took the ring out of the box. His hands shook noticeably as he slipped it onto her finger, pushing it slightly to get it on over the knuckle.

Mel held her hand up admiring the lovely diamond ring that was glittering in the sunlight.

"Is it too tight? I borrowed one of your old rings from your jewellery box for size but I didn't take into consideration that the heat makes your fingers bigger."

"No, it's fine, it's gorgeous really, perfect. When did you get this?"

"Saturday when I came home from the hospital to get you some clothes, I made a small detour. Do you really like it? I saw you admiring one similar to it the last time we went out to Far East Plaza."

Looking at engagement rings had always been a bit of a hobby of hers, as was trying them on when she was alone, but she never thought he had taken any notice of her admiring glances.

Mel was still staring at it, she did like it, she really liked it.

"It looks really expensive, are you sure you can afford this right now?"

"Yes I told you, I'm getting a pay rise Mel, it's fine.

Right I'm off to work, I'll finish as early as I can, I should be able to get home by about five today I reckon."

He bent down and kissed her on the forehead and then tenderly on the lips.

"Rest today and I'll bring something home for dinner."

He walked towards the door.

"I almost forgot, Alison is sending her amah round later, she said she'd drop by at about ten o'clock to clean, make lunch and just generally keep you company, all you have to do is let her in. Call me at the office later if you need to."

God forbid Alison came round to help her in person! But today she was glad to have some help in the house.

"That's nice of her, I'll call later and thank her."

"She's not here, she's gone to Kuala Lumpur for a few days, back Wednesday I think."

"Rob." He stopped and turned. "It's going to be all right isn't it? We're going to be okay aren't we?"

"What a question! Of course we are. We're getting married! Now get some rest. I've set the alarm for two thirty, that's in in six hours' time and that's when you need to take your next pills, so you'll remember," he said, walking out the door, "it's one of the round ones and two of the long ones. Bye."

Mel heard the front door close.

She lay staring at her ring and then at the ceiling for quite a while watching the fan going round and round but she couldn't get back to sleep. She was getting married, she should be feeling happier about it. Not only had she fantasised as a child about marrying David Cassidy with the three Charlie's Angels as bridesmaids and Grease Lightening as the wedding car, but recently, realistically with Rob as the groom.

This was real, this wasn't a game or a dream, she and Rob were finally getting married, so why wasn't she more excited?

Unable to go back to sleep she eventually decided to get up, her wrist and head were throbbing more than ever.

She went into the kitchen and took the carton of orange juice from the door of the fridge, shaking it she realised it was empty so she threw it in the direction of the bin but it missed and landed on the floor. At the back of the fridge she found a new un-opened one. Mel held it in her left hand and placing the edge between her teeth she pulled, the carton ripped open and orange juice splashed all over her nightshirt.

Pouring some into a glass she opened the freezer and took out the ice cube tray, then she turned it over and banged it hard on the worktop, a few cubes shot out violently. Two of them ended up on the floor and the other two she retrieved from the sink and popped them into her glass. Mel drank down the orange juice thirstily and walked back towards the bathroom.

Carefully she slipped her arm out of the shirt and pulled it over her head, turning on the tap she splashed her face and chest to get the juice off.

As she dried herself with a towel she caught sight of the marks on her throat, two small faint purple bruises either side of her windpipe.

She shuddered at the memory of Malcolm with his fat hands around her throat, his grunting and thrusting and his ecstatic expression.

She bit hard on her bottom lip and screwed up her eyes, breathing in and out deeply through her nose.

Her 'cleansing routine' was prematurely interrupted by the sound of the ringing phone.

"Hello?"

"Mel, it's Mum, how are you? I haven't heard from you for a while, is everything okay there?"

Mel hadn't managed to call her before as she had hadn't felt up to it and she hadn't been able to give any thought as to what she was going to say.

"Mum! Hi, it's almost three o'clock in the morning there, what's happened?"

"Nothing's happened Melissa, I set my alarm to call you, I haven't heard from you in a few days and I thought you'd appreciate a call."

'How does she do that?'

She always knew instinctively when Mel needed her. Mel's voice began to wobble.

"Yes I'm good thanks Mum." she lied. "Just got a bit of a cold."

"Yes, I can hear you're snuffly and a bit croaky, you poor thing. I didn't know you could get colds in hot countries! Listen, Gill and I were thinking of coming out to see you at Christmas, just for ten days or so, what do you say?"

"Mum, I was going to call you later on today, there's been a change of plan, Rob's been promoted and he's being transferred to Sydney."

"Australia! We'll that's all very sudden, I thought he had a two year contract!"

"He does, he's still working for the same bank, just in a different office, I only found out last night myself so I can't give you any more details at the moment, I just know that we leave in about four weeks."

"Oh I see, well let me know when you know please, I don't think we can afford to come all the way out there, It'll probably be very expensive Melissa. When will we see you?"

"I'll speak to Rob, we might be able to help you out with flights, he's going to be earning more money so it shouldn't be a problem. If not, the company will pay for flights back a couple of times a year, it's included in the package, one way or another I'll see you at Christmas Mum, don't worry."

Mel had a sudden and desperate urge to be with her Mum, to be cuddled up on the sofa eating Maltesers and watching 'Starsky and Hutch' together like they did when she was a child.

Again tears began to flow.

"Mel love, don't cry, thousands of girls would give their right arm to be in your position, you really should be making the most of it."

Mel looked down at her right arm plastered to just below the elbow and the tears flowed even stronger.

"Listen Mel, you call me when you feel more like talking, and let me know about Sydney. Take care of yourself, your sister sends her love and so does Auntie Lillian, oh and she asked if you could send her one of those silk dressing gowns you sent Gill, blue or red I think she said. Be good and go and get something for that cold, can you get Lemsips out there? Bye bye darling, we love you."

"Thanks Mum, I love you all too."

Mel hadn't mentioned the broken wrist, she hated keeping things from her but she was so far away that some things, most things, her Mum was better not knowing, she would only worry. She decided it would be better to tell her later when she had time to come up with a plausible story.

As for the engagement, she would tell her Mum about it the next time she called her, when she was feeling stronger. Everything in good time, and besides, with the news about Sydney her Mum had had enough information to absorb for one day.

'And so,' thought Mel, 'have I.'

Chapter 25

The rest of the week dragged, Rob, true to his word got home early most evenings but she didn't see anybody else except Alison's amazing amah.

Alison had phoned, as had Debbie a few times to see how she was, but they had never mentioned coming over to visit and Mel didn't think it was the right thing to do to ask.

During their brief phone conversations they had always talked about their trip and how busy they were organising the Asian Expat Tennis Tournament, which this time apparently, was being held here in Singapore.

The poor things were rushed off their feet, but they had sent over a wonderful bunch of flowers and a fruit basket, what more could you ask for!

Mel had the distinct feeling they were all avoiding her.

At least now she was feeling much better. She spent a lot of time just sitting on the balcony and watching the people milling around downstairs.

She desperately wanted to have a cooling swim but with her arm in plaster it was impossible.

It was hot and humid in the apartment and the TV drove her mad, so on Friday afternoon she made her first outing outside the apartment.

Slipping on a pair of flip flops she went out briefly to the mini market downstairs to get some milk and buy a couple of gossip magazines to read. The man and woman behind the counter had looked sympathetically at her as she paid but she was sure that when she left she heard them sniggering.

The magazines took her all of an hour to get through, today even the gossip wasn't interesting her. She had tried calling her Auntie Lillian a few times to wish her a happy birthday but she hadn't replied.

She did however manage to get hold of Alan, Rob's dad, and chat to him for a while. He had had nothing very exciting to say but it was nice to hear a familiar voice.

She had waited for him to comment on the wedding news but he didn't mention it so Mel didn't either, she thought that it would probably be better to hear it from his son first.

She felt quite disappointed that he hadn't been told but then to be fair she hadn't mentioned it to her Mum yet either.

"You know you're too good for my son," he laughed at the end of the conversation, to which Mel had ironically protested strongly.

"Well you've made your bed young lady, so to speak," Alan continued.

"Take care of yourself and my pain in the backside son."

It was seven twenty when Rob finally arrived home carrying familiar boxes from the Mövenpick. He leaned towards her and kissed her tenderly, she leapt up from the sofa and hugged him with one arm.

"You're late tonight," she commented in a sulky voice.

"Hi, how was your day?" he said, ignoring the remark. "I didn't get a chance to call you, I was flat out all day, the Bundesbank cut their interest rates, whole market went crazy. I got you a chicken and pineapple salad with extra fresh coriander, just as you like it."

He held up the boxes and jiggled them proudly.

Mel just caught the bit about the chicken.

"My day was okay, I just stayed here mostly and sorted out the wardrobe and watched some TV. I did manage to get down to the mini market this afternoon, other than that, nothing really exciting. Oh and I spoke to your dad today, he sends his love."

"You didn't mention the wedding did you?" he asked, seemingly worried.

"No of course not, I thought it best to let you do that."

Rob seemed uneasy.

"Is everything okay? You seem bothered about something?"

"Yes fine, I need to go to Sydney next Friday, the twenty fifth I think it is.

"I have to meet the desk manager there and discuss my contract and they've organised for me to see a couple of apartments. I told them that it wasn't a good idea for you to fly at the moment and I'll only be gone until Monday I think."

Mel, feeling disappointed, shrugged her shoulders.

"I would have liked to have seen the apartments, I'm actually feeling much better, I could go for a few days and it would be nice to see Sydney and spend some time together."

"No Mel, I don't think it's a good idea for you to travel right now, and besides I'll be in meetings all weekend, talking shop."

"I suppose you're right, I don't feel much like travelling around there on my own. But if possible don't choose an apartment that's too high up. This one is great but I've always had a bit of a problem being up on this floor."

"What haven't you had a problem with! I'll see what I can do Mel, trust me I'm sure you'll love it."

His tone made her feel uneasy and he definitely seemed edgy.

"Why don't you spend some time that weekend organising the wedding? Call your Mum and tell her about it, I'm sure she'd love to help you. What do you say to a small Christmas do in Sydney? It's their summer so we could do it on the beach and then we could have a bloody big party back home after with all our family and friends, now doesn't that sound good?"

"But that's only three months away Rob, and that would mean that Mum and Gill or your dad probably wouldn't be there!"

"Exactly, it would be a small intimate ceremony. Now you'd better get cracking on the arrangements. I'm going for a shower, please eat something!"

"Are you not eating with me?"

"No I'm good, I grabbed a bite there while I was waiting for yours and I'm not very hungry to be honest."

Mel was taken aback at his sudden desire to get married immediately.

He had never been very enthusiastic about the idea, in fact when anyone had mentioned marriage before he had always come back with some cutting comment or remark.

And how could she get married without her family? That would also mean no wedding dress, she couldn't exactly walk down the beach in a meringue, could she?

All these events, all these changes, made Mel feel that she was on a giant roller-coaster ride but that instead of being thrilling, it was just turning her stomach.

She sat at the table and picked at the salad, it was really delicious as always but her appetite wasn't great either.

Rob came out of the shower dripping wet with just a towel wrapped tightly around his waist. Dancing around the table he got closer to Mel and then opened his towel and 'flashed' her.

"Any chance of a quick blow job?"

He was smiling and waggling everything a few inches from her face.

Mel leaned back out of range.

"I'm sorry Rob but these pain killers are making me feel a bit nauseous and I'm still a bit light headed, do you mind if we take a rain check?"

She had lost her appetite not only for food, it would seem.

Rob tucked the towel back around his waist looking like a child who had just been told he couldn't have a sweetie. Mel couldn't face sex right now, she still couldn't get the image of Malcolm out of her head.

The Friday morning of his trip Rob was up early, his flight was at eleven. Mel had been awake for hours, she had been having trouble sleeping all week and the painkillers weren't working that well any more. Her wrist still throbbed and she had a constant headache.

"I'm going to get dressed and come with you to the airport, I need to get out of the house for a while."

"Don't be silly, that's not necessary, stay here and rest." Rob's tone was insistent.

"God, I've been doing nothing but resting for two bloody weeks, and besides I can call in and see Laurel on the way back, she's not far from the airport, I practically have to go right past her house. She's called almost every day this week to see how I am and I know she's in this morning, her cleaning lady comes on Friday and she told me she never leaves her alone in the house. I'll get dressed, I won't take long."

She went into the bathroom and struggled for a few minutes to get her arm out of her nightshirt. Not wanting to keep him waiting she gave up and went into the lounge.

"Rob. Rob? I need a hand, literally!"

She saw that Rob was on the balcony speaking on the phone.

"No, change of plan, just go through when you get there, okay, gotta go, bye."

"Rob, sorry can you help me out of this nightshirt?" She had joined him out on the balcony.

They both went back into the lounge where he tugged her arm out of the sleeve.

"Who was that on the phone?"

"My boss, just giving me some info on the group down under, nothing for you to worry about, are you ready? I need to get going."

'His boss?'

She retreated into the bathroom and quickly dressed in a light blue boob tube top and white skirt. Not very glam but they were quick and easy to get on and off. Sliding into her shoes she glanced down and grinned proudly at her nicely tanned, neatly waxed legs.

In an attempt to stop the boredom, in the last few days Mel had been making almost daily visits to the beauty salon downstairs and to her delight they all knew her by name now.

She then ran a brush quickly through her hair and applied a bit of mascara. Checking herself one last time in the mirror she noticed that the bruise on her cheek had almost disappeared and the marks on her throat were now just a faint yellow mark, practically invisible under the tanned skin.

She shuddered.

"Ready."

A taxi was waiting for them when they got downstairs.

"Changhi please mate."

The journey was quick as always and Rob held her good hand throughout the trip.

"Now I'm going to be out quite a lot, I hear they've got loads lined up so I'm not going to be easy to get hold of. Also I think it's best if you wait for me to call you, that way we don't pay for the calls, I can do it from the office. That reminds me, the last phone bill was over a hundred dollars, you need to cut down on the UK calls a bit."

"But I don't make that many, Mum usually calls me" she protested, but Rob wasn't listening, he was too busy staring intently out of the window.

The taxi pulled up outside departures and Rob jumped out.

"No need to come in Mel, I'm going to go straight through to the first class lounge and make the most of the free booze and it'll probably be crowded in there and you need to be careful of your wrist."

He leaned over and kissed her.

"Take care of yourself and stay off the G and T's, we don't want any more mishaps."

Mel shook her head, 'Mishaps? Not quite how she'd put it!'

"See you Monday then, my flight gets in at eight pm so if all on time I should be home by about nine and I'll bring you back a Koala."

Rob kissed her quickly on the lips.

"Give me a ring to let me know when you get there and have a safe flight. Oh and Rob, remember don't get an apartment too..."

But he was gone, striding off in the direction of the large sliding doors.

Mel waited a while watching him go, willing him to turn around and wave or blow her a kiss but the doors opened and without even a turn of the head he disappeared inside.

She turned and got in the back of the first waiting taxi.

"East Park Gardens please" she instructed the taxi driver.

As the taxi pulled away Mel recognised the figure sitting in the back of the taxi pulling up at the rank beside her and she frantically began waving as their cabs passed each other.

"Christine," she shouted, realising immediately how futile that was as both her and Christine's windows were closed.

Her frantic arm waving went unnoticed.

Chapter 26

Mel rang the bell.

"Hello, who is it?"

"Laurel it's Mel, can I come in?"

"Oh Mel, yes of course, it's the last house on the right, I'll buzz you in."

Mel walked along a long path, the garden was ablaze with flowers of many colours and varieties. There were four single, three storey houses set back in a row from the path

The end house had a small front lawn area with terra cotta Buddhas positioned randomly amongst brightly coloured orchids and tall red and yellow plants that on first glance resembled exotic bird's heads.

She turned into the narrow driveway and approached the front door which opened immediately.

Laurel was stood there in a plain grey T shirt and matching leggings, she was bright red and sweaty.

She released her hair from its elastic band and shook it with her fingers.

"This is a surprise, I'm afraid you've caught me in the middle of my daily workout, I prefer to exercise here instead of at the gym. Come in, come in."

She stepped aside and Mel passed her and entered the house.

It was beautiful, almost everything in the lounge was white except for a few colourful cushions scattered on the two large leather sofas and there was a huge matching cushion on the floor. Over by the French doors was an enormous plant which took over the entire corner of the room.

Just then Mel heard a loud squawking sound coming from the vicinity of the plant.

"Don't mind Turq, his squawk is worse than his bite."

Mel looked closer and there on a wooden perch on top of a long pole was a large, bright bluey-green coloured parrot.

"Oh wow, he's beautiful, how long have you had a parrot?"

"Actually he's a Macaw, we inherited him from Doug, Tony's predecessor. He was going back to live in Sydney and didn't want to take him with him so when we took over the rent on this house we got Turq into the bargain.

Turq is short for turquoise. His loss our gain."

There was a note of sarcasm in her voice.

"Actually you'll probably meet Doug when you go to Sydney, he's in the office, he's like a slightly slimmer version of Malcolm."

Mel held her breath at the mention of his name.

Laurel moved over to the perch and stroked the back of the Macaw. At her touch the bird turned around revealing a bright orange front.

"G'day sexpot" the bird said in a broad Aussie accent as clear as day.

Mel laughed loudly.

"Doug taught him a lot of choice words, that's nothing! We're trying to teach him normal phrases but we're not being very successful, I think he actually prefers the swearing and blaspheming."

"Screw you" said the bird, underlining the point.

"Would you like a quick tour of the place?"

They climbed the stairs to the second floor where there were two small rooms, one was a single bedroom and the other a small but perfectly decorated bathroom, everything in it was made from light pink marble. The first floor had two more double bedrooms and a larger equally impressive bathroom.

Mel noticed that there was a door off the master bedroom.

"Is that an en suite?" Mel asked curiously.

"No," said Laurel walking over to the door and flinging it open. Then pulling a light switch she revealed a bedroom sized walk-in wardrobe.

Mel stood in awe, that had always been her dream.

On the wall inside was a large framed wedding photo of Laurel and Tony standing with champagne glasses in hand in front of the Sydney Opera House.

Mel couldn't help but reflect on the hour she had spent with him that first night.

She looked away from the photo embarrassed that she was picturing him naked.

They went back down the stairs to the ground floor.

"This you've already seen, there's just the lounge and the kitchen on this floor."

Thinking that was it, Mel went to walk back over to the sofa.

"Hang on" said Laurel, "You haven't seen downstairs yet."

There was another floor?

They walked down another flight of stairs into a large basement.

The basement contained an enormous dining area with a wooden table in the centre which sat eight, and hanging directly above it was an elaborate chandelier.

There was no need for a ceiling fan as it was lovely and cool below decks.

Over in the corner there was a white rattan bar complete with optics.

'That's Rob's dream,' she thought.

Over to the left was a door leading to the laundry room where the amah was busy ironing shirts, she didn't even look up when they entered and Laurel didn't acknowledge her presence either. A camp bed was set up ready for use, over in the corner.

"Sometimes our amah sleeps here to look after Turq when we're away" Laurel said, explaining its function.

They went back upstairs to the lounge where the difference in temperature from the basement was noticeable.

"Take a seat please Mel."

They walked over to the sofa and Laurel looked down at Mel's plastered wrist.

"You poor thing, that must be painful. How are you feeling?"

"Better thanks, it still throbs a bit."

"You had quite a tumble, we didn't notice you were missing for quite a while. It was Harry who found you on the stairs after Malcolm..."

Laurel hesitated and looked around her as if expecting to see someone there.

"After Malcolm staggered out of your room, wearing only his bow tie with blood dripping from his forehead."

Mel stared at Laurel, nobody had ever talked to her about that night before now.

"I shouldn't be telling you all this," Laurel was virtually whispering.

"Alison made us swear not to say anything, you know the code and all that, but after what happened to Sue and then you, to hell with the code, I think you should know."

"How is Sue?" Mel asked with genuine concern. "I haven't heard anything in a while, Rob won't talk about it. What's happened to her? And Dan, what's happening with him?"

Laurel looked around once more. Mel found herself looking around with her.

"It's a long story," sighed Laurel, "let's just say that it all got too much for her. Thanks to her brilliant lawyer she's been sent back to the UK by the judge for long term psychological evaluation. That's legal jargon for she's been locked up in a mental asylum, poor kid."

Mel swallowed hard, there but for the grace of God...

"Dan, on the other hand, is on the mend, he's out of danger and they've moved him to a regular ward. He has a broken pelvis and femur I think it is, and severe concussion. He also had some damage to his spleen and they had to remove a part of it, poor sod." Laurel hung her head in sympathy.

"I don't know really know what a spleen does, do you?"

Mel shook her head

"Anyway whatever it does, he's missing a bit! Basically he's lucky to be alive, but what happened to you was pretty wild too hey?"

At that moment the amah came into the living room.

"Excuse me madam, I've finished everything on the list, do you need me for anything else?"

"Oh thank you Maria, no that's fine, you can go now and I'll see you on Monday."

She walked over and stroked the bird.

"G'day sexpot" he repeated. Maria smiled.

When she had left, Laurel went into the kitchen.

"I don't know about you but I'm parched," she shouted from the other room. "Is it too early for a glass of wine d'you think?"

"I can't drink with these painkillers, it makes me ill"

Mel shouted back sadly. She could have done with a drink right then in anticipation of the rest of Laurel's story.

"Okay, tea it is then, do you take sugar?"

Mel had joined her in the kitchen where everything in there was white too. On the windowsill above the sink was a long row of small black metal teapots.

"No, no sugar thanks. They're lovely," said Mel pointing at them.

Laurel smiled.

"We did a stint in Tokyo before coming here, I started collecting them when we arrived. They weren't very expensive either, I picked most of them up at a monthly antique market in Shibuya."

Mel would have loved to have heard more about Tokyo but the story of that night was still waiting to be told.

A cup of tea in each hand, Laurel walked back into the lounge followed closely by Mel.

Sitting back down on the sofa Laurel picked up the story from where she had left off.

"Anyway, what was I saying? Oh yes, Malcolm staggering out in the nuddy. He told us that you had just gone crazy and that you started hitting him and calling him a rapist. He said he had to virtually sit on you and pin you down to stop you from injuring you both."

Mel opened her mouth to speak but Laurel continued insistently.

"He also told us that when he thought you had calmed down he released his grip and that's when you hit him over the head with something."

That was too much for Mel, she stood up shouting.

"That's not bloody true! I never went crazy. He did pin me down, but with his hands around my throat, he was choking me in some sick, erotic game and I thought I was going to die."

The images of that night, that she had been desperately trying to block out, came flooding into her mind and she began to sob.

Laurel stood up and put an arm around her.

"I believe you Mel, I do, really. A similar thing happened to me, he didn't choke me but he did get very rough. He has at some point with all of us."

Hearing that Laurel believed her was a relief.

Mel continued, still sobbing loudly.

"So, if Malcolm's such a pervert and a bully how come he's in the group? Why hasn't he been kicked out or banned or something?"

She sat back down on the sofa.

"It's very simple Melissa, he's the biggest customer here, he controls the biggest bank and he's almost single handedly responsible for the job success of all of them, including Rob. Without Malcolm's backing they wouldn't have a single customer, none of them. Even Tim needs him on his side, but the problem is that he knows he has this power and knows he can do whatever he bloody well wants."

Mel's head was swimming.

"Thank God we're going to Sydney then."

Laurel took hold of her hand.

"Oh lovely, do you think that's a coincidence?"

Mel looked up at Laurel.

"What do you mean?"

"I mean Malcolm arranged for Rob to be transferred to Australia. He wants you out the way so you don't get much of a chance to say anything to anyone about what really happened. Who do you think it was that put the story out about Sue going psycho?"

Mel sat in disbelief.

"Well then I need to tell Rob, he needs to know."

"Christ Mel, you are naive! Rob knows already, and besides, you couldn't tell him, then he would know we'd had this conversation. Don't say anything to anyone. Promise me Mel!"

Laurel's tone was serious.

Mel nodded. "Of course not, I won't say a word."

"Anyway he's done you a bloody favour, at least you're not going to end up like Sue. And you're going to Sydney, I wish I was going back home."

Mel nodded quietly.

"Listen," she checked her watch, "I don't want to be rude but I have to start getting ready for a lunch appointment with Tony in the CBD."

Mel put down her half-finished tea and stood up.

"Yes of course, thank you for being honest with me, I really appreciate it" she said, wiping her smudged mascara away from under her eyes.

"It's okay, just don't say anything or you'll land me in the shit. We never had this conversation, okay?"

Mel nodded again, then while heading towards the front door she made a small detour and walked over to say goodbye to the bird. Noticing how long and sharp his beak and claws looked she bravely stroked the back of his neck with her finger as she'd seen them do.

"Malcolm's such a pervert, Malcolm's such a pervert" he cried out.

Chapter 27

Laurel looked first at the bird, then at Mel, then back to the bird.

"Oh crap!" she exclaimed with a very worried look on her face.

"Has he ever said that before?" Mel asked hopefully, but Laurel's horrified expression answered her question without having to speak.

"Er, no, never, and with your bloody stupid accent as well, Tony's going to kill me if he finds out I've been talking to you about our get togethers, oh shit! And if Alison finds out too? I'll be ostracised. We're supposed to be hosting the next meeting in two weeks, what if Turq says it then?"

This last thought sent her into a rage.

"Nobody is allowed to talk about anything that goes on!" she was shouting. "You know the rules, we can't talk about anyone, but especially not about Malcolm. I know that Ali hates him as well but we can't, we can't say anything."

"Well, as she hates him too, if she found out would it be so terrible?"

Mel was trying to calm Laurel down, she was now staring wide eyed at the bird in an obvious state of total panic.

"Yes of course it bloody would!"

Laurel was now yelling angrily.

"It's all your fault Mel, if you hadn't come here today with your 'poor me' routine, if you'd have just lay there and let him do what he wanted to do, like the rest of us did, instead of being so bloody dramatic we wouldn't be here now panicking about a stupid talking bird."

Mel was horrified, how could she say such a thing?

"Laurel, that night I was genuinely afraid for my life, that kind of thing has never happened to me before, I didn't know what to do, I'm sorry." Mel was once again close to tears.

"Oh for God's sake! Everything was okay here before you turned up."

Her voice was bitter and shrill and all her frustrations and anger were spewing out all over Mel. That was too much, she felt like she was back in school all over again. Why did she always end up getting the blame for everything?

Mel picked up her handbag and headed for the door, she needed to leave. As she got to the door she stopped, and in an uncharacteristic moment of courage replied.

"It was *you* who started talking to *me* about everything," she shouted back at the enraged Laurel. "I just came here to try and get to know you better, to try to be your friend, you started all this!"

But there was no reply, Laurel was staring silently at the bird.

Mel flung open the door and stormed out into the garden.

"Malcolm's such a pervert" she heard again coming from inside, and to her dismay she had to admit that Turq did a very good impression of her.

Half walking half running she arrived at the main gate and flagged down the first taxi.

Back at the apartment she made herself a large G and T and went out on the balcony trying to collect her thoughts.

'What the hell just happened?'

She took large sips from the glass.

She had been so relieved when Laurel had spoken openly to her about everything, she had finally felt that she had a confidante, an ally. Then, thanks to that bloody stupid bird, everything had changed, she was now the devil incarnate, she had more large gulps of the icy fresh gin and tonic.

She had read somewhere recently that gin, or was it tonic, she couldn't remember which, had medicinal properties, so consoling herself with that fact she decided to top up her half empty glass.

She looked down at her arm, the plaster was now more of a grubby grey colour and on it in red felt pen was Rob's smudged scribbled autograph next to a crude doodle of a penis which looked more like a space rocket - or was it a space rocket that looked more like a penis! - That he had romantically drawn for her.

Rob! She needed to talk to him, to hear his voice, she took a few more large sips and emptied the glass. The doctor had told her it was best not to drink with the tablets she was on, but surely one and a bit G and T's couldn't hurt?

She stood up, and feeling a bit giddy, and walked slowly over to the door.

'Where's the phone?'

She then walked unsteadily over to the table, picked up the receiver and dialled the operator.

"Hello, operator, operator, I need the number for the..."

She stopped, 'What the hell was the name of the hotel he was staying in?' He had told her, the other night while they were having dinner, what was it? Oh yes.'

"The Park Royal or Royal Park Hotel, Sydney, or something like that."

She was now feeling really rather drunk and lightheaded.

"I'm sorry," came the voice from the other end of the phone, "There is no Park Royal or Royal Park Hotel in Sydney."

"That's impossible, it was one of those I'm sure. Sydney, in Australia, look again."

"Sorry, there's no number for this hotel."

And the line went dead.

'What an idiot!'

She dug out the address book from the drawer underneath and with some difficulty, flipped through the pages until she got to 'T.'

'Tony... Trout, who the hell was Trout? And Tim.'

She stared hard at the number written on the page until it came into focus and began to dial.

On the third attempt, after two previously misdialled calls to some irate gentlemen who had told her rather unkindly to 'be bloody careful what she was bloody doing,' the phone rang again and this time, after the second ring, it was answered by Alison's amah.

"Hello, Phillips residence, can I help you please?"

"Hello, yes, this is Melissa, Melissa Harrison, can I speak to Alison please?"

"One moment Miss please."

Mel heard the sound of the phone being laid down and then distant female voices.

After a short time the phone was picked up again.

"Hello, I'm sorry Mrs. Alison is very busy at the moment, she asked if she could call you back in a short while."

Mel heard the sound of the female voices, again, she strained to hear what they were saying. Alison's voice was distinct and then the other, to her horror, she realised belonged to Laurel.

"Yes of course, I'll be in all evening. Thank you."

She put down the receiver and sat uneasily on the arm of the sofa.

'What was Laurel doing there? She was supposed to be meeting Tony! Surely she wasn't telling her everything? She wouldn't!'

Mel slid down onto the seat and curled up in a ball, just as she began feeling sleepy and her eyes were getting heavy the phone rang.

Mel jumped up and, swaying slightly from side to side, like she was attempting to cross the deck of a ship, went to answer it.

"Hello Rob? Is that you?"

Her voice was slurred and the imaginary ship, on which she was sailing, had run into rougher seas.

"Hello, it's Alison, I'm returning your call."

"Oh, hello Alison, it's Mel."

"Yes I know Mel, I called you remember? Are you okay? You sound a bit odd."

"Yes, I think so, I just feel a bit tired. How are you?"

"I'm fine thank you Melissa. Now, listen to me carefully," she said in her serious headmistress voice, "Laurel was here before, she came to tell me that you went round to see her today."

"Yes, I…"

"She also told me that you insisted on talking to her about the last dinner party and all of the shenanigans you caused and she also said you were virtually hysterical and accused practically everyone of all sorts of terrible things, and that finally, she was forced in the end to ask you to leave."

"But I..."

"Well I'm calling because that just can't happen Melissa, you know the rules, I explained them carefully to you. We don't discuss anything outside of those evenings, I explained that" she repeated harshly.

"I only wanted to say that..."

"The rules have to be adhered to very strictly otherwise the whole system falls apart. You have to understand that your behaviour is just not acceptable and that you can't go around accusing people of things and bad mouthing people. I'm sorry to do this on the phone Melissa but the group must be protected and you're a loose cannon, therefore for the remainder of your time here in Singapore it's better if you stay away from us, from *all* of us."

At that moment the money in Mel's patience meter ran out.

"Alison I didn't start discussing *anything*, that was Laurel. I went over to see her just to catch up and have some company while Rob was away. I had no intention of discussing that evening, that disgusting twisted pig or any of your disgusting twisted dinner parties."

She was enraged, screaming down the phone, now it was her turn to let out all her frustrations.

From the other end of the phone there was silence.

She was on a roll and the alcohol was giving her courage so she continued,

"What is wrong with you people? You act all prim and proper with your posh pool parties and your expensive monogrammed clothes, but you're all fucked up, this whole situation is all fucked up."

Alison cleared her throat, her voice remaining calm and severe,

"I always had an inkling that it was going to be a bad idea to let you into the group, but Tim, for some reason that God only knows, insisted that it would be okay. Neither of you are really 'our kind of people' and you obviously have problems Melissa which desperately need addressing. If I were you I would seriously consider therapy, anger management therapy for starters."

That was the last straw, she wasn't going to let the Stellas and the Alisons of this world bully her any more.

"I don't need any bloody anger management therapy."

She was struggling to keep her voice calm so as not to prove Alison's point, but it was difficult as she was hurt and angry, very angry.

"But thanks to you lot" she continued, "and your sick, shagging get togethers I probably do need some kind of therapy *now*! And what's more, if you were any decent kind of wife and took as much care over your husband as you do over your fancy food preparation then maybe Tim wouldn't have needed to start this swapping club in the first place would he?"

That was a low blow and Melissa knew it, but she was trapped in a corner and was fighting back with all her strength.

"And if you were a decent girlfriend Melissa my dear, then your ridiculous, loud mouthed Robert wouldn't be shacked up in some hotel in Penang with Christina right now would he!"

The clicking sound signalled the end of the conversation.

Mel continued holding the phone to her ear, unable to move.

Chapter 28

Melissa leaned back against the wall, the beeping phone still pressed firmly to her ear. That couldn't be true, could it? He wouldn't do that to her. Not after everything else, not after everything she had been through to stay there with him?

Her mind danced around from one scene to another. She flashed back to Alison's pool party, she had noticed Rob talking to Christina for a while in the kitchen and he *had* looked a little strange when she walked in, but then in true Rob style, he was very drunk.

Then there was the dinner dance, he had been standing with her at the bar when she had gone in to find him, but they weren't alone, there had been a group of other people standing with him.

She stood up straight and put the phone back on the hook.

She was still feeling quite drunk so she went through to the bedroom, switched on the ceiling fan and lay below it, staring at it going around and around but that just made the whole room start to spin. Mel closed her eyes tightly and rolled onto her side, she placed one bare foot on the cool floor to try and stop the spinning sensation and the room ground slowly to a halt.

She couldn't believe what Alison had said, why would she be so cruel? She must be lying, Rob had spent so long the other night telling her about his itinerary for the weekend. He had gone into fine detail about what the company had planned for him, a lot of detail, maybe too much now she thought about it.

Oh why couldn't she remember the name of the hotel! She had to phone Rob to speak to him, she was sure when she heard his voice she would know it was just a malicious lie. But how to get the damn number? Someone must know the name of the stupid hotel in Sydney where he is staying, surely! She could call the office in Sydney, directory enquiries were bound to have that number.

She looked at the alarm clock on the bedside table, five twenty.

'Was Sydney two or three hours ahead?'

Either way that that meant it was seven or eight twenty there. Damn, probably everyone would have gone home at this time on a Friday. Then Mel had an idea, Harry, Harry would know, he went out with Rob on Wednesday, Rob would probably have told him then, she remembered he had said it was really posh and Rob did like to boast.

She struggled to her feet and went back into the living room.

She found the address book on the sofa and opened it at H. There was just one name, 'Harry' and in brackets, (Tess).

She wasn't really up to talking to her but desperate times call for desperate measures. She began to dial, she was hoping that Alison or Laurel hadn't spoken to Tess already, but knowing how close these women were she found that difficult to believe.

It began to ring, first, second, third... 'Oh come on!' … fourth, she was just about to hang up when she heard a voice.

"Hello, Harry Reese."

She signed heavily,

"Hello, is someone there?"

"Oh Harry, hi, it's Mel, I wasn't expecting you to be home," her voice was shaky.

"No I've taken a half day off for a medical check-up for the insurance company. If you're looking for Tess she's not here, she went out a short while ago for sunset drinks with Alison, I think she said it was."

What the hell were sunset drinks? Mel felt her ears physically burning.

"No, I'm sorry to bother you but I need the name of the hotel where Rob is staying, do you happen to know the name of it?"

There was silence from the other end.

"Hello, Harry are you there?"

"Yes I'm here, no sorry Mel I don't have the name of the hotel, he didn't tell me I'm afraid."

Mel began to panic, she sensed that Harry wasn't being honest with her.

"Harry please, if you know where he is please tell me, I need to speak to him, I need to speak to him *now*!"

"Mel, have you been drinking? You shouldn't be drinking if you're taking painkillers."

"God, who are you, my mother!" She yelled.

"Mel calm down, I'm just trying to help you."

"Well if you want to help me you'll give me the name of the bloody hotel where he's staying." Mel began crying into the phone.

"Mel, I think you should get some sleep, tomorrow morning I've got to nip back to the office to pick up some stuff, I'll hunt around and try and find out the name for you. I'm sure he'll call you this evening, then you can ask him yourself."

Mel was still sobbing hard and was unable to speak.

"Good night Mel, get some rest."

She walked, dazed, back into the bedroom.

The image of Christina pulling up at the airport was playing over and over again like a stuck mental record.

Punching a pillow hard with her good fist she picked it up and launched it against the chest of drawers which rattled violently causing the photos perched on top to fall over. She screamed out loud and grabbed the remaining pillow, that too was thrown with force in the direction of the chest of drawers. It first hit the wall, causing the photo of Raffles to fall, which on its rapid descent hit the table lamp dead centre, knocking it to the floor where it smashed into several pieces along with the glass picture frame.

She sat on the bed panting heavily from the exertion of her outburst, her tears were slowing to a steady trickle. She struggled out of her skirt and threw it down onto the floor. Even the simplest of tasks, like getting undressed, were so difficult with her wrist in plaster.

She swung her legs round so she was in a lying position, cursing as she did so, at the self-inflicted lack of pillows.

Her nose was running so she grabbed the box of tissues on the bedside table and putting her hand inside she discovered it was empty. She hunted around and found an old, used tissue down the back of the bed, she teased it open, blew her nose hard on it and then discarded it on the floor with the clothing and broken pottery.

She was so tired, her eyes were heavy and she needed to sleep. She laid back down on the still pillow-less bed, curled up in a tight ball and closed her eyes. This time, to Mel's relief, the room didn't spin, her stomach hurt though and it was tied up in tight knots.

After a few minutes with the picture of Christine's arrival at the airport still vividly implanted in her mind, she drifted off to sleep.

When Mel opened her eyes she heard the phone ringing, she got up quickly and went to answer it. As she approached the living room she realised it wasn't the sound of the phone but of the gate buzzer.

She looked at the clock, five past six, she had only been asleep for half an hour.

She walked over cautiously to the small white handset attached to the wall and stood for a while wondering if she should pick it up. What if it was Alison and her gang coming to have another go at her? It buzzed again, twice. She reached for the handset.

"Hello, who is it?" she asked timidly.

"Mel, it's Harry, can I come up? I need to talk to you."

She glimpsed at her reflection in the mirror on the wall next to the handset, what a mess!

"Oh Harry, sorry, it's not really a good time right now."

"Please, it won't take long, and I want to make sure you're OK."

"I'm fine."

"I don't think you are."

"All right, come up."

She pressed the button that opened the gate.

Quickly she dashed into the bathroom and brushed through her hair, which was damp and matted on one side from the salty tears. Then she splashed her face and wiped the mascara smudges from underneath. Finally she squirted some perfume onto her chest and neck and noticing she had one breast half hanging out adjusted her tube top accordingly. Bras were not possible when she was alone, she struggled to do them up with two hands let alone with one!

Retrieving her skirt from the floor, she shook it to make sure there were no bits of glass on it and slipped it on. Just as she did so the doorbell rang.

Running back into the living room, she stopped, composed herself, took another quick glance at her reflection, which was noticeably better, and opened the door.

Harry was stood there in all his glory. He was wearing a blue linen shirt open at the neck and white linen trousers. Mel stood transfixed for a second.

"Can I come in Melissa?"

"Oh, yes of course, sorry." She stepped to one side to allow him to pass.

"Please take a seat", she pointed the way to the sofa, wondering why people always did that, it takes up most of the room, you can hardly miss it!

"Can I get you something to drink Harry?" she offered.

"A cold beer if you have one would be good."

Mel walked a few steps and wobbled slightly.

"Are you all right Mel? Why don't you sit down and I'll get the beer if you like."

"No, no, it's fine, really I'm okay."

She continued on to the kitchen. Opening the fridge door she found a bottle of Tiger beer wedged in between the Perrier water and the mango juice.

"We've got a Tiger beer" she shouted from the kitchen through to the living room.

"That's fine," came a voice from the doorway of the kitchen. "No need to shout!" he smiled.

Mel smiled back.

"Here," she handed him the bottle, "you'll have to open it yourself I'm afraid, I can't work bottle openers with one hand, it's over there in the top drawer."

Harry walked over to the drawer and took out the opener.

"How is your wrist by the way?"

"Okay, I think, it aches a lot but I'm used to it. I really miss swimming though, and I have to wrap it in a carrier bag when I take a shower, which is at least twice a day! I can have the cast taken off in another three or four weeks the doctor said."

"That's good," said Harry sympathetically, taking a large swig from the bottle. He picked up a pen from the side and went back over to where Mel was standing. Gently he took hold of her arm and drew a quick but very accurate sketch of an orchid on her cast then underneath he wrote 'Beauty and the Beasts.'

"So you'll also remember the good things about this place."

Mel was now aware she was staring at him, the smell of his aftershave was stirring up memories and not only S The image of them together reflected in that mirror was etched firmly on her brain. She suddenly felt very self-conscious and a little ridiculous. How could she have a normal conversation with him after that evening? How could she be expected to pretend nothing had happened?

She hadn't felt this awkward seeing someone she had had sex with since her disastrous 'first time' one night stand with Tom at Stella's birthday party three years ago. He was the head boy in the last year of the sixth form at St. Stephen's School and along with Simon Le Bon had been the subject of all the girls' fantasies, and much to Mel's delight, during the party he had very kindly offered to relieve her of the burden of her virginity. He was the most popular boy in the school so how could she refuse!

The night that should have been a dream come true ended very badly when, during a very critical part of the proceedings, she had suddenly felt the full effects of all the cheap cider she had drunk during the evening.

Needless to say after vomiting all over his clothes, which were unfortunately right there on the floor next to the bed in the target zone, he didn't ever speak to her again, and for a while she was known as the "vomiting virgin." She had since decided it had been a kind of divine punishment for being so superficial and easy.

At the time she thought that that was the worst thing that would ever happen to her with a man in bed, now she realised she had been wrong.

"Mel, Mel,"

She snapped out of her trance-like state.

"Listen Mel, I came here to talk to you about something important, let's go back through to the lounge."

His voice had changed and had become serious and cold, a cold that cut right through her, making her physically shudder.

Mel, now filled with dread, poured some neat gin into a glass and took a swig. Harry went to say something but Mel's expression stopped him in his tracks. She led the way back to the lounge and slumped down at one end of the sofa, Harry strategically sat himself down at the other end.

Chapter 29

For a few minutes there was an awkward silence.

"So," said Mel eventually, "let's get this over and done with. What do you know? What do you need to talk to me so urgently about?"

"Okay." He moved a little closer to her. Her heart was pounding and she was trying to prepare herself for whatever was coming next.

"I just think that you should know the truth about a few things."

He continued "I like you Melissa and I don't like to see you being made a fool of, you don't deserve it."

Mel sat up straight,

"What's going on? Does this have something to do with Rob being in Australia?"

Harry looked awkwardly down at the floor for a while before answering. Mel was at breaking point.

Harry reached for his beer but knocked it over, spilling the contents out onto the table which began dripping onto the floor.

"I'm so sorry, I'll get a cloth," he said apologetically, and went to stand up.

"Sit down, leave it! Shit Harry, tell me what the hell is going on, please!"

"Okay, but try to let me finish and above all try to stay calm."

He took a deep breath, Mel did the same.

"Rob's not in Australia Mel, he's in Penang, he's in Penang with Christine, the HR manager."

"I know who Christine bloody well is!" she shouted.

"Try to stay calm Mel, I know this is difficult but please try. Tess told me about your outburst today, and I need you to keep it together."

Mel was too preoccupied thinking about Rob to respond to the comment about today's outbursts.

"The raffle!" The realisation came flooding in. "The bloody raffle ticket, the one that *he* picked out! So it was all fixed. What a bastard."

She was struggling to keep it together and had a desperate urge to punch someone, hard!

"No it wasn't fixed, how could he have known which tickets were hers? It would have been impossible, there were hundreds of them and he didn't put them in the bowl, Alison and Debbie did that."

"Well it doesn't matter how she came by the winning ticket but he certainly took advantage of the situation. How long has he been shagging that bitch?"

"Mel, I can't go into detail about any of this, I just wanted you to know what was going on."

His voice softened slightly. "He does love you, he told me, he's just being a bit of an immature prick right now. The best thing that can happen is that you two go to Sydney together, get away from here, from her and from us."

He moved a bit closer to her, there was now just a small space between them.

"He doesn't love me, if he did he wouldn't be there with her, he'd be here with me." She felt the tears welling up. "All I do here is cry, I'm so pathetic."

"No you're not Mel, you're not pathetic, you're just naive and vulnerable but that can change, you can change."

"We're supposed to be getting married, that's a bloody joke! I'm not going to marry him now."

She finished the neat gin.

"I know you're getting married, that was Malcolm's idea."

Mel almost vomited, she clapped her hand over her mouth to keep it down. On seeing her reaction, Harry, realising that he had said too much, rephrased his devastating statement.

"Well not exactly his idea but while you were in the hospital he told Rob to do whatever it took to keep you happy and get you away from Singapore."

"Oh great, It just gets better and better!" she yelled.

"But he wants to marry you Mel, he spoke to me a few days ago and said that he was glad Malcolm convinced him. He's sure he'll change once you're married. He'll calm down."

"Oh bullshit Harry, you know that's crap, no one can change overnight."

He reached over and took hold of her left hand.

"Just think about it Mel, everything that goes on here, it poisons you, it takes away the boundaries and compromises your judgement."

She looked up at Harry, at this beautiful sexy man sitting before her on the sofa, this man that had kissed almost every inch of her body passionately while he had taken her to fantastical places that she had never been to before.

His aftershave was wafting through the air and his words were echoing in her head; 'It takes away the boundaries, it compromises your judgement.'

What was he trying to tell her? Her head was swimming in deep, dark waters. She was imagining Rob and Christine making love on an exotic beach, the warm waves crashing over them and she was seething with jealousy. He was cheating on her with that skinny, and rather plain looking, bitch. After all the humiliation she had been through thanks to his idea of participating in the wife swapping. She had a broken wrist for Christ's sake as a direct result of his insistence on them taking part in those warped dinner parties. Wasn't that enough? He also had to leave her alone, injured and in pain to jet off with his bloody colleague!

Without thinking, in one quick move, she grabbed Harry's hand that was gently holding hers and placed it on her thigh under her skirt, she leaned in and kissed him passionately, biting him on the bottom lip. He jumped with surprise and pain and pulled his hand back, then he broke free from her kiss.

"Mel, what are you doing?"

He wiped his index finger along his lip and checked for blood.

"This isn't what I meant and this isn't the way to solve anything."

Now, reaching a dangerously high level of revengeful lust, she had become insistent, she put her hand on his crotch area and squeezed hard. Harry jumped again. She went to kiss him again on the lips but he dodged her advance.

"I want you Harry, take me again like you did before, I know that you want to, kiss me!"

She moved in again to kiss him and this time he moved towards her. He put his hands on her cheeks and kissed her back passionately, her mouth opened to allow his tongue inside.

Her plaster cast was getting in the way and making manoeuvring difficult so she slid off the couch and onto her knees.

She plunged her head into his lap and bit lightly on his hardening penis but again he resisted.

"No, Mel stop, this is wrong, please stop."

He pushed her head away.

"You don't want me to stop otherwise you wouldn't have kissed me like that, I can see that you're turned on Harry."

Her hand was kneading the bulge in his trousers. He closed his eyes and tipped his head backwards. Mel smiled, he seemed to be giving in to the situation.

"We can have some fun together Harry, no one has to know, it'll just be our secret." Mel's voice was at its most seductive.

She watched his chest rising as his breathing got deeper and she slowly unzipped his trousers, not an easy task with only one hand, but just as her fingers began to slip inside he blocked her hand forcefully.

"Mel, no!" Now he was the one shouting. "Stop it, this won't solve anything, I don't want to do this now, I can't do this now."

He released the grip on her hand.

"I'm married to Tess. I know, considering what goes on here, it's hard for you to understand, but that's how it is. What happened between us was fun, it was nice but it was just part of the game, that's all it is - a game. It's not about feelings Melissa, it's not real."

She stopped and sat up staring into his eyes once again trying to take in his words and read his real thoughts. To her dismay the cold eyes that were staring back were telling her that he was speaking the truth. How could that not have been real? It certainly felt real, very real.

"I don't believe you Harry, I don't care what you say, you want me."

"Mel, I don't want you, I just got carried away. I'm sorry."

God, she felt so stupid, she had made such a terrible fool of herself.

Mel turned her head away in shame.

"Mel, look at me and listen to me please. You're a lovely girl, you're attractive, witty and sexy but I'm married and almost eleven years older than you. You don't really want me, you're just pissed off with Rob and want to get your own back at him by screwing me, and that may well work for a few hours, but then what? You don't need any more complications in your life."

Her face was still turned away. Gently he turned her head so she was facing him but her eyes remained looking down.

"I don't know what's real and what's not anymore," she was tearing up. "I don't know who to trust. My life is such a bloody ridiculous mess."

"Mel from what I've heard about you, your life was a mess also before. But you're stronger now, a bit older and hopefully a bit wiser."

Her eyes were still firmly fixed on the floor.

"You have to have a solid relationship and be very self-confident to engage in the things that we do here.

Go to Sydney with Rob, don't tell him you know about Christine, just go there and you'll see that things will be better."

"I don't know if I can, he's cheated on me, he's lied to me."

"Yes he has, but you'll get through this, sometimes not everything needs to be dragged out into the open."

Mel looked up at this man who was in her apartment, it wasn't just revenge, she wanted him to do all those

279

things to her again, she wanted to feel all those things again.

As if reading her thoughts Harry spoke.

"Mel, as I said before, you really don't need any more complications right now and neither do I. Think about what I said and consider the alternative. If this ends, if you create a scene and finish with him you'll end up back in the UK, alone. Is that what you really want Mel, is it?"

"Why did you come here this evening Harry? Why did you tell me everything if you didn't want me to do anything about it?"

"I told you, I just thought you should know, I wanted to give you the facts so you could deal with it, so you wouldn't be left in the dark. Now you can plan accordingly. Don't be so permissive, insist he comes home more and don't always suffer in silence."

"I don't always suffer in silence," she said indignantly, "but he's busy with work and I don't like to interfere."

Harry looked over at Mel and shook his head.

"One thing he said to me was that he didn't have to lie too much about where he had been and what he'd been up to because you never ask too many questions."

Mel went to protest but then stopped and realised that he was right. She didn't ask much, she was just happily enjoying being there in Singapore.

Why didn't she ask more? Did she even really care where he was?"

"I was sure you would see sense," Harry continued, "So, can you Mel? Can you see sense? Come on, you haven't been through all this to give up now surely, to lose to Christina, the office bike!"

She couldn't answer him, she just walked over to the balcony and stared out at the setting sun which had turned the sea to liquid gold.

Inside the apartment the phone was ringing.

"Mel, it's the phone, aren't you going to answer it? I should be going."

Reluctantly she came back into the room and picked up the receiver.

"Mel, hi babe, it's Rob, how are you feeling?"

"Rob," she replied, looking nervously over at Harry, "Just a second."

Mel held the handset close into her chest to try to block out any sound and Harry immediately stood up and walked over towards the front door. As he opened the door he stopped and checked his bottom lip in the mirror and combed his fingers through his hair, then he turned and half whispering half mouthing,

"Don't screw this up Mel, take advantage of having the upper hand for once."

He gave a half smile, winked slowly and disappeared through the open door closing it quietly behind him.

In a split second Mel had to make yet another difficult decision, what was it to be; Harry's advice or her first instinct to scream, shout and jeopardise everything once again? "Hey you, here I am, sorry about that, how great to hear your voice."

Chapter 30

"So how's Sydney? How's life down under?"

She was surprised that she was managing to sound quite cheery and relaxed.

"What's wrong Mel? You sound a bit upset, is everything okay there?"

So much for sounding cheery and relaxed.

"No fine, it's nothing, I just feel a bit lonely today and pissed off with this stupid wrist that throbs all the time and stops me from using the pool."

"I know it's difficult but it's just for a few more weeks then they'll take the cast off, try to grin and bear it. And as for you being lonely Mel, you know I wouldn't leave you unless it was really important, business is business."

Mel was now struggling to maintain her composure.

"Excuse me a second again Rob, there's a cockroach running around on the loose and pissing me off and I need to kill it."

She clapped the handset once again tightly to her chest and let out a silent scream. Oh damn, this was so hard, she wanted to yell down the phone at him... 'Lying wanker, cheating bastard,'

"Mel are you there? I have to go, some of my colleagues are waiting for me in the lobby of the hotel to take me to dinner. The guys in the office here are brilliant, so nice and such a laugh."

"Aaaahhh!" she let out a small scream,

"Got it!" she said quickly, stamping her foot down on the floor to reinforce her alibi.

"Sounds like you're having fun," she said, screwing up her eyes and leaning back against the wall.

"You sound like you're having fun there yourself. Yes it's good, but tiring, lots of heavy meetings. I'll call you again tomorrow probably around the same time, will you be home?"

"Of course, where else would I be?"

"Why don't you give Alison or Debbie a call, I'm sure one of them would have you over for dinner."

"I'm fine Robert, I'm a big girl, I can look after myself."

"Robert! If you're calling me Robert then you're not fine. I'll make it up to you when I get home, I promise. Have a nice evening, speak to you again tomorrow, gotta go now, kisses all over."

"Rob, wait, what's the name of the Ho..." But the phone went dead. "...tel."

She just wanted to ask him out of curiosity to see how rehearsed he really was.

She reached for her glass on the coffee table, drained the contents and then threw it with all her strength at the wall. It shattered into a thousand pieces sending little bits of glass flying everywhere.

She was going to have to learn to control her temper otherwise she was going to end up in an apartment that was totally empty except for cushions and pillows, not to mention that she could do herself or someone else real harm one day.

She had to talk to someone that wasn't there, someone in the UK. But who? Who could she trust to be honest with her, who wouldn't judge her, or worry?

There wasn't anyone, not really anyone who fitted into that category. Then she had an idea; Alan, he had always been honest with her, she could talk to him, not about everything but she could ask his advice about this. He was very down to earth and always called 'a spade a bloody shovel!'

She checked the time, it was now almost eight o'clock here so it was almost one o'clock there, perfect. As a creature of habit he always had lunch at home at twelve thirty.

"Hello Alan," she said nervously as he picked up the phone, "it's Mel,"

"Who?" came the reply.

"Mel, Rob's Mel!" That now had an ironic ring to it.

"Yes I know, I'm just winding you up, how are you love? How's it going?"

It was so nice to hear a friendly, familiar voice and Mel fought hard to hold back the tears.

"Oh Alan, I'm sorry to call you like this but I don't know what to do."

"What's that idiot son of mine been up to now? What's goin' on?"

Mel was now crying audibly.

"Mel, don't cry love, tell me what's wrong. Hang on I'm just going to light up."

Mel heard the unmistakable sound of a match being struck and a long puff being taken.

"Right that's better, now where were we, oh yes, my idiot son."

"Alan, Rob's in Penang with another woman, he's gone there with her while pretending to be in Sydney on business sorting out his contract and our apartment for when we move over there and I don't know what to do about it."

There was silence on the other end of the phone except for the sound of another drag being taken on the cigarette followed by deep chesty coughing.

"Mel love, listen to me carefully," he said eventually, "I can't say I'm surprised. You're both young, really young and immature, Rob especially. He's my son and I love him but he's an idiot. You're a great girl and he's lucky to have you, he just doesn't realise it yet, but he will, it's just up to you whether it'll be too late."

"I don't know if I can trust him again."

"Trust is overrated, nobody should really trust anybody. You just need to keep your wits about you."

"So you think I should go to Sydney with him?"

"Mel, I can't tell you what to do, but I can ask you this;

What can you see from your window? Right now what can you see?"

Mel stood up and looked out.

"Well it's dark but there is an almost full moon that's reflecting on the sea and the lights are all on on the tennis courts and in the pool downstairs."

"Okay, and shall I tell you what I can see. There's Mrs. Willis walking in the drizzling rain with her ridiculously small dog who is at this moment crapping on the pavement, a car at the end of the street has had all four of its wheels surgically removed and is now stranded on bricks where it will probably remain until someone sets fire to it and, across from me, some bastard has spray painted the words 'Maggie Thatcher sucks dicks' on the wall in letters three feet high!"

Mel sighed. "I know it's lovely here and it'll be lovely there in Sydney too I'm sure but I really don't know what to do."

"Mel I think you should go to Sydney, give him some time to grow up a bit, and you'll see that things will work out all right, and hell, if they don't you can always come home and I'll buy you a plastic rain hat just like Mrs. Willis'"

They were both laughing. Alan began coughing heavily again.

"Thanks Alan, I'll let you get back to your lunch, you should go and see someone about that cough. I'll speak to you soon hopefully."

"Yes all right and I'm watching the cricket highlights on the news. Oh I almost forgot, I saw your mum at the market the other day, we had a bit of a chat, don't worry she's doing fine without you, coping quite nicely. She's a good looking woman!"

"Yes she is, if you see her again don't mention that we spoke about this please Alan."

"Of course not, ohhhh he should have caught that," he said, commenting on the game. "Bye Mel, good luck love."

Looking around she saw carnage, there was spilt beer on the table and a puddle of it on the floor and there were small pieces of broken glass on everything.

She slipped on her flip flops and passed the hoover around the living room trying to get up all the pieces of glass. She had difficulty moving the furniture one handed but she managed. Then she went through into the bedroom and cleaned up the mess in there.

When she had finished it was still quite early but Mel decided to get ready for bed.

She went into the bathroom and undressed, she was physically and emotionally drained. She took hold of the plastic bag that she left on the side and slid it over the plaster cast, then with the elastic band she sealed it at the level of her forearm to keep the water out.

She opened the tap and the cold water ran over her, causing her to gasp. That felt so nice. She was really uncomfortable with the temperature, it was lucky she would be leaving soon.

She finished showering quickly, deciding to leave washing her hair until the next day. Nobody was going to see it after all.

She quickly grabbed the towel and with the aid of her teeth holding one end she managed to wrap it, albeit badly, around her. She walked out of the bedroom and into the front room, leaving wet footprints in her wake, she went to check if the front door was locked. Satisfied that it was, she went to walk back across to the bedroom. She screamed as her right, bare foot fell victim to a shard of glass that had gone unnoticed over by the bedroom door.

"Ow, ow, ow," she hopped across the room until she reached the safety of the bed, her foot was bleeding quite a lot and she saw she had left a little trail of blood behind her. Looking down, she saw it was a rather large shard of glass that was sticking out of her foot. She reached over to the bedside table and grabbed the eyebrow tweezers that she kept there in the drawer. Then she grabbed hold of the glass and pulled, it slid out easily, Mel looked down, shocked at the size of the piece. The blood flowed faster now from the wound and she shook her towel loose from around her and wrapped it tightly around her foot. She lay back on the bed panting heavily from the exertion. She didn't know if she should laugh or cry, so she did both.

She lay there naked enjoying the feeling of being cooled by the fan. Her wrist and foot were now throbbing and she was feeling desperately sorry for herself.

She wanted to sleep but her mind was full of images of Rob and Christina.

'What a bitch, and an ugly bitch at that. She was better looking than her, wasn't she?' She looked down at her young firm body. God, Christina had to have been at least thirty five years old and had never been married, what does he see in her?

She looked down again at her body with her pert breasts and shapely thighs. Harry had appreciated her, for a few hours anyway. Harry!

Her hand moved skilfully across her breasts and slid down her stomach to her parting thighs.

She laid back and closed her eyes,

'Harry you came back, I knew you would. Take me again now', she whispered seductively.

Chapter 31

The next morning Mel awoke to a strange noise. She got up and looked outside, it was pouring hard, the sea was almost obscured by the heavy curtain of rain. The sky was dark grey and menacing, and the palm trees down in the garden were bowing to each other in the wind and she stood transfixed at the scene below. She had almost forgotten what real rain looked like. Since her arrival, just three and a half months earlier, she had only seen a couple of light, welcoming showers arrive briefly in the evening.

Mel walked a few steps and winced at the sharp pain in the sole of her foot, she had a horrible feeling that there might still be a piece of glass in it.

She slipped on her flip-flops and a t shirt and went into the living room where she opened the balcony door slightly and a breeze blew in, she stood facing the oncoming weather, enjoying the rare experience of the cool wet wind.

Closing the window shut with some effort she noticed the team of groundsmen downstairs around the pool, that morning they were all dressed in bright yellow rain macs and were running around frantically moving tables and stacking sun loungers.

Finally! She wouldn't have to feel bad about not being able to use the pool today, this instantly gave her a sense of relief and she felt herself relaxing.

The rest of the day dragged, she tried to keep any thoughts of Rob and Christine away by immersing herself in a good book. She stopped reading only when the sound of her growling stomach distracted her from the pages.

The rain eventually stopped at about five o'clock and the clouds cleared away just in time to permit a spectacular sunset, the sky was filled with dozens of vivid colours. Mel wished she was an artist so that she could do something creative and capture its beauty on canvas.

When she got to Sydney, *if* she got to Sydney, she would look into a painting course until she found a job, hope springs eternal! She thought.

Still dressed in just a t shirt and having spent the majority of the day on the sofa, feeling cool and reading in silence with the TV switched off she felt strangely and inappropriately at peace with the world.

The phone rang at half past nine, shattering her 'utopian state.'

"Hello?"

"Hi Mel, it's Rob, oh shit sorry, what time is it? Did I wake you?"

She cleared her throat, her voice was a bit hoarse, she hadn't spoken all day and she still had 'morning throat'.

Rob, on the other hand, was clearly drunk.

"No, you didn't wake me, it's only nine thirty here. So how's Sydney today?"

She was aware that her tone was sarcastic, but she figured he was too drunk to notice, and in fact she was right.

"Oh it's amazing, you'll love it, really interesting, and everyone is so friendly. My colleagues took me on a boat trip today, we went past the Opera House. It's lovely, big, white, very impressive."

"Listen Rob, you sound like your colleagues have been maybe over friendly today, you're really drunk. Call me tomorrow evening again if you get the chance."

She couldn't deal with hearing one more lie about Sydney and his made up boat trips.

"Okay Mel I will, I'll call you tomorrow, I should probably get to bed now, I've got another long day tomorrow."

She swore she heard a female giggle in the background.

"Good night Rob, sleep tight." She slammed the phone down. 'You cheating wanker!

Somebody please remind me why I'm doing this again!

The next evening's call was pretty much the same only it came at eleven o'clock and he did wake her up this time. He sounded a little drunk but nothing like the night before.

"Listen, I just wanted to say that there's no need to come and meet me at the airport tomorrow, you stay at home and put a bottle on ice, the plane lands at eight, if all goes to plan I'll be home around nine like I said."

"But really Rob, it's no trouble to come, I could do with the change of scenery, perhaps we could stop off on the way home and get a drink somewhere and you can tell me all about our new home?"

She could sense him cringing at the other end. Mel actually had no intention of going to meet him at the airport but she wanted him to suffer.

"No, don't worry, I'll jump in a cab and be back in a flash. Can we give the going for a drink a miss, d'you mind? I'm knackered, this trip has been non-stop."

"Yes of course you poor thing, sorry I didn't think Rob, I'll just wait here for you."

She felt her hand clenching and her blood was at boiling point.

"Right, I have to get back to sleep myself, sitting around the house all day doing nothing can really take it out of you and I must have turned a hundred pages today."

She managed a small titter.

"Rob, listen before you go, say something to me."

"What, say what to you?"

"You know, something dirty, like you used to when you'd call me from London and you'd tell me what you were going to do to me when you saw me, you remember."

"Mel, it's late, I can't just come up with something just like that."

"Yes you can, you are good at it, the dirty talk, you remember. I need to hear what you're going to do to me when you see me. Come on, say it."

She was fake panting and sighing down the phone and making all sorts of 'oohs' and 'ahh' noises.

Right Robert, let's see just how uncomfortable we can make you shall we? She thought maliciously.

"I can't Mel, not now, I'm not in the mood, way too tired. I'll show you when I get home, it'll be much more fun."

"Oh, all right," she replied in her most dejected voice possible. "But you'd better bring me back the world's biggest stuffed Koala bear, like you promised" she added.

'Good bloody luck finding one of those in Penang!'

The next day Rob arrived home at ten past seven, he strolled in through the door looking more tanned and extremely tired.

"Surprise! I got an earlier flight."

Rob walked over and kissed her. Mel smiled, 'you sneaky bastard!' she thought, 'you had no intention of getting home at nine, you were just worried I would try to surprise you at the airport!'

She had been worrying all day about how she would keep herself calm while he was going on about all his pretend meetings, colleagues and apartments. It was easier on the phone, he couldn't see her contorted expressions, her pillow punching and seething post-call outbursts. But here in this flat, how was she going to contain all her anger? How would she be able to resist pushing him off the balcony?

So when the buzzer went she panicked, she wasn't good at doing 'the calm thing'.

She then had an idea, she decided she would do it for Harry, to prove to him that she was really mature. Rob was bound to go to work and tell him that she hadn't suspected a thing, that she'd believed every bastard lie that had come out of his cheating mouth. And then Harry would see that she had seen sense and was really a strong and rational woman.

When he walked in had been the moment of the biggest difficulty, seeing him there she had had the urge to run over and slap him hard across the face, like a bad old black and white film, but proudly she resisted.

He put his trolley bag down and walked over to her. He grabbed her firmly around the waist and kissed her passionately on the lips. He had never kissed her like that before.

"You're even more beautiful than when I left Melissa, I missed you."

She pulled back to look at him, he looked genuinely happy to see her, and his kiss was full of sincerity. She wondered what had brought about this change of behaviour. What had happened on his dirty weekend away to make him miss her?

"I love you Mel."

He was now standing there teary-eyed looking like a lost child.

He had never said that he loved her spontaneously before, what the hell had happened?

"Rob, you've only been gone three days, what's going on?"

Mel was genuinely confused, she had expected him to come back cooler and more aloof than usual, but he was quite the opposite.

"It's just that I realised how much you mean to me during these last few days, how lovely you really are and how lucky I am to have you."

"That's it", she laughed, "I'm taking you to A and E, you're obviously not well Rob, you must have caught some Kangaroo virus while you were there in Sydney."

"Listen, I look a mess, I had planned to get dressed up and look gorgeous for your arrival. Stay here while I go and get changed and freshen up a bit."

"Stay here," he said grabbing her hand as she walked past. "You look gorgeous as you are."

He gently pulled her down onto the chair.

"Mel, I need to tell you something," He looked worried.

Her heart skipped a beat, he was going to turn himself in! This wasn't expected at all.

How the hell should she react to his news? Should she admit that she already knew, or should she act all offended, hurt and angry and maybe take the opportunity to slap him round the face?

"Mel, I have something to confess."

Just then the phone began to ring, Mel stood up and went to answer it but Rob pulled her back.

"Don't answer it! Leave it, whoever it is they can call back."

His voice was panicky and he looked really worried.

Mel had to admit that she was enjoying seeing him so rattled, whatever had happened between him and Christina must have been pretty bad. That would teach him to bugger off for the weekend with another woman!

She broke free from his grip and walked over to the insistent phone.

"It might be Mum," she said, "I should get it, Rob."

She picked up the phone,

"Hello, hello?" There was no reply.

"Mel just put it down." He walked over to her, snatched the handset and put it back down.

At that moment Mel realised that he must be worried that it was Christina. The situation must have gotten out of hand.

She smiled to herself as 'fatal attraction' came to mind. They had gone to see the film together just after Christmas, scary stuff.

Oh my god, she smiled again, Rob had been away with a 'bunny boiler!'

She was revelling in the moment.

"So what do you need to confess Rob? Tell me all."

She was feeling strong, Harry had been right, having the upper hand for once was a good feeling.

His eyes were still fixed on the phone as he stood frozen to the spot.

He was in obvious difficulty, and Mel was loving every minute of it.

"I need to tell you that…" then he paused and shook his head, "that I wasn't able to get you your Koala bear, I wanted to get it at the airport but I arrived late to check in and had to dash through to the gate. Can you forgive me?"

His tone had changed to a childish drawl.

'What a bloody coward' she thought.

"I don't know Rob, it's a pretty serious offence, I'll have to think about it."

She was being playful but her words were serious. She *would* have to think about it, she didn't know if she could ever forgive him, she just hoped that with time she could forget.

"When we're in Sydney I'll buy you a hundred of them, I can't wait to show you the place, it's beautiful."

"Which reminds me Rob, did you have time to look for an apartment in amongst all your male-bonding crap!"

"Didn't have to, the guy that I'm replacing is leaving us his, it's right in Bondi Junction and it has a roof top Jacuzzi overlooking Bondi beach, how amazing is that!"

Mel had to admit that did sound pretty amazing, she smiled broadly.

"Oh wow! That sounds perfect Rob." She was such a pathetic push over! "So when do we leave?"

She was suddenly desperate to go, to get out of this place that had once held such promise and get away from all its bitter memories and crazy, messed up people.

"We leave a bit earlier than I thought, on the seventeenth of October, just about three weeks from now. That should give you just enough time to get things sorted."

"Rob, talking of getting things sorted, I've been thinking that maybe we shouldn't get married right now, I mean we've got the move and everything and when we get there I'll only have a couple of months to do everything, so I think we should wait a while, what do you think?"

He looked worried again,

"Mel, we need to be married to get you flights home and stuff. The apartment in Sydney is for a married couple's contract. They agreed to give me a married couple's contract because I told them we were getting married soon. How long were you thinking of postponing it for?"

She hadn't given it any thought, she just knew that she didn't feel ready to go through with it now.

"I don't know, I was thinking until the late spring or summer, May or June maybe. I would just like some more time to do it properly."

"I don't know, I'll have to ask, I have to go back over again on the ninth, just for a few days, to have more meetings and meet some more people. I can try and find out then."

You mean go over for the first time, for the real meeting, she thought angrily, and that is precisely why I need more time!

Chapter 32

The next two weeks she mainly spent sorting out their belongings and doing last minute furniture and ornament shopping. She had managed to accumulate a lot of stuff in the months she had been there but the company were paying for them to have a container shipped so it would be rude not to fill it and give them their money's worth, and besides, you can never have too many ceramic elephants!

Rob had gone off on his weekend to Sydney, this time she had checked his destination carefully. He had even written down the name of the hotel which she had rung the minute he had left for the airport to see if they had him down as a guest. The receptionist confirmed that he was booked in alone and that he had a non-smoking, single room with a shower and a view of the Harbour.

Things seemed to be going quite well, their relationship was good and they made love regularly. Passion had made a welcome return and they had found creative ways of doing things so that the plaster cast wasn't a problem. The only problem was that Mel had trouble getting the thought of Rob and Christina out of her head, the picture of them together would usually pop up just at the wrong time robbing her of her grand finale and forcing her often to fake it. She wondered why she never thought much about him with Alison or Tess, why the thought of them together, although unpleasant, didn't upset her like the thought of him with Christine, he had been to bed with them as well after all. What was different?

But what was different was the lying, she knew about the girls, it was part of the game, and let's face it, she had been playing herself.

No, the real issue was that he had probably lied to her for weeks about where he was and what he had been doing and then about his first apparent trip to Sydney; that wasn't a game, or a one night stand, *that* was an affair.

After that first call the phone had rung quite a few more times late in the evening and sometimes in the early hours of the morning but she'd always been met with silence on the few occasions when she had given in and picked up. If Rob was home he insisted that a phone call that late should be ignored, and he always made sure that she didn't answer it.

Then one evening, when Rob was in Sydney, Mel was going through the hundreds of photos they had accumulated and putting them neatly into albums. The phone rang again, she glanced at the clock and saw it was a quarter past eleven. Despite Rob's instructions to ignore it she wasn't able to leave it unanswered, she was worried that it could be her Mum who had never gotten the hang of the time difference.

"Hello, who's there?" But once again she was met by silence.

"Mr Nobody, okay, I'm putting the phone down."

She was just about to hang up when she heard a woman's voice.

"Melissa, it's Christina, from Rob's office."

She sounded drunk, Mel took a deep breath, 'You can do this,' she told herself, 'you're strong enough now'.

"Christina, it's late, what can I do for you?"

"Mel I want you to know something about your dick head fiancé, I think you should know a few facts about your precious Robert."

She was slurring strongly.

"Really Christine, what things would they be? The fact that he was with you in Penang last month and not in Sydney on business, or the fact that he came back from that weekend more in love with me than ever before?"

Christina began to cry into the phone.

"Not quite sure what you did, or rather didn't do while you were there but I think I should thank you, it was obviously just what he needed to come to his senses."

The sobbing grew louder.

"He's a shit!" she screamed, "He used me, screwed me all weekend and then told me on the flight home that he didn't want to see me anymore, that he wanted to marry you. Who the bloody hell does he think he is?"

This last outburst was a bit much for Mel to hear, she faltered slightly not knowing how to respond but then gathering her strength back up she continued.

"I agree that must have been terrible for you, but you're not seriously expecting sympathy from me are you? I'm afraid that's what happens when you decide to have affairs with other people's fiancés. Now you sound like you could do with some sleep, so go to bed Christina and leave us the hell alone."

Mel slumped onto the chair. She was shaking, half from rage half from excitement and her breathing was erratic.

She would never have thought herself capable of that kind of retort. She stood up, looked long and hard in the mirror and smiled at the woman staring back at her.

When Rob returned from his weekend he was full of genuine enthusiasm for Australia. She had even gotten her Koala.

"Oh my God Mel, every time I go there it just gets better and better and the apartment is just amazing, it has a bar in the corner of the living room with optics which they're leaving, not to mention a huge walk in wardrobe in the main bedroom."

He had her attention.

"Does it have a bath or shower?"

"Both, an enormous shower and the bath has a Jacuzzi thing in it! Oh by the way I also asked about putting back the date of the wedding and my new Boss, Doug, agreed to start treating us like a married couple as far as the contract is concerned, but we need to do it by June."

"Need to do it by June," she repeated, "wow, that's romantic" she reiterated sarcastically.

"Speaking of putting things off, let's not have a big leaving party Rob, I would prefer to just slip away quietly, I think with everything that's gone on here it would be better. Do you mind?"

To her surprise he agreed.

"No, all right, if that's what you want. I'll just go out for a few drinks with some of the boys, to the Cricket club. I'm a bit surprised though, I thought you'd be up for a party Mel, you love parties."

Mel shook her head quietly. She used to love parties before she came here and everything took on a new slant.

She couldn't tell him about the row with Laurel or the phone call with Alison or the conversation with Harry. She had been using the fact that she was busy with the move and her wrist as excuses for why she didn't want to go out, but Rob was now getting suspicious.

"Is something wrong? Why don't you phone the girls and arrange to meet up for lunch? You haven't been out for days Mel, It's not good to stay cooped up in here and I'm sure if you asked they'd be happy to give you a hand packing."

More like they'd love to send me packing!

"No it's fine, I can do it, they probably have other more important things to do like getting a facial and besides they might risk breaking a nail."

"Mel that's a bitchy thing to say, what's got into you? Something's happened hasn't it? Tell me!"

No one had called her or been to see her since the call from Alison and so for the second time in her life she'd been 'sent to Coventry'.

It had really bothered her at first, but now she was just thinking of her new home and getting as far away from all of them as possible.

She wondered if there would ever be a time when she would be able to stop running away from things.

"Nothing's happened, they just wind me up that's all, they're all so false."

Rob glared, "Don't be nasty Mel, you should make more of an effort with the girls. Things don't just happen in these places, you have to make them happen."

"Yes, well you're the expert on making things happen aren't you!"

Her anger and frustration was seeping out and it began to show.

"What's that supposed to mean?"

"I would think that was bloody obvious! This whole wife swapping thing, that you insisted on us becoming a part of, ruined everything and it's tainted everything about this place."

She moved in closely so she could look him in the eyes.

"You have to swear that you'll never do anything like that again, Rob, swear it."

"Mel, I don't think it tainted anything, we learned some stuff and had a new experience, why can't you just climb down off your bloody, high moral horse and admit that it wasn't all bad. I happen to have it on good authority that you didn't think it was *all* bad."

Who the hell had he been talking to? She thought you weren't supposed to speak about the dinner parties!

"What! What does that mean? It was awful and degrading and I hated it, look!"

She raised her plastered wrist to eye level.

"Don't start on about that again Mel, let it go."

"Rob just promise me it won't happen again, ever!"

"Mel, I said let it go, drop it! We're leaving, you've got what you wanted!"

Rob pushed the chair angrily into its under-table position.

"Which reminds me, you need to call HR at the office tomorrow to arrange to go there and sign some immigration papers, and when you call ask for Sally."

"Sally? What happened to Christine?" She asked curiously.

Rob's face changed.

"Christine? Oh yes, she's left. Didn't I mention it? Going back to the London office apparently."

"Really, how come?"

She watched as he squirmed, small but visible chinks were appearing in his armour.

"How the hell should I know? Family problems or something I think." He was clearly uncomfortable and irritated.

Mel turned her face away from him and smiled broadly,

'Melissa one, bunny boiler nil!'

Chapter 33

The day before the move Sally sent an army of removal men over who brought dozens of boxes with them of various shapes and sizes. They moved around the apartment expertly packing and wrapping everything up.

Mel felt compelled to mill around and every now and again say, "Please be careful not to break anything!' and then half smiled to herself at the irony.

After a while she felt too guilty just watching them working so she decided to leave them to it and get a taxi into town for one last walk around.

The cab pulled up outside Far East Plaza and she got out, the oppressive heat was on the list of the things that she wasn't going to miss.

She walked inside and went straight to her favourite jewellery stall, the owner, recognising Mel immediately, smiled kindly at her.

"Good day Madam, how are you today? You need something pretty today, is it?"

"I'm looking for something for my sister and my Mum, I'm leaving Singapore tomorrow to go and live in Australia."

"Oh, that's a pity la, but I have a cousin in Australia and she says it's very nice really you know."

Mel smiled, she loved the way the locals spoke. She picked out a couple of fresh water pearl necklaces with matching bracelets and two Cartier copy watches.

'Right! One last Singapore sling at the Mövenpick and then a last stroll down Arab Street.'

In the Mövenpick she found a small table by the window and ordered her drink then she took the jewellery out of the bag and admired the colours in the daylight.

"Melissa, is that you?" Mel heard a familiar voice behind her. She turned around slowly and standing there, immaculate as ever, were Alison and Laurel.

"Hello ladies," she said forcing a smile.

"What a nice surprise. We were just talking about you, we were wondering what had happened to you."

"Really?" asked Mel coldly. "I thought that under the circumstances it would be better if I stayed away, as instructed!"

"Oh Melissa, that's all water under the bridge, things were said on both sides that we now regret, weren't they? We got a little bit carried away I think." Alison smiled sweetly.

Mel actually didn't regret *anything* that she had said during that telephone call, she had meant every word.

At that moment the waitress arrived with her drink and put it down on the table.

"Oh, a Singapore sling, looks good, we'll join you. Excuse me, two more"

Alison instructed the waitress.

Alison then grabbed a chair from the next table, without asking the people sitting at it, if it was taken, and both women sat themselves down.

"So I hear that Christina has gone back to London" said Alison, always straight to the point. "She left in a terrible hurry after her and Rob, well, you know."

"Yes I do know, but as you say, that's all water under the bridge as well, Alison. Rob and I are leaving in the morning to start our new life in Australia and personally I can't wait to go."

Alison and Laurel looked shocked at her tone.

"How's your bird Laurel, Turq isn't it?"

Laurel looked embarrassed, "He's fine thanks, look Mel, I want to apologise for the last time we spoke, I panicked, Tony can be, well, let's say difficult at times."

She brushed back her hair from her face and stroked a fresh bruise on her cheek as she looked over at Alison who in turn looked awkwardly up at the ceiling. Mel was shocked, Tony hit her?

"I was worried that Turq would give away our little chat but luckily he didn't say anything at the dinner party, silly creature."

"Oh that's right, last Friday was the monthly meeting, how did it go?" Her tone was still sarcastic.

"Well Melissa, I'll just say that it was ... it was eventful."

Alison cleared her throat in an attempt to shut her up."

"Oh Ali, under the circumstances what harm can it do? She's leaving tomorrow."

"Do what you like Laurel, I'm just going to the bathroom to freshen up."

Mel was all ears, she took a long sip of her drink and leaned in to hear more clearly. As soon as Alison was out of earshot Laurel began.

"Mel first of all you have to swear that you won't say anything to Rob, he may tell Tony I talked to you and I don't want to make him angry." Her finger instinctively moved up to her bruised cheek again.

"Yes of course," Mel felt sorry for her, if he did hit her then she had had good reason to be panicky and neurotic that day.

"Tell me what happened on Friday."

"Last Friday we were all there at our house, Malcolm and Mary, he never misses an evening, Alison and Tim,

Tess and Harry and us of course. Malcolm was being his usual drunk obnoxious self."

Mel shuddered.

"Anyway, to cut a long story short, Malcolm was joking around about you and your accident, making crude comments about the function of wrists, you can imagine I'm sure, then he said something about you not being woman enough to take a real man or something like that."

"He said what? What a bloody nerve. God he makes me sick." Mel was now trembling with anger.

"So, the next thing we knew, Harry stood up, went over and punched him hard in the face, his nose was bleeding and everything."

Mel sat in disbelief, Harry stood up for her!

"Why did he do that?"

"Honestly I thought maybe *you* might be able to tell *me*."

She raised an eyebrow and looked hopefully at Mel.

Mel shook her head, she genuinely couldn't say.

"Anyway, as you can imagine, all hell broke loose. Malcolm started threatening Harry with getting him fired, Tim tried to calm things down and ended up being threatened by Malcolm as well and then Tim told Malcolm exactly what he thought of him." Looking nervously over in the direction of the bathroom and half whispering, she continued.

"Even Alison threw in a few choice comments herself, in fact she really let him have a piece of her mind!"

Mel was listening in disbelief at Laurel's story.

"So if Turq does ever blurt out that comment about Malcolm again, it could be accredited to several people."

"So the evening finished there? Nothing else happened?"

"Well nothing else happened, as far as what usually happens no, but after Malcolm stormed out, with an apologetic Mary in tow, poor woman, Tess and Harry…"

Just then Alison came back from the bathroom.

"Where are our drinks? I have to be getting home soon, I'm having my new sofa delivered this afternoon!"

Mel was champing at the bit, "What about Tess and Harry?" she asked in her most nonchalant voice.

Alison looked angry. "I don't know if it's a good idea to discuss it Laurel, do you?"

"I don't see why not, if it was me I'd want to know."

"If what was me? What on earth happened?" Mel's voice was not quite so nonchalant anymore.

"Well if you must know Mel, they were rowing about you" Alison said caustically.

"About me? Why?"

"You really don't know? Alison said in disbelief. "Your arrival here was like a stone in our millpond Melissa, and the ripples have been emanating ever since!"

"How, Alison? I don't understand."

Mel was perplexed to hear this poignant statement, she didn't consider herself important enough to have had an impact on anyone or anything.

"Well the fact is, Tess began accusing Harry of having a thing for you, she was furious."

"She even accused him of having an affair with you" Laurel added, sounding quite excited at the whole idea.

"Why would she think that? Someone's got her wires dangerously crossed."

The girls were looking at each other, it was clear they were now revelling in the delivery of gossip but neither were sure how far they should go, they were constantly looking at each other for support and approval.

"She was under the impression that he sneaks out to see you, she said as much."

At which point Laurel continued, excitement level rising with every revelation, "She said, well screamed actually, that he went to see you on the weekend that Rob was with you know who in you know where!"

Mel was stunned, Tess seemed so together, so sure of herself.

"Of course Harry denied it."

Both were staring avidly at Mel trying to judge her reaction.

"But something told us he wasn't telling the truth."

Again, more staring. Mel was in difficulty, what should she say?

Obviously if he had denied it then she probably should too.

"But then," grinned Laurel, "he admitted coming to see you."

Mel swallowed hard, "He did?"

"Yes, but he said nothing happened."

Alison and Laurel were having a verbal tennis match, passing the conversation from one to the other, almost a perfect rally.

"Well, it didn't!"

"Oh please Melissa! How is that possible? My God, if Harry came to visit me at home and I was alone I would strip him down and eat him alive."

Alison closed her eyes to better picture the scene. "Ummmm" she murmured.

Mel was taken aback by Alison's public confession and show of weakness. What was going on? Everybody seemed different today, it was like she had stopped for a drink in the Twilight Zone.

"Well I didn't strip him down, as you put it! Yes okay he came over, but we just talked, he knew I was alone and he was worried about me, that's all."

"Well if you really believe that then you're a bigger idiot than I thought you were" Laurel scoffed.

"He obviously has a thing for you! Tess asked him to look her straight in the eye and tell her that he wasn't interested in you at all."

"And?" Mel's heart was racing.

"And... he looked away and told her not to be ridiculous, sure sign that he clearly *is* interested in you, little Miss innocent!"

Alison's tone had returned to its former bitter self.

"That's when Tess stormed out as well, so as you see the whole night was a complete bloody disaster. I wouldn't be surprised if the whole thing collapses around our ears, the end of the club, what with Sue, you and now this episode."

"Probably just as well, the whole thing was getting pretty boring anyway, same ol', same ol'" commented Laurel.

Mel sat staring at her drink still patiently sitting there in the glass. Unbelievable! Now she was leaving, the reason for her exile was no longer!

The two girls finished their drinks and stood up.

"What a pickle!" Alison said sarcastically, and threw fifty dollars on the table.

"Oh well Melissa, Sydney tomorrow, lucky you! Away from all this mess, most of which you yourself created."

Mel detected a distinct note of bitterness in her voice and just a pinch of jealousy maybe.

"Never mind," she continued with a sigh, "I'm sure we'll clean it up."

"Or get your maids to!" Melissa said under her breath.

"Anyway Mel, we have to dash, as I said I have a sofa being delivered and then we're off to Korea for the weekend to buy some antique furniture and I still have to pack."

She leaned over and kissed Mel on both cheeks,

"Ciao my dear, the best of luck in Australia, hope you find some peace in Sydney, oh and try not to fall down any more stairs."

She picked up the pen that was on the table and drew a large question mark on Mel's plaster cast and signed her name underneath. As she did so, she noticed the orchid drawn on the other side.

"Harry's favourite doodle, Beauty and the Beasts." she read aloud. "Oh dear, perhaps you're not going to find that peace after all."

In the taxi on the way back to the apartment she kept thinking about what Harry had said to her about it only being a game and then about what he had *not* said to Tess last week at the dinner party. Melissa was confused, very confused. She was leaving with Rob tomorrow, finally he was being the man she wanted him to be, attentive, passionate and above all present. Harry was here and the club was probably going to be dismantled, but Harry was just a crush, she'd get over it. She'd made a fool of herself enough lately and it was time to make the best of what she had and stop searching for more.

Why was everything always so complicated?

When she arrived back at the apartment the men were still wrapping and packing. She went through into the bedroom which was empty except for the bed and chest of drawers. The bedside tables were bubble wrapped by the door. As she looked down at the space they had occupied she saw a piece of the broken table lamp sitting there. She remembered the anger and frustration that had led her to its demise. How would she ever be able to trust him completely again?

She decided to call her Mum, it was time for some honesty and a few home truths.

"Hi Mum, just calling to say that we're all packed up here and ready to go."

"Oh that's good, I expect you're excited about Sydney, don't forget to call the minute you get there to let us know you're safe."

"No I won't, I promise. Mum listen, I need to ask you something."

"Oh yes me too, I've booked the flights for me and Gill for Christmas, I couldn't really afford it so I decided to cash in my insurance policy and luckily we managed to get a fairly cheap deal, the only problem is the deal was only valid for a couple of days so I had to make a quick decision and they're not refundable. I did try calling you a couple of times in the evening but nobody ever answered so I took a risk and booked it, I hope that was all right Mel? You did say we could come."

'Rob and his damn not answering because of Christina!'

"Yes Mum, of course it is but you shouldn't have cashed in your insurance policy though, we could have helped you out."

"It's fine, I've always wanted to go to Australia, and I wanted to see you. We're coming on the fifteenth of December, we thought we'd stay with you for a couple of weeks or so and then go and see my friend Linda in Melbourne for New Year and then, if we have any money left over, maybe travel around a bit. I'd love to see that big rock they have that changes colour. What do you think?"

"Yes, sounds perfect, I'll tell Rob, I'm sure he'll be pleased."

"Lovely, now what did you need to ask me?"

"Nothing, it doesn't matter. I'll call you tomorrow when we arrive, it'll be about midday there and remember Mum there's a nine hour time difference."

"Oh yes of course, is that ahead or behind?"

"Sydney is nine hours ahead of you."

"Right, let me just write that on the calendar. Got it. Okay love, have a good flight and I'll speak to you tomorrow. I'm proud of you Mel, bye for now, love you."

Mel went to walk through to the bedroom when the phone rang again.

'Oh Mum, what did you forget this time?'

"Hi Mum, what's up?"

"Mel, it's Harry."

Shit.

"Hello Harry, how are you? If you're calling to speak to Rob I'm afraid he's not here right now."

She was aware that she was trying too hard to sound chirpy.

"I know, he's just popped in here to the office to speak to Tim. He's in the conference room, I actually called to speak to you."

"Oh okay, that's nice." She was sounding like an idiot. 'Pull yourself together Mel!'

"How's the wrist? When do you get the plaster off?"

"Just ten more days the doctor reckons, I can't wait."

"I bet, Mel listen, I need to tell you something before you leave tomorrow." He paused.

"I just want you to know that I liked making love to you, I didn't want you to leave thinking I'd used you. Things go on here and after a while you become desensitised, you don't think and you don't feel, but with you it wasn't like that."

Mel's heart felt like it was about to explode.

"Melissa you're vibrant, kind and sexy and you're far too good for this place and probably too good for Rob. I may be out of turn but I just thought you should hear something nice for a change, I just thought you should know."

Mel was in the all too familiar situation of being speechless.

"Mel, are you there?"

"Yes, I'm here, thank you Harry, that's... that's... I don't know what to do with that."

"It's okay, you don't have to do anything or say anything, maybe I shouldn't have said anything either. Take care of yourself Mel in Sydney and keep well away from people like us. I'll miss you."

Double shit!

The next morning when Mel woke her heart was heavy, she sat there watching Rob sleeping, and she was torn once again. Torn between what she thought she wanted to do and what she felt she had to do.

She leaned over and grabbed hold of the packet of photos that were still on the floor next to the bed.

Rob had asked the guy who'd been living in their new apartment to take pictures of the inside and outside of the apartment in Sydney. Mel looked through them for the tenth time since they'd arrived by post two days earlier.

It was lovely and the view from the roof, as Rob had said, was amazing, you could see the whole of Bondi Beach, golden sand and blue ocean as far as the eye could see.

Rob opened his eyes and turned over in the bed,

"G'day Sheila, time to leave," he smiled, "Sydney, here we come, cobbers."

"Rob, don't do the accent" she begged him.

He leapt out of bed.

"Come on, we've still got an hour before we need to leave for the airport, let's go down and get some breakfast, I'm starving."

They dressed, prepared the last of their things and left the suitcases ready by the door. Mel looked sadly around the almost empty apartment one last time.

They went down to the restaurant below and had a breakfast of pancakes and fresh fruit while sitting outside and watching the people in the pool.

"I'll miss this place" Rob exclaimed a little sadly.

"Yes, me too." Mel sighed a heavy sigh.

"Oh come on Mel, you hated it here, you were miserable."

"I didn't hate it here Rob! Actually I loved this place, this actual place is really beautiful. What I hated was the sordid way people live here, so ridiculous and false. We were sucked down in to something awful and almost drowned in it all."

"Mel when you say sucked it gets me going."

Rob was laughing but Mel wasn't.

"Rob I'm serious, God you can be so childish sometimes."

He looked dejected.

"And you can be a real bore sometimes Mel, try being young for once and not so uptight! When I met you, you were fun, remember?"

She did remember, so what went wrong?

They finished their breakfasts and stood up from the table.

"Okay, that's it, time to go. I'll run up and grab the cases, you go and flag us down a cab."

Rob walked around the table and pulled her close into him.

"It'll be all right Mel, you'll see, everything will be better, trust me."

On the airplane they were directed to their seats in first class.

Mel, who had never been in first class before, couldn't believe the size of the seats.

"Oh Mel, did I tell you that I saw Malcolm yesterday evening? He had his nose broken by a cricket ball, he had two black eyes and he looked a right mess."

Mel stopped looking and flicking through the in-flight magazine. Harry had broken his nose! How hard had he hit him? She smiled and looked out of the window.

Rob took hold of her hand and squeezed it,

"I thought that would cheer you up! Let's get some champagne and toast to our new adventure."

Mel continued looking out of the window at the line of palm trees in the distance.

What was she doing?

Just then a tall hostess, with legs up to her armpits, arrived with the drinks trolley.

Rob eyed her lecherously up and down.

"Champagne? Miss? Would you like some champagne?"

Rob took the glasses from the hostess and handed one to Mel.

"Cheers", said Rob, raising his glass, "here's to us."

The airplane began slowly backing away from the gate.

"To us," repeated Mel.